THE LAST

ZOMBIE OCEAN BOOK 1

THE **ZOMBIE OCEAN**

The Last (Book 1)

The Lost (Book 2)

The Least (Book 3)

The Loss (Book 4)

The List (Book 5)

These and all Michael John Grist's other books can be found at:

www. michaeljohngrist.com

To hear when the newest book is out, and get access to special deals and giveaways, sign up to the newsletter-

www.michaeljohngrist.com/newsletter-sign-up

for SY

PRE-APOCALYPSE

1. MAYOR

One day and two nights before the zombie apocalypse kills every person I ever knew, I become mayor of Sir Clowdesley.

Sir Clowdesley is a cozy little independent coffee shop in the Flatiron district of Manhattan, on 23rd street and 2nd Avenue, decked out with soothing shades of teal and raw wood shelving. I come here every day to make storyboards, drink decaf lattes, and perpetuate the routines that have kept me alive this long. Now I've become mayor, which is dangerously exciting.

I lean back from my laptop in the mezzanine area of the shop, called the 'library' for all the donated books lining the walls, and watch the little twinkling Jeo badge revolving on my phone's screen.

MAYOR

I feel flush with pride. Baby steps they said, when I was finally released from the hospital. This feels like a baby victory.

I survey the low bustle of hipsters I have come to rule, spread out on mismatching vintage sofas and benches. They wear skinny jeans and neck beards and plaited ponytails, all clutching phones like the sawn-off hilts of swords in a war. I suppose I look much like them, a 28-year old artist with dreams of becoming relevant, though I'm now their leader.

I sip my decaf latte and shuffle through the Jeo option screens. It seems Sir Clowdesley have made a few mayor's rewards available, so I can bestow such favors as free coffee, reserved seating, and double-speed Wi-Fi upon whomever I please.

I don't know anyone here though. I've avoided the Clowdesley chat room so far, to keep the headaches at bay.

> Who wants a free coffee? I have five to give away. Make your case.

I type and send the message, geo-locked to the Clowdesley coordinates. Across the room I hear a few low chimes jingle as my decree arrives. The first answer comes within moments.

> I'm pregnant. Baby needs caffeine.

I reward this bold soul with a cup of decaf. I watch out for someone to rise, a pregnant lady perhaps, but MichelleGondry42 doesn't seem to want to claim his/her prize just yet. No problem, I slap a sixty-second countdown on it to flush them out.

A skinny guy by the window springs up out of his bucket leather seat and hurries over to the counter, holding up his phone like the Olympic torch. I get a kick out of that.

> God wants me for his messiah. Coffee will fuel his second coming. His wrath will rain down on the unjust.

Double espresso. I do the timer again and now a portly girl in skinny black jeans makes her dash to the counter. This is probably too much fun.

"So you're the new mayor, huh?"

I look to the side.

Shit.

It's the gorgeous auburn-skinned waitress, standing there looking down at my phone. Immediately my heart starts to race. She's some kind of coffee-nut blend as rich as hazelnut cream, Afro-Caribbean with a French touch to her eyes, with these lovely dark ringlets of hair that circle down her cheeks. I've noticed her many times. I've been coming here every day for months.

Shit.

"We haven't had one for a while," she goes on. "The spec is set pretty high."

I put the phone down and smile, belying the terror I'm feeling. "It's the culmination of all my plans."

She snorts. "You are in here a lot. It would probably be me, for all the shifts I do, but they don't let staff on Jeo."

I shrug. "I'll bring it up with the council."

She laughs. Her eye-whites are truly sparklingly white. "So what are you doing here every day, writing a novel?"

I follow her eye-line to my laptop computer on the table, open on a page full of text.

"Ah, yeah," I say, "it's not a novel, actually. It's storyboards for a graphic novel. I make them here then I do the art at home."

Her eyes light up a shade brighter. "Really? I'm into comics. What's it about?"

My smile goes wry. "Zombies."

"Ha. That's cool. Do they run?"

I laugh, then rein it in. This is the closest I've come to flirting since the incident, and my head is already starting to twinge with the pressure. "They do. Do you want to see some panels?"

"Panels is like pages? Sure."

I lean to the laptop, swizzing the word processor screen away and bringing up my latest work. I full-screen it and angle the display so she can better see.

Her jaw drops a little. This and mayor makes it a great day.

"You are kidding me?"

I go all bashful. "No, it's mine. It's the penultimate panel, actually, I'm brainstorming what to do with the last one."

She leans over my shoulder and studies the screen closer. It's a view of New York from high up, around the 30th floor of the Chrysler building, but everything is destructed fitting the post-apocalypse; all cracks and weeds and toppled skyscrapers with leathery corpses strung on telephone wires.

The zombies are there too, but they're heaped in the middle at the Times Square intersection, in a tower of contorting limbs reaching up many stories high. They look a bit like they did in World War Z, climbing up to pull down a helicopter, but in my image they're climbing toward nothing we can see.

Drawing it laid me up in bed for a day. I could barely move for migraine-twinges and thinking I was going to die. It's worth it though.

"This is amazing. But what's going on?" Her breath touches my neck as she leans closer. My pulse starts to race. Not good, really, but I

5

can't slam the laptop and run off now. "What are they trying to get at?"

I swallow down my dry throat and spit out words. "That's the question. At this point all the humans are dead, so it's just zombies left. You'd think they'd roam around mindlessly with no brains left, but in fact they stack up like this. I'm not sure if I should give the reason for it in the last panel, or sort of leave it open."

She leans back. "OK, like a cliffhanger. So do you know what they're climbing for?"

"Yeah. It's not aliens or anything. They're not climbing up to the mother ship."

She chuckles. I should probably stop this now while I'm ahead. I don't. "I'll show you if you like," I say. "I'll be here tomorrow. I come in here most days."

"I know."

There's a bashful quiet. Of course I've seen her before, for the past five months, but I had no notion if I'd registered on her radar. We never talked, and really I'm not supposed to be talking to her now. It could kill me. I should just shut up.

"Dinner," I say instead. It comes into my head and I say it. "I'll show you at dinner tomorrow night. There's a great modern French spot nearby, they do logarithmic art on the walls and they have a cat that sings for its supper. My treat. I'll show you the panel. You render judgment."

Her left eyebrow raises a fraction. "A date? I approached you, though, it's true. I suppose I was asking for this."

"I'm the one asking. I think it'll be fun."

She laughs. "Points for opportunism, then. And for being the mayor. What if I say I have a boyfriend?"

"Then you'll have to buy the comic yourself. No free peeks at the last page."

She laughs again, and her bright eyes narrow, appraising me. "Well, you seem OK. No scurvy, rickets, nothing like that. It's a deal. Give me your phone."

I hand it over solemnly. She taps on it deftly then hands it back. "I'm not in here tomorrow," she says, "but we can have dinner. The cat better sing. I want good logarithms."

"Only the best."

She raises the eyebrow a little higher. I'm not entirely sure I know what a logarithm is, so I hope she won't ask. I saw it on a flyer.

"Lara," she says. "That's my name."

"Amo. It means love in Latin. My parents were hippies."

"Amo the mayor, OK. I'll see you."

She turns and goes. There are other people's novels to check on, probably, and my constituents to serve. Also they profit-share here, there's a career path and everything, which has got to be motivating. Next month Lara could be the manager, next year the world.

Ah shit. My heart is racing. This plus mayor is probably too much excitement for me to take. I sincerely hope I don't fall into a coma and die.

A year ago I fell into a coma and died.

It lasted for two weeks, and in fact I died many times, with my heart stopping and all brain function fading. Many times they somehow brought me back. I don't remember any of it and no one knows why. When I woke up it wasn't because of anything the doctors did; the fit or infection or whatever it was had just passed. It left me with a severely weakened heart, and a severely weakened mind.

"Think of it like diabetes," my doctor said, a serious Indian man with bright red glasses, which I found galling. Who wears bright red glasses when they go to see a man coming out of a coma? It's not a catwalk, man. "Your brain and body chemistry has changed," he went on. "Now you have this condition, you can't go back, and one lapse could lead to serious complications."

My head was already starting to hurt. The first twinge of many, many more. "Complications like what?"

"Like more comas. Like death. Honestly, we don't know."

I was sitting in my hospital bed in a lovely clean white ward that looked out over Central Park, a bright green contrast against the hospital's sterility. My family had all come in and out hours earlier, quietly of course, bringing bobbing foil balloons in the shape of skeleton and zombie heads, and now my doctor didn't have a goddamned clue what he was talking about.

"So I need to avoid death," I said, squinting against the rising pain. "How do I do that?"

He actually took off his glasses then. I suppose this was sincere. He wagged them in his hands as he made his points.

"Your family tell me you were under a lot of stress when it happened. You're an artist, yes?"

I gave a little nod.

"Art is tricky. It does things to the brain we don't understand. You don't seem to have any other risk factors, nothing genetic, nothing in your system, only the stress of what you were working on. Was there anything else stressful in your life at the time?"

I cast my mind back, but I couldn't think of anything. It was work; I was making the panels for my biggest project yet, an anthology horror piece I was editing that several online stores had already agreed to feature prominently. I'd set it up, bringing eleven other artists on board. It was a big deal for me.

"There was pressure, but not overwhelming. I can't think of anything else. I guess I just collapsed while I was working on that?"

He sighed. "You won't like to hear this then. I'll put it bluntly. We think you may be allergic to art."

"What?"

He held up his hands. "I know, that's not possible. But your brain is highly abnormal, Amo. Over the course of your coma we've studied you a lot. Some of the best researchers in the country were here, trying to untangle the maze of contradictory data. For all the world it looked like your brain was a fever map, with lights flashing on and out, changing constantly. Some areas seemed to burn out, the ones we normally ascribe to creativity, then just as quickly they reformed. We thought we saw cancers growing, we were ready to operate, but they receded. You died and you came back multiple times. Your brain is essentially entirely new, having regrown itself many times. We don't understand it at all. You'll be a case study for years to come. I honestly don't know how complications will manifest."

I sat there dumbly.

"So I can only advise," he went on. "I'd advise you to avoid stimulation of any kind, particularly any kind of artistic endeavor, plus the parts of the brain associated with romantic love- they lit up some of the brightest. It was like fourth of July in your head."

I frowned at him. He seemed to regret that last phrase. He put his glasses back on and nodded, as though confirming something I'd said.

"Don't do art," he said. "Don't fall in love. It's what I have to advise. I'd prescribe you drugs, Xanax or another sedative mood-stabilizer, but I've no idea what that might do with your fragile brain chemistry. We can't take the risk."

I mull this over. No art? No love? "So what can I do then?"

"You can recover. Read old books you've read before. Boredom is your bandage."

"What about movies?"

"If they're very dull, or old. Black and white would be best. I have to also advise you against any act of sex. The stimulation could trigger a relapse. However it may be wise to masturbate once a week, as clinically as you can, to avoid any kind of hormone build up. Again I'd prescribe for that, but I don't think it wise. There's too much risk."

I stared at him. Already the first of the twinges was beginning to kick in. "You want me to masturbate clinically?"

He shifted uncomfortably. "As clinically as possible. Use very soft porn if you must."

"Because if I get too excited, I might die?"

"Or worse."

"Or worse? What could be worse than dying?"

The doctor shrugged. "Some would say a never-ending coma is worse. I've never been in a coma so I wouldn't know. I imagine if you never wake up though, then you may as well be dead. It's just a horrible, powerless delay."

"I woke up this time."

"You did. Who can say, really?"

"Who can say?" I repeated, then slumped back on my pillows, with the twinge in my head ramping up to migraine proportions.

2. CERULEAN

For the last hour at Sir Clowdesley I fight off the headache, but it comes anyway, rolling over me in waves. I close my eyes and pretend I'm listening to music, when in fact I've got nothing but white noise coming through my headphones.

Lara pops in and out of my thoughts, bringing twinges of excitement. I can't believe I actually asked her out, taking such risks. It has been an exceptionally boring year.

I leave Sir Clowdesley at 7pm, checking out as mayor before I step through the door. New York awaits me, and 23rd street is chilly for spring, getting dark already. The faint smell of diesel and pizza hangs in the air, mingled with sweet orange blossoms from Madison Square Park a few blocks over. Cars buzz by angrily, a pedestrian flood flows with them, and I fold smoothly into their mass.

Halfway to the subway my phone vibrates in my pocket as a message slots in. I fish it out and bring up the notifications. It's a message from Cerulean, my Deepcraft friend.

```
The darkness awaits! Fresh bric-a-brac available.
```

I smile and tap out a quick reply.

```
                    Ready to do my duty.
```

I take the stairs to the subway and descend to the 6-line platform, filled with sweaty commuters irritable after another day's work. Some guy wearing a big headset has his techno playing too loud, and a few complaints have already been fired onto the station's Jeo-locked bulletin board. They can't make him turn it down, but they'll all feel better for venting.

On the platform an advert scrolls lazily across the tunnel wall, for the big superhero movie they've been building to since 2016, the concluding part to the trilogy that took the world by storm: Ragnarok III. They say everyone's going to die. It looks great, but I don't suppose I'll be watching it. I try every now and then with tamer movies that pop up on Saturday mornings, but when I feel a twinge I switch off.

I get on the train and ride it home. Podcasts talk to me about crafting techniques in Deepcraft and the latest mods. It's soothingly mundane. Did I know an augur can drill platinum but it can't drill titanium deposits? Actually I did.

The train arrives in Mott Haven, South Bronx, and I get out. On the street the air feels clearer, with few skyscrapers looming overhead and Willis Playground just across the way. It's a nice place to live.

Soon my redbrick tenement building is in front of me. I rent a room in the top back, a tiny rooftop garret fit for a starving artist, all I need and can afford. I enter and go up the stairs to the fourth floor where my room is tucked into the eaves.

The sloping roof cuts it in half diagonally, with a big skylight and a little window at the end. On the walls I have my street art; a few Banksy prints including the one of the guy throwing a bunch of flowers, a fake Space Invader space invader in yellow and green tile, and one large print of the vinyl faces on Mumbai rooftops by JR.

Other than that there's my bed, chair, and desk with top-range computer; last vestige of the days when I had a little money to reinvest.

In the kitchenette corner I brew a cup of decaffeinated green tea and warm up some frozen spaghetti bolognese. I don't eat much these days; I just don't have the appetite. I take a hot sip of green tea while the microwave blasts the food. The bitterness is refreshing, and the tannins will surely help with my brain's ongoing detox.

I slot into my chair, tuck into the bolognese, and bring up the darkness. Cerulean is already in there waiting for me. I slide my view screen goggles over my eyes and enter our shared world: a Yangtze shopping fulfillment warehouse, in a private Deepcraft mod.

Deepcraft saved my life. Before Deepcraft though there was Yangtze, and that saved my life too. I owe my life to lots of weird little things.

It was two months in to my convalescence after the coma, hiding out in my parents' dark Iowa basement, reading old comics and in-line skating around the dehumidifier and ping pong table, when I realized that I had a choice to make: man or mouse.

"You'll be with us again soon," my mother would often say, when she brought down my lukewarm milkshakes or diet mayo tuna sandwiches. "Coming back to the land of the living."

I appreciated everything she did, but it pissed me off. I'd been through this terrible thing and here now it was continuing. My brain was weak, my body too, I could hardly stand to be around other people and TV made my brain twinge like crazy, but I wasn't some feeble dying goat incapable of doing anything for myself.

"Baby steps," my doctor said when he discharged me. "Think of it like mental rehab. Your brain has to get re-accustomed to stimulation step by baby step."

So I got a job.

I researched the least mentally demanding work out there, in the dullest, darkest environment, and came up with picker at a Yangtze online shopping fulfillment center. They're the people who collect the stuff we order on the website, who labor all day in vast windowless warehouses that cover about a square mile each.

I applied and they took me on. Two days later I turned up and nodded through a twinge-inducing but mercifully brief induction. The supervisor gave me a simple gizmo called a 'diviner', which I was to follow as it flashed left-right directions through the warehouse. I picked up the stuff it highlighted then put it on conveyor belts for the packing department, ad infinitum, like a rat in a maze.

I loved it. All day I walked down dark climate-controlled shelving corridors, making no decisions for myself, just following the diviner to pick up limited edition basketballs, sets of tea knives, greetings cards, self-published books from the cranky print-on-demand machines, talking teddies, butt-shaped pillows, and so on. Whatever the diviner demanded, I collected.

It was a lovely monotony. I got back into some kind of physical shape, and built up my stimulation endurance. If any order was too weird, I'd try not to look, and count backwards from one hundred to distract myself. I got good enough that the twinges mostly went away and my thinking cleared up.

I got so good at the job I could anticipate turns even before the diviner told me where to go. With all that extra brain-space, I started to notice the other pickers. They were all weirdos. Hank for example was a bitter redneck who got 'stranded' in Iowa after his community college kicked him out for selling weed, and he washed up on the fulfillment center's shore to make ends meet. In lieu of completing his studies he'd signed up for an online 'sexual mastery class,' and often would try out conversational gambits on me when our paths intersected through the warehouse, like lonely little ants at a scent-trail crossing.

"So when she says her name, you say, 'You should speak a little louder, you must be the shy one in the group'," he told me once.

"It's embarrassing her," I said.

"Right, it's putting her on the spot, meaning you control the spotlight. It's cool stuff man, neuro-linguistic programming from the top artists in the game."

"Does it work?"

"I haven't tried it yet."

Bobby was six foot seven and really into North Korea. Sometimes he wore the red star of North Korea on a T-shirt he'd clearly printed himself, as if daring our overlords to kick him out. I don't think the supervisor ever noticed, he probably thought it was a basketball shoe logo.

Linda from Arkansas was working her way around all the Yangtze fulfillment centers in the US, for a travel memoir she was writing.

"It's like the travel book by the guy who hitch-hiked round Ireland with a fridge," she told me once. "You've got to have a gimmick. This is my gimmick."

I loved it. Here were weird people, all with their own strange aspirations just like me, and I was handling it. When I needed time apart, I'd turn at a crossing when it looked as if we were going to intersect. A simple shrug of the shoulders and a point to the diviner would explain all.

The gods are rerouting me, that shrug said. It's just my fate.

It was Lucy on the print-on-demand machines, that clattery

industrial corner of the center where books were baked in great X-ray like kilns, who put me onto Deepcraft.

I liked to stay near the printers for as long as I could before the sound made my brain twinge, watching pages slip in and out of the runners, forming up gradually into newly birthed books, their binding still tacky. These were dreams being made, just like my brain was rebuilding itself.

"I print my own here," Lucy told me once. She was a chubby girl with poorly dyed blue hair. We all called her Blucy. "I write romance with Amish vampires in the post-apocalypse. It's a big niche. They let me print them at cost."

I nodded. She showed me one of her books. The cover was awful, just clip-art of something representative of each of those genres horribly overlaid.

I made her one much better that night, stretching my brain's limits to the max. I had twinges for the following week, but she went wild for it. She invited me to play Deepcraft with her.

"It's just like digital Lego, Amo, you can turn down the danger and everything so there's no random events like falling into lava, no roaming zombies, nothing to make you scared or set off stress alarms, just a sandbox to build in. I make weird ruined worlds for my characters to live in. I think you'd get a kick out of it."

We went in together at her place, viewing one of her post-apocalyptic worlds through split-screen. It was funny to see the broken elevated roadways and tattered skyscrapers she'd envisaged built in chunky 3D blocks. Her ruins were fun and bright, like her writing. The game itself was intuitive and repetitive, involving grinding out ores by digging, then crafting them into tools and materials to create buildings.

It was fun. At home I built a miniature version of the fulfillment center; lovingly stacking up the long clean corridors, fitting it with low lights, stocking the shelves with whatever weird products I could craft, even hand-coding the mod for a diviner.

At the same time I started making covers for all Blucy's books. She never paid me, but she put me onto her writer friends who wanted covers, and they did pay. The work ran me down, but then I'd go in Deepcraft and grind out ores for hours, add to my fulfillment center, and wander it in a trance. In god mode I added non-player characters modeled on my co-workers in real life, who wandered its corridors endlessly online, forever doomed to think of little nuggets of information they wanted to pass on.

It was wonderfully soothing, and it sped up my recovery so much that I was able to make more covers. I had enough cash and energy after eight months to quit the picking job and go full time with the covers.

"Don't go," my mother said, when I told her I was heading back to New York. "That place broke you. I couldn't bear for it to happen again."

My dad patted me on the shoulder and stood by.

I came back to New York on a Greyhound, quietly defiant. I worked on art that would've bored me to tears before. I went to Sir Clowdesley's as mental therapy to build up my tolerance. I crafted goods to sit on my Deepcraft warehouse shelves, even opening it up for others to run online and critique.

On one of those runs I met Cerulean.

"This is bullshit," Cerulean says calmly, as we stand side by side in the darkness, our name for the fulfillment center. His character is a red and green parrot with a little pirate on its shoulder, which is his idea of a joke.

His words pop up as a speech bubble over his head. He's pointing at one of the shelves, on which there's a rack of colorful videogame-style mushrooms that are glitching through the shelf base.

"I spent hours making these, and now this. What kind of damn mushrooms are these?"

I chuckle. Cerulean can get very upset about the smallest things. It's not funny really, more a part of his condition, but still I have to laugh.

"It's just bits," I type.

"Shit bits," he returns. "Shitty little bits."

We walk. We have our diviners synced. We do this for hours, most nights, ever since I opened the darkness on a public board and Cerulean found it. After a few weeks of glimpsing him hovering constantly just at the edge of my vision, we talked, haltingly at first, but in time the story came out, and we realized we had more in common than just about anyone in the world: we'd both died multiple times.

"I met a girl," I tell him.

He stops his parrot in the act of reaching for some generic Ken doll-alikes. "What?"

I explain.

For Cerulean this is great and juicy gossip, because Cerulean spends all day in the darkness. He died in a coma too, just like me, but his coma hit while he was about to do a high-level dive at competition, on track to become an Olympic competitor. Unconsciousness hit at the edge of the thirty-foot dive platform and he fell, breaking his back and half-drowning in the pool before anyone could get him out.

He's much worse off than me, essentially a paraplegic, and far more sensitive to stimulation. Now we are each other's support systems.

Cerulean's pirate is stomping excitedly round his feathery shoulder as I finish explaining.

"That is crazy," he types. "Mayor and a date?"

"A lot happened today."

"Are you coping OK?"

I shrug in the real world. "I'm OK now. I twinged pretty hard after I invited her, and I'm worried about what might happen on the date, but yeah."

"Damn. You're a brave man Amo, I couldn't do that. But maybe it's just what you need."

I laugh. "If I don't die."

We walk again. Our diviners click in synchrony. Up ahead Hank is coming for us. He'll probably tell us about a new pick-up trick he's learned, replete with a link. I actually programmed him to do that, so his character doesn't get completely dull; he's really just the outer skin on a few blog feeds about picking up girls.

I need less of that topic right now, thank you. I steer me and Cerulean left.

"In other news, I've decided what to do with my comic."

"The last panel?"

"I'm going to use it," I say. "I've finished it, and I promised to show it to you first. Can you handle it now?"

"Hang on a second." There's a pause before he goes on. "Just taking some aspirin. OK, hit me."

I hold out a piece of paper in game. He takes it in his wing.

"Feast your eyes," I type, "slowly."

He raises the paper. I wait. Right now the image will be unfolding across his screen. His brain will probably twinge quite hard. I hope it's worth a headache.

"Oh man," Cerulean types.

I bring the panel up too. It's another image of the tower of zombies in Times Square, but seen from a different perspective. This one's not from thirty stories high, floating clean above the fray, but right down in the dirt of rotten bodies.

The angle is tilted sharply, looking up through a frame of zombie flesh to the tower, all the way to the empty sky, where there is a hint of a shape written in the clouds, which might be the face of the hero's wife. It's a purposely faint resemblance, written in cottony wisps.

She was lost to the infection near the beginning of the book. Even the hero himself succumbed pages earlier, beaten down and chased through the streets of New York, dying in an ignominious alleyway behind the theater showing Cats.

In this final panel we see through his zombie eyes, and what he thinks is his wife in the clouds.

Cerulean speaks.

"Jesus, Amo, this is beautiful. I can almost not handle it."

I get a twinge of emotion, because this image means a lot to me too. I think it came out of my coma. After I woke I felt like I understood the hunger of the zombies, these creatures I'd been sketching and painting for so long. I realized that no matter how much they consumed, it could never be enough. There weren't enough brains in the whole world to fill the holes carved out of them.

"I feel just like this," Cerulean says. "I'm like this sucker at the bottom reaching for clouds, but it's all an illusion."

I clear my throat. I pull away the goggles for a minute and rub my eyes. I've been keeping this to myself for months. My brain starts to twinge. I put them back on.

"I need to walk the darkness," I type.

"Me too."

We walk side by side. Occasionally our synchronized diviners click left or right and we follow to collect. It helps.

"It felt like this for me too," Cerulean says eventually. "The coma. I was diving, but it was a dive that never ended. I knew if only I could hit the water clean then everything would be all right, but I couldn't, and I never did get clear."

"You did, Cerulean. We both came out of it."

His parrot avatar laughs. "Not me. I'm a cripple Amo; I'm just like this guy. I can't even get out of bed. My mom has to clean it up when I piss in my pants."

There's nothing to say to that. "I'm sorry. I didn't mean to make you feel sad."

"Screw sad, this is better. I'm in awe, Amo. This is beautiful. Now let's just shut up and work."

We work. We walk. I think about Lara. Despite Cerulean, or maybe because of him, I start to feel something different from my usual mixture of fear, guilt and self-pity.

Fulfillment. Finishing my comic is a big thing for me, and Cerulean's reaction inspires me. My brain twinges with mixed emotions so hard I think I might pass out, but I don't care. This is what life is for.

Only after we've completed the full circuit do I notice Cerulean has logged off already. I don't blame him. I log off myself, and roll from my chair into bed. I am exhausted. I am excited. Things are changing for me, and tomorrow is going to be a wonderful, terrifying day. I can't wait.

3. LARA

I wake up at 7am and get to work. I don't eat breakfast and haven't since the incident, but a brew of detoxing decaf green tea gets my brain gently firing. Slotted into my chair I start the next round of book cover bids, like a farmer out sowing seeds on fallow ground.

Around mid-morning Cerulean messages me.

> Sorry to bail on you last night. Amazing. My head is splitting now, but at least I'm not bored. I promote you to supervisor.

I smile and reply.

> First order of business, fix those mushrooms. I'll catch you in the darkness after the date.

He answers in seconds.

> She'll love you. Good luck.

He logs off. I do some more work, some light exercise, then think about some lunch, but I'm still not hungry. My doctor thought it was strange, an outgrowth of my broken brain, but after plenty of tests they found I wasn't starving, I wasn't even losing muscle mass, so there was no real problem.

"Like I said, you'll be a case study for years to come," he said as he discharged me, with his red glasses off. "Maybe in your brain lies the key to solving third world hunger. Or even the next diet fad."

I need to plan for the date.

I bring up the French restaurant on the Internet, it's called 'Rien', meaning 'Nothing,' which is just fabulously avant-garde. It's a bit out of my price-range but I can afford to splash out. I dig into their About page and find that the singing cat is actually a mechanical automaton that works on similar principals to a Roomba hoover, patrolling the floor and singing for his supper. Guests toss him a few crumbs and he moves on.

The logarithmic light show has a guest video jockey tonight. I click through and book a table for two at seven, then I bring up my phone and open the notes folder. There lies Lara's number. I don't give myself any time to prepare, I just punch it in.

After three rings she answers. "Hello?"

"Hi, it's Amo, we met in Sir Clowdesley yesterday. How's it going?"

I can hear the smile in her voice. "Ah, the zombie mayor! Have you got your art ready to show me?"

Zombie mayor is not a good nickname. "I've got it. I've got a booking at the French place too, Rien, at 7."

"OK great. I can meet you outside, I checked it out. The cat looks fun."

I smile. "Yeah, I think so. I'll see you then."

"See you Amo."

She hangs up. I slump back.

My heart is hammering, there's sweat on my temples, and my head is starting to twinge hard. Crap. I'm going to die.

I flop off the chair to the floor, with my eyes throbbing sharply already. I drape the video screen goggles over them and plug in my earphones. I don't log in to Deepcraft; I'm too close to the precipice even for that, what I need now is nothing.

In the silence and dark I count down from a hundred. I flex each of my fingers in turn, then my toes. This is the worst it's been for months.

An hour passes, two, and gradually the twinges ebb. My breathing eases and my body unclenches. I lie there wondering how on earth I'm going to sit at a table with this woman.

I don't have an answer. I'm just going to do it.

I get back to work making covers. I need my routines. By five I'm hungry, so to satisfy the dinner routine I warm up another batch of bolognese and eat a few mouthfuls only. I'll be eating again in two hours.

I get dressed. Agonizing over what to wear is not a profitable use of my limited mental resources, so I go with my standard smart casual: gray flannel pants, dark cotton shirt, brown loafers and dark gray sports coat.

I pack my bag with my laptop. I head out the door.

It's a gray day outside and getting dark already. I ride the train, see more posters for movies I can't watch, and get off. I arrive early and wander up to Madison Square Park with my jacket hood pulled over my head. I kill time wandering for ten minutes, and then head back.

This is not a baby step. This is an almighty leap, but I'm tired of rehabilitation. I'm ready to live or die.

Lara is standing in front of Rien already. My heart is booming. Excuses for why I might have to suddenly turn and run away pop into my head, but none suffice. I'm on this course now. Orange blossoms flutter down around me in slow motion, like a samurai heading for war.

I walk up to her with flowers in my hand, bought around the corner. She's wearing a smart cream blouse and twill orange skirt, with her mass of curly black hair condensed and twirled atop her head like a modernist sculpture. A strong twinge is setting in.

She smiles to see me.

"You look beautiful," I say, that truest cliché. "These are for you."

She takes the flowers and laughs. "They're gorgeous, thank you, Amo. You clean up good."

I smile. "Thanks. And they're Caribbean Lilies. I've always liked them."

She lifts the flowers to her nose. They are delicate frondy things, with many weaving purple buds tucked within a bed of long petals. I smelled them already, they remind me of coconuts.

"This is a good start."

I smile. "It can only get better. Shall we?"

I present my elbow. She takes it, sending fireworks up into my brain. I stride us into Rien.

Inside it's a classical French restaurant with a modern twist. Most of the walls and floor are polished concrete, dressed with soft down-lights and oddly placed squares of inset industrial metal, giving the impression there are a dozen hidden alcoves tucked into the walls. The techno cat is a gimmick really, hardly better-looking than those walking dogs of ten years earlier, but the lightshow is already rippling across LEDs embedded in the screen-wall. They flow and ebb like the soothing wind in Deepcraft.

It takes all my concentration to address the maître d'. We sit down at our table. The twinge is already a storm between my temples with Lara at the eye, and everything else is a gray swirl. She's talking, and I catch myself thinking how awful it will be for her if I collapse and die now. Will she ever get over it?

I push back. In my mind I step into the darkness. I put my mouth on autopilot.

"I'm from Iowa," I tell her, answering a question she possibly asked. "My folks have a little farm, they used to raise pigs but now it's just grass for feed. When I was five years old I wanted to be a pig cowboy, riding a pig around the plains. That's actually true. Then I wanted to be a football-player, then an artist, and that's what I've been doing ever since."

"I can imagine you riding a pig," she says. "Painting zombies from pigback."

I chuckle. "It's not only zombies. I do book covers too, all kinds. I used to have this great idea for a graphic novel about a graffiti artist like Banksy who becomes a superhero. Maybe I'll do it one day."

She nods along. "Who doesn't like Banksy? I think that'd be fun. He'd fight crime and leave social justice tags at the crime scenes."

I laugh again. My left temple feels like it's going to pop, but at least it's only the left. "What about you? Where are you from?"

She taps the flowers in their vase. I hadn't noticed the waiter bring a vase to put them in, but I guess that happened. "You were pretty close with these. I'm from St. Kitts in the Caribbean originally, but I barely remember that, we left when I was just a kid. My mom was French Caribbean, my dad was in the navy, so I'm a navy brat and I grew up all over. As for childhood dreams, I wanted to be a princess, then an astronaut, and somewhere along the way a bank manager or a lawyer. Now I'm a barista. I'm sort of happily floating along."

My eyes prickle and my brain is stewing. "It sounds nice."

"It is. I went to law school for four years, passed the bar, but the stress burned me out. I took a coffee course and ended up at Sir Clowdesley, and I haven't looked back since."

I nod. "I know something about burning out. I was hospitalized for a while, and the doctor said I might be allergic to art."

She laughs. "That's not even a thing."

I shrug. "For about six months I couldn't paint a thing without migraines. I can't watch movies now because they're too much art. It's getting better though."

She studies me appraisingly, looks to the panel and back. "So you really do suffer for your art."

I laugh. "I suppose. I hadn't thought about it that way. Anyway, give me your hand."

"What? Why?"

I want to change this conversation's direction, that's why, but I'm not going to say that. "Can I see it just a second?"

She frowns, then cautiously extends her arm across the table, which is bare wood. They haven't even given us any cutlery yet, and of course there's no tablecloth. Rien means nothing, after all.

"You're not going to read my palm are you?"

"Better than that." I take her hand. More fireworks shoot in my head, rising to a crescendo. Her nutty skin is warm and smooth. What am I doing? I don't really know. I'm being carried away. I cast my mind back for something Hank at Yangtze once told me about the immutable laws of attraction.

"This skin tone is probably between Fawn and Isabelline," I say, tapping the back of her hand. "I know that because I'm an artist. Have you ever heard of those colors?"

She shakes her head. I wink. "They're both kinds of brown." Before she can pull her hand back I turn it over and tap her palm gently. Classic Hank move. "This is between Ecru and Fallow. Have you heard of those?"

"Are they kinds of brown?" The sarcasm drips off her.

"Very astute, they both are. According to some ancient peoples all colors have a meaning. If you combine these two colors," I tap her palm and the back of her hand lightly again, "you get a kind of equation that predicts your personality and your future."

"So what's my future, oh seer of color?"

"Happiness," I say, and smile sincerely. I look in her eyes and just keep on making it up. "Everything you want. All good things for you, Lara."

I hold her gaze a moment longer than is comfortable, then let her hand go. She gives a little start, like she's waking from hypnosis. It wasn't anything like that though. It felt more like a blessing. I don't know where it even came from.

"Order for me, would you," I say, while she's still looking slightly confused. "I've got something in my eye."

I barely manage to get up from the table. The room spins and threatens to wash out in gray. The pain has been mounting since we met on the street, and I feel like a volcano about to blow. I weave my blurry way between the tables and chairs and into the toilet, where I flip down the lid and slump on the seat.

Tears leak from my eyes. I can't take this. It hurts too much. I'm out there talking nonsense, and the darkness doesn't help. I feel like I'm going to throw up. How can I eat like this, when I'm so far from hungry?

I drop to my knees on the toilet floor and rest my head against the wall. I squeeze my eyes tightly shut and wish for an angelic host to come beaming down through Rien's roof and airlift me out. That would be awesome.

Then as if in answer to my prayer, my phone buzzes in my pocket. I barely know what I'm doing, but I ease it out. I read the message.

I'm in the darkness, running. I just stood with Blucy for twenty minutes, doing nothing. The air is cool and the corridors are long. You're here with me, Amo. We're running this thing together. Our diviners are firing off like crazy, and we're getting it all. Potato dolls, plastic mop handles, Leatherman wrenches, whatever it calls for, we get it.

We can't be stopped. We're in this together. Breathe clear and get it done Amo. This thing is not going to take us both down with it. You out there and me in here, we have this.

I suck in a breath. Of course it's from Cerulean, that glorious bastard. I push out a breath and tap on my phone.

Sorely needed that. Thank you. Slumped in the
toilet freaking out. I'm going back in!!

The hammer in my head is still clanging and twingeing, but I can face it a little longer. I get up and brush down my knees, thankfully only dust. I wash my hands thoroughly. I go out.

She looks up brightly when I arrive. The mood feels different now; even I can sense it through the fog in my head. She's serious now in the same way she was flippant before.

"I ordered you mushroom spaghetti," she says. "Garlic bread. Are you OK?"

"I'm better now. Thanks for ordering, that sounds great."

We sit in companionable silence for a time, watching the light show. The video jockey is playing it understated, working ripples of color that threaten to become clear shapes but never quite do. Sometimes the images look like clay on a potter's kiln rotating, but with bumps bulging in and out in strange organic ways. The cat rumbles over and mews a Britney Spears song at us. We toss it scraps from our starter bread, which it hoovers up then continues on its way.

Our food comes and we eat, delicate dishes painted with dots and strokes of colorful sauce, more relaxed now. We talk about art and the décor of Rien, about life in New York, the subway, the orange blossoms, our parents, but there's an undercurrent to everything now, a lovely balance of comfort and tension that makes the pain in my head just manageable. This is promise.

She twirls a strand of dark hair idly round her little finger. Her bright white eyes fix on me a lot, and I like it. I reach my hand across the table, and after sipping her wine she lets hers drop to rest beside mine. I stroke her finger with my thumb. Heat zings between us, and we're both melting. These are the hormones that I'm not supposed to have, and they are electrifying.

We talk about ambitions and holidays we've been on. She likes taking long walks on the beach. I'd like to paint that. She'll make us a cup of coffee from hand-roasted beans when we come back. I'll paint that too. We get through starters and main. It fills me up, but I keep eating. She's looking at me differently now. Perhaps I've passed a test, but I don't know what. The bigger test is still coming. She brings it up when we've finished our bottle of wine.

"Are you going to show me, then?"

I smile and bring out my laptop, setting it on the table. One of the waiters comes to clear away our plates helpfully. I swizz the screen around.

"It's not such beautiful fare for dinner," I say. "Forgive that."

"I want to see."

I bring up the penultimate panel again, full-screen, then point to the right arrow on the keyboard. "You can click it."

She studies yesterday's panel for a long moment, the tower from above, the ruined city, then clicks, and studies the final page even longer. Finally she looks up at me.

"I get it," she says. "I like it."

She takes my hand. I did not expect that. And weirdly, instead of making the burn go up in my head harder, it takes a chunk off. I let out a gasp, as the weight starts to come loose. A great chunk of it is calving away like Arctic ice, terrifying and exhilarating.

"You lost someone," she says. "I understand that. I know what that's like, and what it's like to want them back."

I can't stop my eyes from welling up. The chunk of my pain falls into the water and is gone, leaving me paralyzingly free. I can breathe again.

I nod imperceptibly. I didn't just lose someone over a year ago, I lost everyone: my friends who couldn't understand why I was blanking their calls, my girlfriend who couldn't be with me in silence, my parents who stopped treating me like the adult son they were proud of and instead saw me as an invalid child to be treated with kid gloves, but most of all I lost myself. I lost who I was in the face of the twinges and the coma and the fear, but maybe that's somehow changing back now.

I take her hand in both of mine.

"It's just zombies," I say.

She laughs. There is emotion in her eyes too. Another chunk of pain and pressure starts to fall away. Is this my mind or my suffering, I don't know, but I dive into it. I lift her hand to my lips and kiss it gently. She gives a little gasp.

"Let's skip dessert," she says.

I leave money on the table. We hurry down the streets together. We kiss on the subway, at first tender but growing passionate and hungry. I don't know what is happening to me. Everything really is changing. I run my fingers through her curly hair and she whispers in my ear something about colors and lust. The street rolls by and the tenement block comes and goes, then we're in my room and moving as one, and the last of the walls of pain that have barred me in for so long come tumbling down.

I hold onto her and she holds onto me, both undergoing our own transformations. She is lovely and deep as an ocean. Perhaps I am something the same for her, two lost souls crossing in the dark of the fulfillment center, finding fulfillment in each other's embrace.

I kiss her ear. She presses hard against me. We move together like the waves, in urgent rhythmic motion.

That night the apocalypse strikes.

APOCALYPSE

4. OUTSIDE

I wake up a new man.

It's hard to describe the feeling lying on the rumpled sheets with Lara pressed against my side. Faint morning light is filtering in through the blinds on the skylight, there's a tingling sensation all across my body, and the constant sense of pressure in the back of my mind is gone completely.

I can't believe it. It feels like an extension of a dream into wakefulness.

I get up slowly, rolling my body forward. No customary warning twinge comes as the first stimulation of the day rolls in. I rub my eyes but no pain awakens there. I feel good. It's a miracle.

I turn. In the dim light Lara behind me looks beautiful with her curly hair spilled across the pillow. She mumbles something and snuggles into the covers.

I sit on the side of the bed and run a hand over my head. It's still all there; no brain-shaped chunks have come out in the night. I don't know what is going on. Has sex saved me when it should have damned me? That was anything but clinical.

I pick up my pants, crumpled on the floor nearby, and fish out my phone. The charge is down, but there's a message topmost in the notifications from Cerulean.

                Are you even alive? Call me!!

There are a few missed calls on Skype too. I chuckle, then plug the phone into the charger and roll smoothly to my feet. He's being dramatic, and eager for gossip. Another half an hour won't kill him. I put on my clothes, socks and shoes, and go to the door.

Down through the building I emerge into the street. It's quiet at this early hour, and there's a chill in the air; 143rd street near Willis, overlooking the scrubby dry Willis playground, just a few streets over from the Mott Haven historic district. There are cars on the road but none of them are moving, stopped by traffic probably. I duck into my hoodie, tuck my hands in my pockets, and stroll down the sidewalk. My breath makes clouds of steam in the air.

At any minute I'll wake up. I can't stop thinking it. I focus on my feet. If my feet are still here, it has to be real. Clomp clomp they go, clomping along the sidewalk. The twinges will hit at any minute, I'm sure.

I round the corner onto Willis, crossing in front of the neighborhood bodega. The lights are on inside, with stacks of Bud Lite in crates in the window, but I don't see anyone come for their morning swig. The awnings are up so they're open, probably in the back getting stock.

I go by. A shorthaired terrier is shivering tied by the leash to a newspaper box. He looks at me plaintively as I pass. I figure I'll buy an extra croissant and hand it to him. Do dogs like croissants? All this is unreal.

I reach the coffee shop, a 24-hour Starbucks, and push through the glass door. It's not a patch on Sir Clowdesley inside; there's no stacks of donated threadbare books, no warm feel of a weird little community, it's all so corporate.

I go to the register and scan the blackboard in back for prices. They usually put the decaffeinated somewhere tricky in the corner, surrounded by swirly chalk effects like they're trying to disguise it. Dare I go with a regular latte, or is that courting disaster?

I lean on the bar. The barista must be out back checking something too. Only the low whine of an air conditioning unit circulating hot air breaks the stillness. I survey the place; it's empty too. Not a soul. I see a few haphazard coffees spread around on tables, the nearest one half-drunk.

This is getting weird.

"Hello?" I call.

No answer comes. I walk along the bar, looking for a bell, but there is none. I shout, "Hello" again but nobody answers. Maybe they've all gone out for a bit, maybe a cigarette break, en masse, out the back?

My heart speeds up. One possibility leaps to mind.

I exit the coffee shop and jog out into the street. I see it now, where before I was too dizzy to really notice. The few cars have actually stopped, flat in the road and not at the traffic light, some lilted at weird angles like they were haphazardly pulled over. None of them are moving, and there's no one in them. Across the road a BMW with gold hubcaps has gone through the window of 'Billy Ray's' pawnshop. Its taillights flash on and off soullessly.

Normally this much would set me twingeing hard, but I'm still in the clear. I look all around, studying the unkempt bushes of Willis playground, the windows of studio apartments on the redbrick tenements' first floor, but there's no sign of anybody.

Nobody's here.

My mind races. Could I have slept through some kind of terrorist attack, and everybody has fled? Sweat prickles down my back, and through unconscious habit I start to count back from one hundred, but still no twinges are coming. This has to be a dream, and I don't like it anymore.

I start to run.

"Hello!" I shout as I jog south down Willis toward the bridge. "Anybody?"

I think I see a glimmer of movement behind a curtain on a second story apartment but it's gone. There may be figures in the park, but when I try to focus on them they blur away amongst the trees.

I blow into the intersection with 142nd panting hard, and see the wreckage of a car accident just round the corner. A blue Chevy saloon is resting at a crazy angle on its roof, its front all dented in, next to a yellow bulldozer in the middle of the road. I reconstruct the impact in my mind, following the sparkling pattern of smashed glass and black skid trails burnt onto the road.

Smoke gushes up through the car's chassis, and there's a strange scratching sound coming from nearby. I look up and down 142nd, where normally there are people chatting and strolling, reading papers, checking their phones, but now it's empty but for more abandoned cars. They are scattered randomly across the four-lane blacktop, several crashed into each other, some nudged into walls, one punched through the window of the Halal meat place.

Smoke rises from them in near silence.

My mouth is dry. I can hear the click of the traffic light overhead, shifting in and out of sync with the scratching from the upturned Chevy. I notice I'm standing in the middle of the intersection, but no traffic is coming. The road is jammed with cars and trucks left like slaughtered buffalo on the plains.

"Somebody help," I shout, but nobody replies. I'm alone.

I run to the Chevy and round to the driver's side, waving through the thick black smoke that fogs around it. I lean closer and my eyes sting, but I can pick out a figure on the asphalt, trying to drag itself free from the driver's side window. There's broken glass on the ground and a dark puddle of what must be blood or oil spreading around him; a guy in a blue denim shirt with long brown hair. He's pulling to get out and the scratching sound must be the seatbelt tearing.

"Hang on," I call to him, "I'll get you out."

He looks up. His eyes are so pale through the smoke I think I'm looking into balls of ice. The pupil at the center is dark but the iris is drained of all color. It freaks me out. His jaw wags and blood spills down his chin.

"I'll get you out," I call again, though I can barely breathe in the smoke. I press my sleeve up to my face, squint my eyes tightly shut, and plunge closer. I get my hands on the guy's arms, in his hot wet armpits, and pull. I lean my weight all the way back and drag on him. His hands patter helplessly off my thighs but he doesn't come free. The scratching sound gets louder.

It must be the seatbelt. I contemplate ducking in and trying to clip him out, but he's so close already, and I don't like the way the car's starting to tick. We have to get clear. His head nuzzles against my knee. I put one foot up against the car body and tug with all my strength.

There's a sharp ripping sound, like Velcro unzipping, and he comes free. I stagger back with him trailing in my arms, so much lighter I can't regain my balance. I fall hard and smack my butt firmly on the concrete, dropping the guy at the outer reach of the smoke.

"Shit," I cry, rolling over. My whole butt's gone numb, I must've twanged my coccyx, and now my legs have gone trembly. I get onto my knees and shout to the guy.

"Are you OK?"

I see his weirdly white eyes emerge from the smoke first. There's blood running out from under his hairline and down his pale gray cheek and chin, staining his shirt. He's crawling to me on his chest, hand over hand, dragging himself near.

It comes to me as a cold flash that he's got no legs. I double-take, thinking maybe he's a veteran or a diabetic, maybe he never had legs, but now he's over halfway out of the smoke I can see the trail of black blood oozed out behind him like a slug trail. His legs were there but they're gone. I blanch, get to my shaky feet, and back up.

"What the hell…?" I mutter.

He keeps crawling. I back up more. He has no legs and no pelvis either. His lower body is wholly gone, ending at a ragged line across his middle, like torn chicken meat. A lump of flesh spits out of his open belly and straggles behind on a strand of purple gut like a sad little kite. I gag. I take another step back, but still he's crawling toward me.

"Hey buddy," I say, pointing with a trembling hand at the organ he's left behind. It looks like a crushed pink ping-pong ball. "You left, uh…"

I stop talking. His blood is everywhere. I finally get what just happened; I tore him apart. He was sawing himself through the window and I finished the job. Now he's coming for revenge.

"Holy shit," I blurt, as he snatches up at me with his bloody hand. I bat it away and take another step back. "Buddy look, I'm sorry, I didn't know."

It is a ridiculous thing to say. He's still coming. It isn't possible; it has to be a dream.

He's a goddamned zombie.

I walk backward and he follows, like some messed up waltz. For each step I take he lurches closer. I watch with sick fascination as more guts unspool from his belly. Of course I've seen this a million times before, in movies and TV shows and in my own comics. It looks really realistic, is all I can think. The words 'great special effects' roll numbly through my mind.

About twenty yards back, the Chevy bursts into flames.

The blast wind smacks my face and flutters my clothes, but it doesn't throw me through the air. The door does fly though, scything like a Krull blade and cleaving the guy in two like sour cheese, before taking off and pinging away over my shoulder. Fire singes my eyebrows and something punches me hard in the arm and I go down.

Shit. I roll back to my feet and see the car's indicator lever sticking out of my shoulder. It is actually stuck into my left shoulder. The zombie half-man is still nearby, grappling toward me with his one good arm. He's left the other one behind, along with all his spools of gut, slit diagonally apart by the door.

I stagger back in shock, looking at the indicator lever sticking out of me. There's blood running wetly down my chest and belly, darkening my hoodie. What the hell? Dizzy ideas come through the fog, that maybe I should push it left, push it right.

Click click.

I yank it out. It comes easily, looks like a screwdriver in my hand, then I drop it. It hits the concrete and rolls. The guy is using his jaw now to propel himself closer. His head bobs up and down like a swimmer going under for breath.

"I mean," I start to say, though I have no idea what I mean to say. The car is burning hard now, with fire rising high, and the chassis has ruptured and warped. "Just a second."

I stumble away from the burning wreck. Twenty feet clear I realize I'm limping and stop. My legs are fine. My left hand is clamped to the indicator-wound but there's hardly any blood coming now. Smoke is drifting finely everywhere. Something catches my eye, and I see a jumbo jet spiral out of the sky.

I track it from high up, spinning like a ninja's shuriken star. The wings tear off and the fuselage breaks apart so it descends in pieces, raining seats, engine parts, and bodies. They're wriggling like maggots. Fire breaks out from a sputtering engine before it falls beyond my field of view, behind the redbricks to the south somewhere near the bridge to Manhattan.

BOOM.

The blast shakes the ground though it was at least a mile away. A fireball rises briefly above the 'Pimpin Ridez' moped shop.

The zombie half-man is nearly at me again. His trail of blood is so full and thick I can barely believe he's got anything left inside to drive him on. Put a shell on his back and he would be a grotesque snail.

I snap myself out of it and start running back down Willis Avenue, toward the bridge to Manhattan. Zombie apocalypse or no, there could be survivors. I dodge around cars, trucks, and motorbikes left driverless. In glimpses down intersections at 141st and 140th I see a maze of vehicles in disarray, some burning, some upturned. A few buildings are on fire too, but there are no wails of fire trucks drawing near.

As I pass through 139th I look to the sky expecting to see F1s or Stealth Bombers closing in, at least helicopters, but there's only the corkscrewing contrails of the plane that fell.

I cover half a mile in five breathless minutes, emerging past barren Pulaski Park to the Harlem riverside like a cork popped from a bottle, to survey the Mott Haven bridgehead to Manhattan.

The Upper Manhattan skyline is on fire. Black smoke rises from many points, forming a miasma that hangs over the city like cigarette fog in a jazz bar. Several of the nearby skyscrapers, bland buildings that aren't famous, have been damaged. There is a visible gout missing in the top corner of one, and something is burning on the upper floors of another. It looks like the city has been sacked by barbarians.

I shake myself and look across the bridge. A chunk of the white support scaffold has ruptured, and the railing beneath it has been swept away, leaving trailing metal fenders pointing down toward the Harlem River. The falling plane must have hit it like a bomb.

There are chunks of fuselage and wing hanging amidst the scaffold like garish Christmas decorations, while other pieces of wreckage lie spread over the blackened asphalt, some of them belching thick black smoke.

And there are zombies. My jaw drops. They cover the bridge like sand on a beach, a herd of hundreds doddering step by step toward Manhattan. A horrible resurgence of my artwork rises in my head. Are they going for the clouds? Are they going to form up into a tower and reach for the skies?

They see me. One by one they turn their ice-white eyes on me. I hold up my hands like I'm pacifying an ornery drunk, as if that will somehow help. "Just a second," I actually say.

They start running. Their bodies flex and lope expertly, and damn fast. Some of them sprint.

I turn tail and sprint back up Willis. Intersections flash by with the thunder of their stampede gaining behind. Am I really running from a zombie horde? Back past 140th I toss a glance over my shoulder; leading the pack is a guy in a three-piece suit, splattered with dark blood. Yes I am.

I break stride for a second to reach into my jeans for my phone, but of course it isn't there, I left it to charge. I remember Lara, she's in my apartment now. Shit.

I crank up the speed. I vault over the bonnet of a red Porsche jammed in headlight-to-trunk with a garbage truck. I dodge round another crawler on the ground. I run up the hood of a beat-up old Volkswagen and down the other side.

The Subway station passes by on my right. On 141st I hit the southern edge of Willis Playground. I pass back through the intersection on 142nd and pinpoint my snail-zombie from his bloody trail. I jump over his head. This is ridiculous. My breath comes hard but my legs feel good, and the lack of a twinge still is amazing.

The last stretch to 143rd and my apartment passes in a blur. I wheel left at the bodega and I'm back on my street, with the lead guy maybe fifty yards behind me.

I hit my tenement with the keys already in my hand. I jiggle them into the lock and dive into the hallway, slamming the door behind me. I stand for a second panting in the hallway.

It is so quiet in here it freaks me out. Then the door takes a massive thump as the guy's body hits it. I literally jump in place. I cast about me for something to reinforce the door with. This hall is so empty! There's an ancient dark pipe running round the skirting board into a heavy metal radiator mounted on the wall, but that's no use at all. There are shelves filled with the owner's chintzy bric-a-brac, the kind of Delft doggies and Portmeirion plates we sell in our fulfillment center. There's a mirror, there's three doors leading off the corridor, and there's a little side-table and a chair.

THUMP.

The door rocks again and that must be the next in line. It's followed by a steady drumbeat as more bodies pound on the door. How long can it hold? I grab the side-table and push it up haplessly against the door. It looks utterly forlorn, far too small and light to do more than perhaps keep a cat out.

I grab the chair and stack it next to it, but that will do little more. I get frantic as more bodies impact, and the smacking of their dead white flesh on the wood becomes a hailstorm. They'll pummel the door from its brackets in moments, I'm sure.

I go to the first door on the right, the owner's flat. She must have furniture I can use, a sturdy chest of drawers or something.

I try to kick the door open but fail. My foot hurts from the impact. I try again, growing more frantic as the hailstorm becomes a thunder. How many zombie body battering rams can my door take? I kick again, then throw my shoulder into it, before I remember the landlady keeps a key under the rug. I drop to one knee and flip up the frayed Persian and voila, key. I open it up.

The door leads directly into a dark and dank living room full of heaps of junk stacked high to the ceiling; a hoarder's paradise. It smells of moldy plaster and old newspapers, likely because there are tall piles of newspapers and magazines tied in coarse string bundles filling the room like pillars.

This is my salvation. I grab a heavy block of newsprint in each hand and carry them down the hall to stack at the door. It is weirdly reminiscent of building with blocks in Deepcraft. I make ten frantic trips more and build a wall of solid paper bricks three wide and seven high in the entrance hall.

My chest heaves up and down with panting, but at least the thumping from outside is muffled now. Will it hold? It might. If it's anything like as strong as the door to the landlady's room, it will. Either way I'm hanging by a thread.

Lara.

I run up the stairs. Any day of the last year I would have been collapsed on the floor disabled by twinges, but today I feel vital and alive. On the top floor I shuffle the key out and jiggle my room open, then step back into familiarity.

It's almost quiet up here, with the thumping four stories distant. My room's soothing smells are on the air; green tea, bolognese, fresh sheets, but Lara is not here. I look to the bed, to the desk, even out the window, but she isn't here.

"What the hell…" I mumble.

In her place the bed has been made and there's a note lying on the pillow, written in neat handwriting. I snatch it up and read it three times.

> ```
> I had a great time. You have my number. Good luck
>          with the zombies. Lara. xx
> ```

I sag to the bed and laugh. This is utterly crazy.

My phone rings. I pick it up and see it's an incoming Skype call from Cerulean, with a history of thirty-three missed calls. I've had his number for all these past six months, but we've never actually spoken.

I slap answer and hold it to my ear.

5. PHONE

"Cerulean," I say into the receiver, "holy shit, Cerulean you're alive."

A moment passes and he says nothing, during which time I feel like I'm falling, then his voice comes through, weak and high.

"Amo?"

"It's me, I'm here, shit I saw your message earlier, I thought you were talking about the date then I went outside and damn, it's been crazy, the girl's gone, the whole city's been turned to zombies, what the hell is going on?"

"Amo," he says again, his voice getting clearer now, a deep Midwestern drawl. "I'd just about given up, I've been calling and texting you for hours. You say you went outside?"

I take a deep breath. Abruptly tears start coursing down my face. Shit, this is Cerulean, and it's our first time to talk.

"The twinges are gone. I went out to get coffee and the world's gone crazy. They're everywhere. They chased me up and down Mott Haven. Planes were falling from the sky, New York is burning. What's going on?"

"Calm down. Amo, I know. I've been watching it all night, it started around midnight and it spread across the country in hours. They were calling it a disease vector carried on the gulfstream, until it got them too and most of the news outlets went out. Twitter went down while they were trying to evacuate, but most people were at home asleep in their beds. The whole country's gone down, I'm surprised the internet is even up still, phone service and texts went down hours ago. I thought I'd call you until my uplink went dead, and then..." he trails off.

I stifle my tears and stare wide-eyed out the window.

"The whole country's gone down?"

"They're all zombies, Amo. This thing is instantly virulent, one breath and you're infected. You've seen them so you know. I saw them on the news; there were videos up on YouTube before that went down too. A few websites are still working, so I Googled everything I could find and downloaded it to our shared drive on your computer. You'll need to know this stuff, I've got reams on the prepper lifestyle, survival tactics and strategies, how to make weapons and how to find weapons, how to rig a generator and hotwire a car, siphoning fuel from a station, all that kind of stuff. It's good I did because Wikipedia has just gone down, I guess they didn't get enough donations."

He gives a scrappy laugh. I'm struggling to catch up with everything he's saying. My heart's still pounding from the run.

"What are you talking about? Cerulean?"

He takes a deep breath. "Amo, I'm cured too. The twinges are gone and I'm thinking clearly. I'm not a zombie, but everyone else is. You said everyone you saw in New York is a zombie? They're all zombies, as far as I can tell. Now you need to survive."

"Sure, but-" I begin then trail off. There's something missing. "What about you?"

He laughs. "My brain got better but I'm still a cripple, buddy. Where do you think I'm going to go? I'm busting for a piss but is my mom going to come down and take me to the toilet? More likely she'll come down and tear out my throat. She's banging on the basement door even now, she's been at it all night, her and a few dozen others. It sounds like they're pulling up the floor overhead, actually."

"What the-" I start. "She's a zombie?"

I can hear him smiling. God I love Cerulean. That fit, handsome, paraplegic bastard. His mom's upstairs coming for him and he's been calling me all this time, trying to save me. "Of course she is, and it's not to bring me a batch of midnight cookies."

I get to my feet, deciding instantly. I look around the room taking stock of what I'll need. "Where are you? I have your address here somewhere. I'll come get you. I'll get you out."

He laughs softly. I picture the only Cerulean I've ever seen images of on Google, the dark young man on the dive platform or the medal stand, full of confidence and in his prime, ready to take on the Olympics and the world and make them his own. "Don't be silly, Amo. You'll never get here in time. The basement door's been iffy for years; it won't take much longer for them to get down here. They'll come through the floor in a day or two anyway. Don't worry about me, I've got a syringe here and I know what to do with it."

The blood drains from my head and I go dizzy. I'm still looking round my room urgently, like there might be an answer here when there cannot be.

"What do you mean, you've got a syringe?"

"It's all right," he says. "Sit down. Are you somewhere safe, Amo? Are you in your room, are you barricaded in?"

"I don't-" I begin, then look at the door. I can hear them thumping faintly from downstairs. "I'm in the tenement. I blocked up the front door, but there's probably hundreds of them out there now. I don't-"

"Block up your room," he says. "Do it now. Wedge the bed against the door, wedge something against that if you can. They're not smart but they're persistent, and you're in no state to take to the streets again. You need to lie low and get your head straight, Amo, if you're going to get through this. Do you hear me?"

"I-"

"Deadbolt the door and wedge it in. Use everything you've got. Do it right now. I'll still be here. Put the phone on speaker and do it now. I want to hear it happening."

I take the phone from my head and stare at it blankly for a moment. I don't know what I'm supposed to do.

"Amo!"

I remember and click the button for speaker. I hear the distant sound of Cerulean's home somewhere in the Midwest filter into my New York apartment. There is his breathing and the sound of an air conditioning unit, circulating round the cement basement that's been his prison cell since the incident.

I shake myself and look to the bed, then the door, and start moving to bring them together. The bed drags noisily out of the recessed wall. I push its headboard flush against the door. The board is a metal lattice that reaches three quarters up the height of the door, so even if one of the zombies get in the house and successfully punch a hole through the door, they'll still have to get over the headboard's metal slats.

"I've done the bed," I shout to Cerulean. "I'm getting the desk."

"Good. Don't damage your computer, you're going to need that."

I lift my monitor carefully off, then drag the desk to the tail of the bed. Laid end on, it fits almost perfectly between the bed and the wall, wedged into place. It's going nowhere. They'd have to bend the bed's metal frame or push it through the wall to get in, and I don't see either of those happening. That's more force than human bodies can muster.

I drop to the floor by the side of the bed and start to shake.

"I've done it," I say to the phone, turning it off speaker mode and holding it back to my ear.

"Good, good. Now you need to relax. We can talk about something that really matters. How did your date with the Tomb Raider girl go?"

I laugh beside myself. I scratch at the wooden floor with a fingernail.

"It went fine. It went great. She came back here, but she's gone now. The note she left Cerulean, it's mad."

"Call me Robert," he says. "That's my name."

More tears pour down my cheeks. "I know. OK, Robert."

"Are you crying? Come on old buddy. Pull yourself together. It's not the end of the world. Just the end of most of it. You said she's gone?"

I laugh. I rub my eyes. "I don't know. I think so, yes she's gone. She left a note, it said 'Good luck with the zombies'. She was talking about the comic, but Christ, look at this shit Cerulean. I mean Robert. Where the hell is she now?"

"Probably running halfway down Manhattan, if she's not already infected. Calm your ass down, Amo. What are you going to do for her now? She'll either get safe or she won't, on her own. You're lucky you're alive. You know how many people out there who're immune? Do you have any idea?"

"No idea. I didn't see any. Maybe her?"

"Maybe her. On top of that there's me and there's you. I've not seen any others, Amo, not any at all. Every live video feed I saw got corrupted in seconds, because the people filming it were infected. It's the most virulent thing ever. It's like that cat in the box, the second you open the box to see if it's alive or not, it drags you in so you're inside the box too. There's no time to report out."

I laugh through my tears. "Schrodinger's cat. I don't think that's how it works."

"Whatever. Listen Amo, it can't be a coincidence that it's me and you, and maybe her. Did she have the same condition as us, did she have a coma then recover like us?"

I wince as I try to recall. "She said she burned out. I don't think she was twingeing though. I don't think so."

"Well maybe you'll find out. Perhaps proximity to you conferred immunity. I'm pretty sure we're immune, Amo, because whatever is hitting them now hit us a year ago. Do you follow? Some lesser strain hit us, but it acted like a vaccine, so now we're safe. We went blank, we died multiple times, but they brought us back. Maybe if we hadn't been brought back, we'd be like these others out on the streets now. We got saved."

I shudder. I'm grasping at straws now.

"You're alive," is all I can say.

He laughs. "I am."

We sit in silence for a while. My room comes back to me. I look up at my Banksy picture, the guy throwing the flowers. I wonder, is Banksy a zombie now too? Is Space Invader?

"I can come for you," I say. "I'll get a nice car and make it there in a day. I'll drive all night."

"That's a lyric from a song isn't it?"

"Stop it! Tell me your address and I'll come."

"No you won't. Why in hell would you come here Amo, to see my bitten-out corpse laid up in a bloody cradle stinking of methadone and shit? I'll not have that. I won't be alive by then, Amo. Understand that. Accept that, and we can move on. I've downloaded everything I can think of to your computer, plus a few extras I've had the time to come up with. The fulfillment center will be a bit different. I think it's going to be pretty important to you, going forward, or for a while at least. There are some new routines. You'll figure it out. Until then we can talk."

I sag. "I want to come."

"I want you to come too. Don't you think I'd love that, if you could come charging in now and rescue me from this mess? But you can't. It's not going to happen, so let's move on. We've never even spoken before, have we? Hi, Amo, I'm Robert. I'm a freak just like you. We might be the last two people alive in the world."

I laugh. "Hi Robert, I'm Amo. It's good to meet you. I don't want you to die."

"So tell me about the date," he says. "Tell me everything."

I do. It starts off jerky and unclear, but soon I'm rolling. He laughs as I pull the move inspired by Hank on her. He goes quiet when I bring her home. He listens while I pull the guy apart out on Willis Avenue.

"It's a good memory, on the whole," he says. "You'll need to hang on to that, Amo. You will, won't you? She might be alive out there. You might be able to find her. Hold on to that. You'll put out some flags and let her now where you are. You'll figure this thing out and make it right. I know you will. You've always been resourceful, and smart, and so damn charming."

I laugh.

"It's good you can laugh. Don't forget that Amo. Don't you dare feel guilty. I want it to be you, not me. You're a good man. You're the best friend I've ever had. I want you to get good things out of this and become better for it. There's always room to grow. When I lost my legs and I knew I could never dive anymore, I just about gave up. Then I found this weird guy who'd built a weird mod on Deepcraft, and he welcomed me in. He loaned me a diviner and we fulfilled stupid orders together. I saw the world through him, and I'm still seeing the world through him now. Amo, you're going to be OK."

I find I'm gulping at the air.

"Get yourself solid. Research the stuff I sent. Find a safer place than your apartment, a bank or something downtown, something this girl Lara can find, and start clearing the streets around. Make a base and she'll be drawn to you, Amo, if you're offering safety and something worth having. That way you'll find the others too, the ones like us who are lost somewhere across the country and don't have each other like we've had each other. I know you will. You'll make good things out of this."

I gulp back tears. I can hear the thumping through the phone getting louder.

"She's almost through the door isn't she?"

"She is. It's all right. I've got the syringe loaded with my methadone, enough of a dose to knock me right out. I won't feel a thing. It's better this way Amo. I wouldn't stand a chance on the road. I was never good in a wheelchair."

I sob into the phone. "How long?"

"I don't know. A minute, maybe five? I've already injected it." His voice starts to go woozy. "You'll stay on the line won't you? You'll wait with me."

"Of course I will. Robert I'm sorry."

"Don't be sorry. You're here with me. We're in the fulfillment center, running it together. I've got legs again, Amo. We're keeping up with the orders. We're one step ahead."

The tears are coming freely. I hate this. I want to reach through the phone and save him. I want to save my friend, but I can't.

"Goodbye, Amo," he says fuzzily. There is a crash through the line, and his mother must have breached the basement.

"Robert," I say urgently. "Robert."

"She's coming. I won't feel a thing. The darkness is so close. I'm going to turn the phone off now Amo. I don't want you to hear this. Goodbye."

The phone clicks dead. The sound from his distant basement fades at once. My last link to Cerulean is severed.

I lean back against the bed and cry, curled around the phone like it's a dagger thrust though my belly. I have just lost everything and everyone I love.

6. ESCAPE

I come back to myself and it's bright still, with early spring light glowing in through the skylight right onto my face. I don't hear the zombies, they're not banging on the downstairs door. I look up at the sky and wonder if it could all truly be a dream.

I don't have a headache, no twinge at all. That is a wonder I can't help but be glad for. At least Cerulean had that too, in his final hours. At least we got to speak.

I look at my phone. It's not even mid-day, I guess I slept for only an hour or two. In the corner there are no signal bars, but the Wi-Fi symbol is still there. I click through to the Internet but the pipeline is empty and I get missing server messages. I click through each of my tabs on the phone methodically, social media, email, news, and they all erase themselves away.

Perhaps I'll never see them again. Pushing the back button in the browser doesn't recapture them. The Internet is gone.

I double click the button and the phone pings.

"Hi Io," I tell the screen. Io is the name I've given my phone's generic AI assistant. Io and Amo, it was a kind of lame joke, I suppose.

"Hello Amo," she says.

"My friend just died. His name was Cerulean."

"I'm sorry to hear that."

"Me too. Now the whole world's gone to shit."

"That sounds difficult."

I laugh. "Yeah. But Lara might be alive. I don't know where she's gone though."

"I hope you find her, Amo."

I put the phone down. I need to think clearly.

I get to my feet and go to the window.

The street is filled with zombies. Seeing this is like an ice water shower. There are hundreds of them, all pale-faced with bright white eyes looking up at me. It chills my blood. They don't groan or rasp, they just stare. I open the window and I can hear them breathing, like a lapping tide. They jostle and sway like bits of wreckage caught on a wave.

I hold my hand out like the Pope giving benediction. Their ice-white eyes track me. It makes me feel dizzy and I step back. I drop to the bed and the springs crunch comfortingly. Lara's note is still there.

Good luck with the zombies.

It's a good joke.

I sit there slackly for a while, adjusting. My art doesn't matter now. Nothing really matters, now that everyone is dead. There's no sound from the city; no rescue helicopters are coming, because they're all gone. Cerulean saw it, and it's really over, the zombie apocalypse.

Lara though may be alive. I have to find her. That thought gets me up and moving.

First I need to prepare. My shoulder throbs where the indicator lever hit me, so I'll deal with that. I pull back my shirt to study the wound. It's capped by a stud of dried blood, which I nudge away. The hole beneath is puckered and sealed already, with only a slight red ring of inflammation. I rub it gently; it feels OK. I rotate my arm and it works well enough. I put two sticky bandages on top and call it a day.

Next I go to my computer on the floor, and swizz the mouse. The soft chime as it wakes up comforts me, telling me the power grid isn't down, though it probably will be soon.

I open the shared drive with Cerulean and survey the contents he downloaded. It was less than a gigabyte of stuff before, mostly texture maps and crafting patterns, but now it's packed to the gills and close to its hundred-gigabyte limit.

I scroll through the contents and find a mish-mash of html webpages, pdfs, videos and books about the 'prepper' lifestyle; people who spent their free time preparing for a coming cataclysm.

Judging from the titles they are mostly about basic survival; securing sources of food and water, finding and reinforcing shelter, sourcing weapons and using them in combat against 'hostiles', sourcing power and fuel and using these to employ vehicles, computers, walkie-talkies and so on. I notice that preppers like the word 'source' a lot.

I go to the desk and pluck out five thumb-drives, which I use all the time to back up my art. I slot them in to the computer and set the contents downloading. The prepper Bible needs to be portable.

The computer says it'll take at least an hour. I slump back against the bed, and a sound comes from beyond the door as if in response.

I freeze. I look. The door is sealed but the sound is still coming, a wheezing right outside my room. Is that…?

My blood goes cold. I listen to the low susurrus of breath rise and fall like one giant lung. I get up quietly and go to the door, then lean over the bed and put my eye to the spyglass.

Holy shit. They are in the corridor, packed five wide all the way back to the stairs, so tightly they can't move, like wieners in a vacuum-packed casing.

I jerk away. I back-pedal across the room until I hit the wall.

I'm trapped.

I make green tea.

It's gratifying that the kettle still works. I spoon green dust that smells like freshly mown grass into the cup, and pour boiling water atop it. The smell of bitter tannins wafts into the room, and I hold the cup in my shaking hand. There is solace in such routines, even though my brain may no longer need them to survive. They've saved me before, and they can save me now.

I'm barely even thirsty, but I sip anyway. I try to think about practicalities objectively, one at a time. I look at my phone; it's 11:33. Plenty of daylight left. Wherever Lara is it can't be that far.

I need to plan. I bring up my phone and click the app for Jeo. My geo-location still works, though the map it's built upon doesn't refresh. I am a blue dot in the midst of the gray blur of New York, pointing southeast. Good to know.

I'm not hungry, but I make up a bowl of cornflakes with crisp cold milk. I'll need fuel. I sit on the bed and eat it, trying not to think of

Cerulean's voice on the phone. I try not to think of what remains of him now, in his basement.

I start making up a pack, adding my laptop, a kitchen knife, a water bottle, some clothes. What else do I really need? I add my comic, Zombies of New York, to the USB download tray, plus the latest build of the fulfillment center. I add my phone and laptop chargers like I'm packing for a trip.

The computer chimes, signaling the transfer is finished. I put the USBs in my pocket. I look at my bag and think about where I'm going to go. I think about Lara, and where she would go. I don't know anything about her, not really. Her folks live in upstate New York somewhere, but that could be anywhere. She lives in Brooklyn, but that could be anywhere too.

The computer blanks out abruptly. My phone chimes to say it's been disconnected.

The power's gone out. I toss the keyboard and mouse away, useless now. There's only one place I can go where she might conceivably be.

Sir Clowdesley. It helps that I'm still the mayor.

First I experiment. I smash the glass out of my window and toss mugs and plates down at the zombies' heads, but that doesn't do a damn thing. Mugs bounce off their heads in shards, and plates, no matter how hard I Frisbee them down, just buckle whichever one they hit for a few seconds.

Next I try my computer, contained within a 33" monitor. It's heavy, edged, and I won't need it anymore.

"Goodbye old friend," I tell it. I take aim and hurl it out the window. It hits a male zombie on the head corner-first, staving in his skull. There's a nasty crunch and he goes down bleeding. Then he comes right back up.

I feel nauseous. He's looking right up at me. He still looks like a person despite the gray skin and white eyes. He's dressed like a salesman with his tie neatly knotted at the throat. Now black blood discolors his white shirt.

I turn to the side abruptly dizzy. I just tried to kill someone. It doesn't seem to matter that he's already dead, I still feel sick. Is he even dead? Could be they'll all recover in a day or two, and I just tried to kill one of them.

I bend over and breathe heavily for a while. Shit. Perhaps I'm not cut out for murder with a monitor. The sweet scent of orange blossoms on the air only makes it worse. I pant until I'm feeling better.

At the least, I learned something. Caving in their skulls doesn't kill them. Good to know.

It's past two. I've got my bag and my USBs. It'll never be any easier or better a time than now. I survey my room a final time, then I move the chair beneath the skylight, push it wide open, and climb out onto the roof.

It's chilly here but sunny. The roof is red slate and thankfully dry, so I'm not slipping on moss. The zombies start to breathe harder down below. From higher up they look like an ocean of grayish heads. To the south the skyline of Manhattan rises over the blocks of tenements. Still there are no jets or helicopters in the air.

I have a loose plan, and for it this bit needs to be quiet, and fast. I slide awkwardly up to the roof's sloping crest, with my bag on my back. At the crest a line of stacked ceramic tiles runs like a monorail, which I hold onto as I pad along the roof, looking down into the square back yards behind each tenement house.

Three houses over I see the first parked motorbike, a black and chrome beast which is surely more than I can handle on a first outing. I've never ridden a bike before, plus there's no skylight into the garret for easy access, so I slide on. Two buildings further on there's a pastel green moped on a kickstand, much more my style, and a skylight in the roof.

I try to pry it open, and to my joy it's already unlocked. I peer in checking for zombies, but there are none. It's a rec room with a drum set in one corner and some workout weights in the other. I dangle in from the skylight frame, then drop to the carpeted floor with a soft thump.

Breaking and entering.

Remembering something from a movie I saw, I go to the weights. The dumbbell bars are just about right, and after I slide the weights off one, it fits in my hand perfectly as a club. I creep to the door and creak it open.

The corridor beyond is mercifully empty. The house smells like toasted bagels, and there's a large poster of Bob Marley's face on the wall. I tread lightly to the stairs and start down. The inhabitants like pictures of Bob Marley, and flowery wallpaper. I pass by four bedrooms, two for kids with the names of the inhabitants written on hanging signs.

Jemima

Janiqua

It's not a tenement then, but a single family. They must be rich. I hope they're all out. I pad down with my senses on high alert, straining for any sound. By the ground floor my heart is going crazy.

I pad over the tiled corridor toward the back yard. I open it up, onto a classy kitchen with a polished granite breakfast bar, bright plastic stools, and a full-length glass door through which I can see the moped in the yard. I start toward it, then see someone standing off to the left by the sinks, with his back to me.

"Uh," I say, involuntarily.

It's a guy in a bathrobe, with long dreads. He turns, and I see he's wearing blue pajamas beneath the open robe. His skin is a gray tan and his eyes are ice-white.

An awkward moment passes.

"I'll just," I start, perhaps intending to finish with 'let myself out,' but he doesn't give me the chance. With his robe fluttering behind him he charges.

"Shit," I mutter and try to get my dumbbell club up in the air. He hits me before I can bring it down and slams me back against the half-open door, which crashes shut with a juddery slam.

I try to bounce away but his weight pins me and his outstretched fingers claw off my hoodie, his mouth is open and for a second his cheek hits my cheek and I freak out completely, spinning a frantic elbow into the side of his head.

The force knocks him down to his knees, and I leap away and kick him in the head, the same way I'd kick out at a rat, not really wanting to touch it. I connect and his head whacks to the side but it does nothing but slow him briefly, and he keeps coming.

"Goddamn shit," I curse, because now my foot hurts and I'm penned in and all I've got is this damn metal club.

I bring it down on his shoulder, too squeamish to go for the head, and with a horrible crack his collarbone crumples in. He doesn't give a shit though, and rises to his feet smoothly, leaning in.

I drop my weight low and shove him in the breastbone as hard as I can. It's enough to send him tumbling into the bright stools at the bar. There's another crack as his skull bounces off the sharp stone edge, then there's blood pouring down his back and spreading across the floor.

My legs go weak. He's on his knees and I kick him in the chest, driving his head back into the marble again. He manages to snag my jeans leg with his hand, pulling me off balance. I bring the bar down on his forearm with all my strength. The heavy metal snaps through the bones like they were made of Graham crackers, and his arm distends like a marshmallow.

I feel like I might puke. He barely notices. He tries to use his broken arm to get to his feet and instead bends the bones back the other way against the floor. I gag as his now-useless appendage flops like a fish. He looks at it, pushes off the stub of forearm bone so hard it pierces the skin and blood starts coming out there too, and gets onto his feet.

He's like a Terminator. I kick him pathetically in the thigh and hit him again with the bar in the other shoulder. Another cracks rings out as his other collarbone snaps, and now both his arms sag uselessly at his sides. He gets to his feet with them dangling weirdly in front of him.

Shit shit shit, this is too messed up. I want to go back to my room. I notice he's wearing fluffy red slippers with faces on. It's too much. I back up frantically and he follows. His blood is everywhere now, dribbling down his neck and spilling out past the white knob of bone sticking through his forearm, puddling across the dark floor tiles.

I grab the kitchen door and plunge back through it, slamming it behind me.

The hall beyond is lit by a half-light cast through the glass by the front door. I stand with my back to the door, panting and holding tight to the handle, waiting for him to try and force it open. Of course he doesn't. He thumps and shuffles against the door like a zombie. His blood leaks underneath. He hasn't got any functioning hands to open the door with. He hasn't got the brain for it either.

Still, I don't let go of the handle, not even while I puke, not until one of his kids comes bounding down the stairs, Jemima or Janiqua or whatever, her ice-white eyes pinning me like a bug to the door.

7. RIDE

I can't do this.

I let go of the door handle and dart to the left as the little girl rounds the bottom of the stairs. I barrel through another door without a second to think and slam it hard behind me, shaking the walls with a loud bang.

How many goddamn zombies?

It's the living room, with two sofas facing each other, a big-screen TV at one end and a faux fireplace at the other, a coffee table, a big piece of Orwellian-looking art on the wall, and scrabbling around in the middle are two more of them.

Shit. Jemima/Janiqua thumps at the door behind me, her dad thumps in the kitchen, and now I'm looking at the mom and the other kid, and it's horrible. I should have stayed in the goddamned kitchen.

They've got crusty dark blood round their mouths, spattered with bits of purple and pink gut. The mess of it spreads to their throats, their hands, their forearms, dressed in pajamas both. The girl has a weird yellow cartoon character on hers, and there's a big splodge of quivery meat right on the creature's stupid yellow face. Their dark hair clings in ratty bands to their chins.

"Oh God," I murmur.

They look up at me. I crane my neck to see what they've been eating. On the floor, fouling the taupe carpet with its well-chewed red and black viscera, lies what looks like half a tortoiseshell cat.

I puke a little in my mouth. Now I see the clumps of brown and black fur sticking to their cheeks. Oh lord. They rear up and come for me, and I start moving. I get one of the sofas between them and me, and they circle round after me, thankfully both coming the same way, and I go round ahead of them.

Shitting ridiculous, is all I can think as we run round a second time, then a third, with them straining to reach me. I have to time it just right so they're both almost on me, or I risk having them come round both sides at once and pincer me.

I scour the room for a way out. The dumbbell bar hangs slackly in my hand, but I'm not doing that again. There's a dining room stretching out into a conservatory beyond the sofa, overlooking the yard, but I have just a few seconds lead time on them, not enough to open the door if it's locked.

I go round the sofa and they follow.

"Wait a second," I bark at them. It has no effect. "Jemima, Janiqua, mom, just wait a damn second!"

Nothing. I get it in my head that maybe I can herd them, and start planning how I'm going to shove the coffee table here and the sofa there, like constructing a maze, but I was never good at Tetris and I can't figure it.

We hit the fifth time round.

"Arrgh!" I shout, and break for the dining room. They follow. I hit the door with time enough to try the handle, of course it's locked, then I'm back to circling, this time round the gorgeous redwood dining table. They clatter after me, and I pull a chair out and tip it over.

The mom hits it hard in the shin and goes down, then the kid follows. It takes them a second to get back up. I use that time to throw another chair at them.

"Sit down!" I shout at them. "Just take a goddamned seat!"

The chair bounces off the mom's shoulder and she falls back, collapsing on her daughter. I throw another chair and another, shouting inane one-liners like, "Have a break, take a load off!" until all eight chairs are resting on them or either side of them.

A brainwave strikes and I shove the table sideways over them, pressing hard against the chairs and locking them skewed against the thick mahogany dresser against the wall, with the mom and daughter tangled up in them.

The Last

I stop and pant. I drop and look under the table. For now they're tangled in each other's limbs and the chairs, reaching out toward me still, but any second they'll break free.

I run to the living room, snatch up the coffee table and carry it back. I slide it under the table and press it up against the chairs as well. I drag the green sofa over too, pressing it flush against the head of the table and bracing in the chairs. I get the TV and press it in tightly above the coffee table. I throw cushions from the sofa to cover them up.

I stop and pant some more in the middle of the now-empty living room. I just made a zombie fort. The furry remnants of the cat stain the carpet by my feet. My dumbbell bar is there and I pick it up. The fort makes creaking sounds, but I don't think they can get free. Maybe they never will.

I creep past them to the back door. It's made of glass, and there's no key apparent. I cover my eyes and hit the glass with the bar. It bounces off and sends a jarring reverberation up my arm, so I hit it harder with a stabbing motion like I've seen on TV. It smashes. I open my eyes and pound, crack, and kick the rest of the glass through.

I step outside. Now I'm outside.

I look into the kitchen, where the father zombie with the broken collarbones is pressing up against the back door. His face leaves bloody smears on the glass. I can see his snapped right collarbone jutting up underneath his robe. I turn to the side and throw up again, hot and acrid.

To the moped. It's a beauty, sitting there on the brushed concrete, bright and limpid as a lily pad. Beside it there's a tiny work shed, a low bank of withered tomato plants, and a big plastic trunk spilling over with kid's toys. I go to the yard gate, slide open the bolts, and put my head out into the backstreet beyond.

Empty. That is a delicious sight. The alley runs left and right in cracked asphalt, at one end meeting Willis and at the other turning onto 143rd.

I duck my head back in and close the gate as quietly as I can. Probably it's only a matter of time before they find me. I dart back to the moped and pat down its front, finding the ignition keyhole right at the top of the front wheel's upright axle, set within a classy walnut bevel.

Of course there is no key. I don't have a clue how to hot-wire it.

At the kitchen window I press my face up close and look for the key. I scan the walls for little hooks, the sideboards for little dishes. The zombie father's face thumps against the glass in front of me, obscuring my view. What an ass.

I slide over and look, soon enough spotting the most likely candidate: a papier-mâché soap dish in the middle of the breakfast bar, within which a tangle of keys and chains lie.

The idea comes easily.

I tip up the yard toy box and carry it back into the living room. With one hand I open the door to the corridor beyond, and with the other I hold up the box. Little Jemima/Janiqua is standing there looking up.

I put the box on her head like I'm cheating at a carney game; dropping hoops over spikes in the back of a cruddy stall, then press down. Her legs give out and she crumples to the floor. I set the box on top of her and weight it down with the TV stand. She thumps but she's trapped.

I open the front door and look out. Hello, horde. They are crammed in to the right, still staring up at the roof of my building where they last spotted me. I look only long enough to see there's a bit of clear road between me and them, in front of the library, and maybe enough.

I jog back inside, open the kitchen door, then run. The dad lumbers awkwardly after me, his arms swaying like pendulums. I dash out the front door and he follows, out into the street in full view of the horde, where I wait for him to catch up.

Crazy. The horde notices me and members start to peel off at a sprint. Seconds remain before they hit me, and he's still barely clear of the door. I run at him then dart to the side, vaulting over the low green fence and cutting in behind him for the door.

I make it with seconds to spare and slam the door. They hammer against it and I run on, I've probably got moments only, so finding the key is essential. In the kitchen I snatch up the papier-mâché tray and splay the keys out onto the breakfast bar.

Smeared blood and crushed cornflake crumbs mingle on the counter top. I pick through the keys rapidly; house, house, shed, maybe car, another car, surely moped? It has a lime green fob the same color as the moped. I snatch it up, try the kitchen door and thank Buddha it opens. The thumping gets louder behind me and I sail through into the yard, closing the door behind me.

I straddle the moped and fumble to turn and waddle it to the yard gate. I fumble to get the key into the handsome slot. I fumble to open the yard-gate, backing up the moped to let it swing inward. I turn the ignition key, and just as a resounding crack comes from the front of the house, the engine revs into life.

It is the most beautiful sound I've ever heard. I squeeze the handle for gas hard and the moped takes out from under me like rocket, jetting off and throwing itself forward into the alley and me flat onto my back.

"Ugh," I say, as the wind smacks out of me. Sprinkly stars flood across my eyes, black beckons, and I dimly make out a throng of zombies running through the kitchen, to hammer up against the door.

The glass fractures like ice cracking. Dizzily I watch them, beating at the glass kitchen door just yards away.

They look so sad. Their faces and eyes are just dead. I feel like crying, that so many of them have become like this and there's nothing I can do but run.

"I'm sorry," I whisper, because I can't help them, and I'm going to leave the little girl in her box forever. The mom and daughter will stay in that fort until they rot and become trickles of mess on the carpet like their poor dead cat. The father will wander limp-armed around his own home with all his family lost, because of me.

A shard of glass skitters out of the door and hits the ground next to my face. That gets me moving. The glass door cracks outward and the flood pour through, drawing bloody stripes down their faces on the jagged glass.

I jerk to my feet and leap through the gate, slamming it behind me. The moped is thank god still revving on its side, and I pull it up, get on tentatively, and squeeze the handle just hard enough to sneak a squirt of gas into its firing chambers.

It picks up. I stay on. Together we spurt off in an amateurish zigzag down the alley, followed by a crash and a tide of zombies seconds later.

Jesus shitting Christ.

I burst out onto Willis like a bat out of hell, a good half-block ahead of my zombie comet trail. Turning south I zip past the right turn onto 143rd in a blink, briefly glimpsing the mob still flowing away from my apartment, then I'm gone and flying down the silent road, pushing sixty in a thirty zone.

I whizz through the intersection where the Chevy exploded; it's just a black and burnt-out skeleton now. The dark slug-trail of the guy I tore in half is still there but he's gone and so am I.

Wind whips in my hair, and I weave in and out of standing traffic. Yesterday this much stimulation would have killed me. I blink dust out of my eyes and focus on the road, already past 140th and closing fast on the Harlem River. There are a few zombies straggling through the intersections limply, a big guy in a brown jogging suit and a young girl wearing bright red spectacles with her hair up in a 70's bob. I swerve to pass them by. They pick up running after me, falling into my wake like jet skiers behind a speedboat.

I blast through intersection after intersection with no red lights to stop me, 139th, 138th past the gourmet deli where a food truck has knocked over a fire hydrant and there's a wide pond of brackish water.

137th, 136th, the streets pass by like postcards. Jutting out from the gas station on the corner of 135th a white semi-trailer truck lies halted across most of the road and I veer around it, only to drive almost directly into an old lady zombie. I bank hard and nearly throw myself from the moped, pulling to a stop on the hard shoulder.

I pause to catch my breath. Maybe a minute ago I was in the house and now I'm here. A tall tenement rises to the side and a flash of movement inside catches my eye. There, perhaps on the fifth floor, someone's banging against the glass. I study the building's façade and pick out more of them, trapped like prisoners in hundreds of stacked cells, looking out at me and hammering on the glass.

Can they see me? Seconds later the glass on one of the high-up windows goes out, falling like a spray of twinkling light, followed by a body. I catch flashes of a dark naked male, then he hits the cement with a disgusting wet thump. A second later he gets up, ruptured and bloody and with his neck broken at a hideous angle, and starts shuffling for me

More glass smashes. Bodies rain down from above like cats and dogs. The old lady hobbles closer. I rev the moped and race on, up onto the overpass by 134th. Pulaski Park whizzes by again, empty basketball courts baking in the morning sun, and I thump onto the bridge. There are no zombies milling here now, they're all at my house.

I veer around the tipped delivery truck and a few abandoned cars.

Halfway over, with a fresh salty breeze blowing down the river, I come upon the wreckage of the plane fuselage, lying across most of the road. The oval tube of the plane's body is blackened by fire.

A zombie child bursts out from behind a car and I yank the handlebars left. For a moment I think I'll go off the bridge where the railings have been scoured away, but I get the moped under control and race on, leaving the child running behind.

Scattered around the fuselage lies all manner of charred wreckage: narrow food trolleys spitting up plastic ready-meal trays, in-flight magazines like a drift of glossy snow, broken bodies, some of them crawling. There's a bank of seats tipped upside down, and zombie hands wave out from underneath like legs on a millipede. For a surreal second I imagine the bank picking itself up and coming hurtling after me, running on hundreds of zombie arms.

I angle for a slim gap between the fuselage and the edge of the bridge. I'm not getting off and creeping through on foot now; there's too many of them behind me. I duck low on the moped, rev the engine, and cut through the gap like Evel Knievel through a ring of fire.

Whoo!

The road is clear beyond. There are zombies, but I'm getting good at the moped now and evade them easily. I take it down off the bridge and onto 1st Avenue, into Manhattan proper. This is probably the stupidest thing I've ever done, driving into one of the most densely populated urban areas in the world, but whatever, I ride on. I flash briefly on Rick Grimes riding his horse into Atlanta and laugh.

I'm on an iron steed. A lime-green moped. When they make the movie of my life it will look pretty silly.

I squeeze the accelerator and accelerate south. The streets are nearly deserted here, but for a preponderance of eighteen-wheelers, and I figure the infection must have hit some time deep in the middle of the night for them to be so many of them, with so few commuters and so many people trapped in their houses still, wearing pajamas.

I speed under the green copper bridges on 125th and 124th, past a night bus, a cop car, the wreckage of a downed helicopter lying in a bonfire-like heap of shattered glass and twisted metal pilings, torn from the face of a nearby skyscraper.

Thomas Jefferson Park whizzes by on my left, the Metropolitan Hospital on 99th on my right, where zombies wearing white gowns wander in the parking lots. They all pick up my trail and follow along. Around 94th street I hit the canyon walls of skyscrapers that will flank both sides of the street all the way down to Coney Island, boxing me in.

There are more of them on the streets now, rising up like floodwaters: businessmen and women heading home late or coming into work early, revelers in lurid makeup and skin-tight tops enjoying a walk of shame that will last until their bodies rot into the ground, a fat guy in a sumo diaper, his great gray haunches quivering with dead meat.

I round a long stretch limo on 92nd, quietly ticking in the rising morning heat. Down 87th street I glimpse a horde wandering down a beautiful, tree-lined avenue. Everything is so surreal and seen like postcards. A KFC near 90th has its doors wedged open by the husk of a dead dog, its entrails splayed across the sidewalk in a dark inkblot of dried blood.

Through the 80s and into the 70s I go, through the 70s to the 60s until on 65th street outside a gorgeous little sandstone church I spy the pale tide of a herd ahead, and pull sharply right. I speed three streets over to Lexington Avenue, clear of the swarm; god knows what they were gathering for. Another survivor?

Down Lexington I put the pedal down, hitting eighty through a school zone, past Bloomingdales with its flags out on a long clear stretch to the sea. I've never seen New York so empty except in movies. The odd zombie stumbles along like a latecomer to the party over on 1st, and I whizz by. The streets are narrower here, three lanes wide and claustrophobic. My knuckles ache from clutching the handlebars so tightly. There's blood on my hands and sleeves.

Around 56th street I catch my first glimpse of the Chrysler building's crenellated top, unbowed, jutting confidently above the other buildings. It follows me all the way down to 42nd street. On 40th I hit another horde and swing left over to 2nd Avenue, then juice it the rest of the way down to 23rd and past the Subway station stairs. There I swing right, racing along my old commute route, and halt the moped bang in front of Sir Clowdesley.

Bizarre.

Clowdesley looks like a New Orleans bar from the outside, all weathered brown wood and Nemo-ish spiral copper designs, with a perplexity of Hard Rock-like literary merchandise pasted to the windows and decoupaged to the walls.

The Last

I jump off my steed and stride up to tug on the stout wooden door, only to find it's locked. I tug harder as if that'll make a difference, but it doesn't.

I press my face to one of the windows to look inside. It's empty of course, with no sign of Lara. That doesn't mean anything though, and I've nowhere else to go. I pull my dumbbell bar out of my pack and smash through one of the windows. I can only hope it's high enough that they can't climb through. I scrape the frame clear and drag myself in.

I've reached Sir Clowdesley!

I sit at one of the wooden window seats in my favorite old haunt, which I am doubtless now mayor of for life, and catch my breath, thinking about all the mad, horrific, disgusting things I just saw.

Level one cleared.

POST-APOCALYPSE

8. CLOWDESLEY

It is surreal to be here.

I look into the shadowy interior, up the stairs to the cozy library where I used to sit and dream about zombies, and marvel at how nothing has changed. The air still smells of fine-roasted Jamaican beans. If I close my eyes I can hear the clatter of the baristas whacking milk froth off their steamer sieves.

It was only yesterday. Now there's no one left to govern.

I get my breath back and stand up. There's plenty to do, and Lara might come at any minute. I make purposeful strides, formulating a new plan with every step. I need to get secure, I need to put up a flag for Lara to see, and I need to figure out what the hell is going on.

First things first.

At the coffee bar I lift the hinged counter section and go to the door in back. Inside lies a pokey little office; desk, chair, a few neat gray filing cabinets and a thumbtack-studded corkboard with all kinds of notifications. It's darker here, lit by only sunlight from the front windows. I hold up my phone in flashlight mode.

Lara

She's on the work-rota Tuesday through Saturday.

I rustle in the desk and come up with a roll of duct tape and a few marker chalk pens. An idea pings into my head like a twitter notification, and I bring it up.

Approved.

I climb to the coffee bar and find the release clip to pull the blackboards out. There are four of them in total, a lovely coincidence. Each is about a meter square, and I lay them out on the floor.

A zombie rolls up to the broken window like it's a drive-thru booth, a red-haired lady with crusted blood down her throat.

"We're closed," I tell her. She doesn't listen. I drag one of the big sofas over and upend it in front of her face. It covers the window almost completely.

Good enough for me. She thumps against it and I tune her out.

The blackboards are covered in stuff about coffee; gentle boasts, bits of art, prices, wit. I spray the boards down with liquid detergent and smear the old chalk trails off using a bar rag. They come away in rainbow sweeps, leaving a pure black canvas behind.

I reflect on the infinite possibilities it offers. I am an artist, after all.

I write my message one huge letter to a board.

L A R A

Four boards for four letters, like panels in a comic. I paint them in bright yellow, which really pops against the black. I add a message on the bottom of the first board.

> I'm inside, Lara. It's Amo. If I'm not here when you come, please wait. I'll be back.

Finally I draw a quick cartoon zombie at the edge of the last panel, all pale-faced and white-eyed, for fun. It's standing at a door and staring at the doorbell with its jaw hanging down, to take the edge off the reality. It's not funny, but it looks, what, poignant? Irreverent?

I put the boards up across the windows. They lean nicely against the wall above the windows. I tape them steady with duct tape. The zombie lady outside tracks me, whacking whichever window I'm standing behind.

When all the boards are up it's quite dark inside Sir Clowdesley. I cover the last window with bits of paper from the office, and the zombie lady stops thumping so much. That's good information to have.

I stand and look into the darkness. I bring up my phone and double-tap it. Craziness has already invited me in, and right now I need to hear another voice.

"What now Io?"

"To what are you referring, Amo?" she answers.

"All this." I spread my arm to take in the dark and empty coffee shop.

"I believe we're in your favorite coffee shop. Aren't you mayor here?"

I chuckle. Io is pretty good at liaising with other apps, even with the Internet down. "I am."

"All hail the mayor," she says puckishly. "You have coffee to hand out today."

I snort a laugh. I have all the coffee in New York.

"I'll get right on that," I say. I pocket the phone and the hammer. It's a much better weapon than the dumbbell bar, which I slot into my bag next to its twin.

Moving on. I need to get secure. Ideas race through my head. Paper bales didn't do a thing. Doors and windows don't stop them. I need something sturdier, a wall of some kind.

I glance around the dark shop. I've got a few shelves, some tables and chairs, enough to reinforce the windows maybe, maybe enough to stop the flood at the door, but what good will that do me if a flood is all Lara sees?

She won't come near Sir Clowdesley if it's thronged with bodies. I need to clear a space so she can see my sign. I need to press outward and reclaim the street.

Nothing in here can do that. But I have an idea of what might.

I climb the stairs into the dark of the library mezzanine. The familiar smell of old, well-worn paper surrounds me, mingling with the rich aroma of ingrained coffee. It feels like safety. In the corner lies the wood-paneled fire door in the corner. The emergency light above it glows a dull green.

I stride over with my dumbbell club in my hand. My heart hammers in the silence. A simple twist of the lever in the handle unlocks it, and I jerk backward and it swings open smoothly.

Beyond there's a nondescript stairwell lit by emergency lights. Cold dank air streams over my face. Raw concrete steps spiral upward in a tight oblong.

"Hello?" I call.

No answer comes. It makes sense there'd be no one on these steps in the middle of the night.

Across the way are the toilets and the glow of another emergency exit. I walk over, depress the emergency bar and swing the door open. Light floods in, and I step out to a tiny and ancient loading dock, about a meter tall above the ground, like a balcony onto the inner square of a New York block, fully enclosed by buildings. It strikes me like a peaceful oasis. A cracked and weed-sprung road leads twenty yards away, overshadowed on all sides, then stops dead at a wall.

It's a remnant, I suppose; a donut block in the middle of New York, with a road that would have once allowed resupply trucks in and out, now sealed up by buildings. I eye the surrounding structures. They all have windows and doors facing this way. There is not a single zombie about.

I found my escape route. Through this tiny forgotten access road I can enter any building in the block, and exit at any point I like on 23rd or 24th, 1st or 2nd Avenue. It's a good thing to have.

I duck back inside.

The stairwell takes me up, winding. The air is clammy and cold. The door to the second floor doesn't open. I give it a few desultory hits with the bar, accomplishing nothing but putting tiny dints in the metal handle. I keep on up. The third floor is locked too, but the fourth floor door opens readily.

It leads to a bright modern office, with glass partition walls lining a gray-carpet corridor leading away parallel to the floor-to-ceiling windows on the left. Fresh light rinses over banks of desks, computers, and the occasional whiteboard to either side of the glass corridor. A fern wilts slackly in a ceramic pot by the door, a coffee machine and water cooler face me in a tucked-away culvert, and a wooden door chock skitters away when I accidentally kick it.

It looks like the office of a tech firm, or maybe a telesales depot. Do we have those in New York? I don't know. Probably they have their logo and a receptionist up at the far end; there must be a lift too that I've never seen, perhaps connected from one of the adjoining buildings.

I pad along the fuzzy gray carpet, peering left and right into both sides of the office through the glass walls. Cords run everywhere like tangled veins, for phones, computers, printers, all redundant now.

I stop in the middle. There's nobody here, but more building material than I could have hoped for. The desks look solid, and I'm pretty certain I can craft a zombie-proof wall out of them. I start planning the procedure.

Then I hear a shuffle. It's coming from the far end, where a fuzzy gray partition rises flanked by more ferns, beyond which I guess lies the reception and the door to the lifts. I set my feet and slide the pack off my back. Seconds later a fat dead guy emerges.

My heart does a belly flop. He pops out of cover at a lurching run, bouncing lightly off one of the glass walls, his glowing white eyes targeted on me. There's dark blood down his white shirt and staining his navy jacket. His black tie is askew like he's tried to hang himself with it and the rope broke, twisting at a painful angle. His neck is flushed red, his feet slap the floor, and there's a glinting silver shield at his waist.

He's private security, probably patrolling the floors last night. I spin but there's no time to run back for the stairwell, and I can't cede this building anyway. I need these desks, and besides this is not a mild-looking family standing in their pajamas, this is some asshole I've never met made-up like Halloween, packing heat and picking up speed like a damn bull charging. He wants to eat me, for god's sake. I'm not going to play patty-cake with him.

I start running. I redouble my grip on the dumbbell bar. When we're about ten feet apart I launch myself into the air, feet first and held out rigid. For a second I fly, then I impact the guy's chest full on and punch him off his feet. My heels catch on his chin and send me somersaulting through the air past him. Before I hit the ground, I have time for just one thought:

I dropkicked the shit out of this bastard.

Then I hit the friction-burn carpet and crack my side hard, roll and smack my ankle bizarrely off the flat glass, and wind up lying on my side with my wrist throbbing. What the shit? That was probably the stupidest thing I've ever done. It was also utterly awesome.

I think this for about two seconds, until I get up and see another security guy coming at me from behind the divider, while his buddy shakes the fall off and starts to run too. Shit, what are they breeding back there?

I bolt up and turn to the glass to my right. One good stab with the bar and jagged clumps of it come down, another smack affords me some clearance, and I leap through seconds before they smack chest-first into each other.

I spring up on an office chair, which then reclines weirdly, like some asshole hasn't even taken the time to set it in a proper position, twisting my ankle. I fall onto the long bank of desks, smacking my knee on the edge and catching myself bodily on a monitor, which then folds back so I smack my face on a keyboard.

My teeth crunch, I bite my lip, my gut and chest spark with pain where the monitor top hit, and a hand grabs at my feet.

"Shit!" I yell, and scrabble away with the pain forgotten. I roll into a chair on the other side of the bank and then out of it again, so now I'm standing on a twingeing ankle with two fat mall cops wheezing evilly at me. Finally, to put the cherry on top of the cake, they split up and come for me round either side of the desks.

I look around desperately, remembering how little my computer did to the zombies outside my tenement. There are actually the same brand of computer here, which seems ironic.

There's one more long bank of desks and I climb up onto it. Monitors are the only thing I can use, and even if they don't kill them, they might buy me some time. I run to the end of the desks, toward the guy I dropkicked. I pick up a screen just as he comes near, and throw it with all my strength. It arcs beautifully towards him, a perfect shot, then catches on its cables with a crack and spins, swinging hard back toward my feet.

I cry out and leap away, dancing for my balance as it crunches onto the desk and the screen shatters. I get my balance back standing in the middle of the far bank on a keyboard and a mouse-mat, again with nowhere to go. Both of the fat zombies are right in front of me now, blocked only from grabbing my legs by a row of wheelie office chairs.

This is utterly stupid.

I snatch up a Bluetooth wireless keyboard and Frisbee it at the nearest of them. It cracks off his mouth and his head recoils but it makes no difference. He stumbles through the chairs blindly, reaching for my feet.

I bring the bar down edge first. It buries in his eye socket with a horrible slurp and a geyser of gray goo. I gag and pull back, but the bar is lodged now and I just tug him closer, pulling myself off balance.

As I'm about to fall into his embrace, I push away, relinquishing the bar. He staggers back with blood and gray matter gushing down his face, but he doesn't go down. The other one is through the chairs now and almost on me.

I run two steps then jump for the aisle between the banks, where I back away tipping chairs over between us. They stumble over them. This is better. I get some clearance and space, and at last they're both following me the same way. I could do this all day.

At the bank's edge I grab another monitor, unplug it swiftly, and hurl it at the nearest one. It hits him edge-on in the face and breaks open his nose and his eye-socket. He falls back for a second and the one with my bar in his eye comes on harder. He looks a horrible mess.

I unplug another monitor and throw, but miss. Shit. I run halfway down the other bank, tipping more chairs, and toss the next monitor. It hits him in the neck with a gristly crunch and he goes down, this time staying down to gurgle and spit. OK. I unplug three more monitors in advance of the guy with the broken jaw reaching me, then hurl them at him in fast succession. One misses, one hits his head, and the third time's the charm with another crunch and gurgle in his neck.

He goes down. My arms throb. I stand there and pant. I wipe my hoodie over my face, coming away with blood and gray juice. The office is silent again but for my breath and their palsied, bubbly rasping.

I stand there and wait for it to stop, but it doesn't. I pick my way over cautiously. The bar guy is looking up at me with his one good eye. His fingertips reach toward me, but his arms lie slack.

It is too creepy.

I walk along the desk to the other one. He's just the same, a caved-in throat and a motionless body, but eyes that track me. It's horrible. I've killed them but they're not dead. Do I have to kill them again?

I back up and start to shake. I clamber over my own alley of tumbled chairs and round to the hole in the glass. In the corridor I stand and shudder. I can't believe this shit. How many times? I start back for the fire door, thinking maybe I'll go down to Sir Clowdesley and get some coffee and wait for Lara, but what am I going to tell her about this?

"Yeah I half-killed two of them upstairs, I just left them lying there like those creepy paintings in a haunted mansion. It was too creepy to deal with them, and I couldn't handle using the desks to make a wall with them watching me. What do you mean you'd rather go survive alone than do it with me? It'll be fine, I have moral compunctions."

She flies off on an albatross. She rides a unicorn out of town.

Shit. I rub my eyes and stamp my feet. They haven't moved. I haven't moved. It's between them and me, and it has to be me.

I start back. I go to the one on the edge first, with my bar in his head. 'You can keep it, pal,' I feel like saying, but this is no time for levity.

I nudge his head with my foot. It lolls to the side with no control. I nudge it back the other way. I can't think of a way to make this less disgusting, or less of a horrible memory. I've painted zombie head explosions a hundred times in comics, but it's never so visceral as when they actually look just like regular people, only paler. I can smell the tangy blood and the bitter salt of brain. I can see it oozing out in live-motion before you.

Monitor? I don't like the thought of feeling the weight crack through his skull and mulch his brain. The fewer senses involved the better.

So, gun.

I edge around him. I nudge his arm but he doesn't respond. He's like a seed planted in the office, waiting to sprout. I stand on his right hand. I pin his left beneath a chair. I put a chair on top of his face, in case he suddenly rears up. I reach to his waist belt, and unclasp the button on his holster.

The gun comes out easily, and rests in my hand smoothly. It's affixed to his belt by a coiled bit of rubber tubing, but I can deal with that. I stand up over him. I study the gun. It looks simple enough, though I don't know shit about guns. It's heavy and gray with no branding anywhere. I look for a safety button, and see a little sliding lever with a red inner bit showing.

I'll guess that means the safety is on. I click it over. I kick the chair away, and point the gun at his staring face. It would be so much easier if he weren't looking at me.

"Look away," I tell him.

He doesn't. He stares at me like a dog. His mouth opens and closes. The bar in his face bobs obscenely.

I pull the trigger. The gun cracks slightly in my hand, the report sounds out with nothing like the bass rumble you see in movies, but more of a piercing tenor pop, amplified by the contained space.

My ears buzz. If any nearby zombies didn't know I was here before, they do now. Maybe Lara heard it too. As for the guy's face, his head, his brain, I don't want to talk about those things. It's a mess. His one good eye is still there, crumpled inward by the force of the shot and the ricochet off the floor, looking like a bloody gray toad, but at least it's not staring at me anymore.

Wait, it is. I feel his hand twitch under my foot. What the…?

I stand there in horrified silence for several minutes, waiting for whatever this is to end. Death throes? It doesn't end though. His brain has been mulched, but he's still trying to reach for me.

I aim the gun at his throat. I pull the trigger again.

Flash, bang, bloody mess. This time he is dead.

I puke a little. I get my shit together. I go over and execute the other through the throat. One shot and done.

I unfasten his belt while I'm still in shock. I unfasten them both. I take both guns with their cables and blood-spattered belts trailing behind me like empty leashes, until in the gray corridor I put them down, drop to my knees, and have a mental breakdown.

9. DESKS

Things speed up after that. It's business time, and I can defer the horror to later. It helps to move. I shoot out the glass to the street outside; it takes three bullets, god knows how many each gun holds, to put a nicely cracked hole in the big panes.

I smash the rest with hurled monitors. Glass rain falls outside and a blast of cool air rushes in. I walk through crunches of glass to the edge and look down. Already there are some twenty or so zombies lining up at the Sir Clowdesley entrance, baying for free coffee.

Ha, no, but they are thumping against the glass.

"Hey!" I shout. They look up at me. "What's up?"

They amble over and stand beneath me, five stories down. Perfect. This is much better. There'll be only the sound and hardly any of the proximity or the visuals.

It takes me a while to figure out how to unhook the first desk from its fellows. Little near-invisible catches on the underside inner rim are the secret. I unspool the cables running through it, then toss the desk contents out the window: monitors and computer towers. They each make a pleasing crunch and smash on the concrete outside.

I don't even look to see if I take out any of my groupies. Who cares? They'll get it in the end. This is just the resource-gathering stage of the game, grinding out my tower defense before I set to crafting.

It helps me to think of it in Deepcraft terms. There are zombies in Deepcraft too. I'm building my tower against zombie invasion. I'm just playing Deepcraft.

Dragging the desk up to the edge of the window is a good workout. It just fits through. I push it out halfway until it's on the balance point, like a truck on the edge of a cliff. Outside there are plenty more zombies hobbling closer, a fresh horde of dead New Yorkers.

I shove the desk. It grates over the edge and dives. There are about seven zombies beneath it when it hits, and they all get crushed. A smack, a crack, and the desk tips away, clearing the impact zone.

I don't look at the bodies too hard. They look just like crushed people, like crushed bugs with their bodies burst. They didn't have to be here. This is my damn tower. I can't have them here when Lara comes.

I start clearing the next desk. I do a quick count. There are thirty-one desks in the office in total. I imagine what kind of ring-fence that can make around the exterior of Sir Clowdesley. If I stack them atop each other and weigh them down with all the rest of the crap I've got in here, that will make a wall sixteen long. I envision a semicircle desk-fort-wall around the door and windows, then I expand that vision. I imagine sealing off a whole section of the street.

I'll need hundreds of desks. But this building has about a dozen floors. All of those will have heavy office furniture. I can tip them all out, my raw materials, then go down, clear, and build up my wall.

It's just Deepcraft.

I get to work. I shift desk after desk. At some point I hear frantic barking from below, and watch as a pack of running zombies chase a dog down the street. The dog is lathered with scummy brown sweat, and the zombies run like Neanderthal man, like they were born to this, their feet slapping the asphalt.

Poor dog. There's nothing I can do for it. Its barks echo away down 23rd headed for a messy death somewhere.

I don't stop shifting desks until it's well into the afternoon. They pile up like messy dominos outside, with bodies crushed amongst them. They almost reach all the way across the street already. Some of them crack on impact and the metal frame pulls away from the wood. Each one crushes one or two zombies into the mix.

I look back on the office, empty now but for the two dead security guards and plenty of bits of trailing cable. A company just got downsized. The smell of decay and baking road-tar blows through the window.

I go over to the guards. I don't look at their pulped heads and necks, I just grab the first one and drag him away by the feet. He's harder to move even than the desks.

Out the window he goes. I don't stop to watch his body smack and roll. I tell myself it's just another desk. The next one goes. I stand at the window and look west along 23rd. The stink of dead bodies is rising up now, a kind of butcher-shop blend of blood and guts. The sun has already descended below the canyons of the city, and the sky over the buildings is leering toward a blast furnace orange.

I have to do this whether there's enough light or not.

I pick up the two guns and belts and strap both around my waist. I have to buckle them to the tightest notch, never before used by the two fat guys who wore them before. I realize I'm thirsty.

The stairwell to Sir Clowdesley is cool and dark. It doesn't know any of the bad things I've just done. I come down and back through the coffee shop, where I pick up a bottle of water from the unrefrigerated fridge section of the bar. It's cool and I drain it.

At the window I'm happy to note my blackboards are still there. I peel away the sofa covering the broken window, my muscles throbbing warmly, and see the redheaded lady still there. Somehow she survived the rain of desks. I point the gun at her head and pull the trigger.

Bang.

Her head blows open and she is flung off her feet. I peer through the window to see her getting up. I aim one more time and shoot her in the throat. She goes down permanently, gurgling.

More zombies come over at a steady lope, drawn by the sound. I climb through the window to meet them. A guy in a black nightclub shirt with bloody stains all down his thighs, a homeless-looking kid without any shoes and filthy blackened feet. They've gotten grayer already. There's dried blood on their teeth and round their lips, where they've been eating; cats, dogs, at one point I thought I heard a horse whinnying before it fell silent. It must have run across the bridge from Queens. Probably people too. I haven't seen any other people.

I shoot the guy in the brown suit in the neck. After three shots, only two of which hit, he goes down. I get the kid in two.

I start dragging desks. I get a good rhythm going, starting at the left side of Sir Clowdesley and laying them out. The first time that I get blood or some other cold slick liquid on my hands I freak out and rub it away on the desk, leaving bloody finger trails. The second and third times I ignore it.

I press on, running backward at a fast clip pulling each desk behind me, scraping loudly along the road. I tip them over on their sides, so the smooth surface of the desk faces outward. I get four lined up, the first quarter of a semi-circle, and more zombies come.

Another dirty kid, a guy in a bathrobe, a cop packing heat, a girl with a fast food apron on. I drop them and rescue the gun from the cop's holster. Now I have three.

I get twelve desks down, and it's properly getting dark. It gets harder to pick out the zombies as they come near, with no streetlights. Still I can hear them clacking and slapping their drunken feet nearer.

Bang bang bang, my guns report. I get sixteen desks out from the pile's periphery, then I have to start salvaging ones buried in the midst of half-dead zombies. Here there's an arm half-cloven through, emerging through a crack between two desks, the fingers still twitching toward me. I reach in and shoot the owner in the throat. I do that four or five times.

I start to wonder how many bullets I've got left. One of the mall cops' guns clicks emptily as a blood-smeared Goth guy in ripped leather jeans and a drooping Mohawk comes charging for me. I panic, drop the gun and snatch up one of my others. It takes four shots to put him down.

I pile up more desks atop the sixteen. They've heavy but I slide them on top one end at a time. The wall stands high enough that I can't see over it now, only through cracks. It's dark, but I hear them slapping against the impromptu barricade. They can't get at me except through the narrow slot I use to drag in the desks.

The last few drag wetly, tearing over crushed bodies. Many of these are still alive, but unable to get up due to broken bones and bodies. They lurch and grope for me like a nest of octopus tentacles.

I get the last desk out and up. I turn and see one more zombie creep through the corral. It's a lady in a low-cut white dress that has slipped to reveal one ample gray breast. She jogs unevenly toward me, one of the heels on her shoes broken away, making an uneven clopping sound. I shoot her in the throat from point blank range, and she lies down like she just got tired, flat on her back, and gurgles wetly to a second death.

I pull her dress back up to cover her chest. I haven't got the energy to pick her up and push her over the wall.

In the darkness I amble the wall's half-circle courtyard with my phone flashlight on, stumbling on bits of broken computers and monitors. I toss them under the desks to weight them down. Zombie palms slap the desk wall like hail. I'm done though.

I go for Sir Clowdesley, past my moped, and crawl in through the window. I shut it up with the sofa.

In the library I hunker down on one of the sofas with lots of pilfered cushions spread around me, in the dark. It's even cozy like this. I eat a packaged BLT sandwich, drink one of the lukewarm banana milkshakes before it can go off, and drain another bottle of water.

Outside their thumping is a low cacophony. Exhaustion creeps up over me and I put my head down and sleep.

I wake cold and unrested to silty gray morning light. It takes a moment to realize I'm in Sir Clowdesley, and why. I look around the library; there's no sign of Lara. At least the twinges are at bay, though my arms and shoulders ache. I lie still for a moment, straining to hear the chop of helicopter blades or the friendly loudspeaker hail of a soldier calling for survivors outside, but there's nothing.

I'm alone in this.

I get up and go groggily down the stairs, with one of the guns and belt wadded in my hand. I pull back the sofa and peer out of the drive-thru window.

The redhead is still lying there in a mess, the weak light making her wounds look ghastly. The others I killed are there as well, spotted like strange gray mold risen through the paving slabs. Blood has set in dark puddles like blackcurrant jelly. Looking at them makes me ill.

Overhead the sky is miserable. I bring up my phone and look at the screen blearily. 11:16. I slept right through the alarm. It's fine. I feel sick. I push the sofa to the side, grab a sandwich and a bottle of water, and sit to a desultory breakfast. The bread is mushy. The sell-by-date is two days past. I keep eating though I don't even feel hungry.

What now?

I hawk and spit out of the window. I think I'm getting sick. I can hear them mumbling away at the desk wall, but it's holding.

The Last

I bring up the gun. I try to un-attach it from the cable, but it seems to be part of the haft's molding, rubbery black plastic encasing the metal. I turn it over, careful to point the muzzle away from my face. I click the safety back and forth, trying to remember if it's on when it shows red or off.

I look for the button to eject the clip. Ten minutes later the clip slides out smoothly. I never owned a handgun, but I've fired my friend's, when I was back in Iowa. I pull the slide forward, revealing one coppery dark-nosed bullet in the breach. I tip it out awkwardly, then let the slide roll back.

Now the gun should be empty. I click safety over, aim out the window, and fire.

Click.

I eject bullets from the clip and count them; seven shells remain. I feed them in and slot the clip back, work the slide to feed one into the breach, then put on the safety.

I fasten the holster-belt round my waist. I put the sofa back.

There's more work to do.

The fifth, sixth, and seventh floors are all offices, and their doors to the stairwell open; a cubicle farm for a travel agency, a call center, and the admin hub for an upscale bridal service. In the travel agency I find tourist maps of New York and pocket one. On desks I see personal thingamajigs; here a Jessie doll from Toy Story, there a Totoro, pictures of family in fun stylized frames, faces that are all gone now.

I smash out the windows and send their desks raining down. Today I'll aim to expand the space I have. Across the street there's a 7-11 which will have all kinds of canned food and drink. They'll have a lighter so I can warm the night with a fire. I don't know what I'll use for a brazier, but whatever. Maybe I can shell one of the milk steamers and use that. I'll make a chimney out of rolled plastic picnic tarps. I have lots of ideas.

Desks rain down all through the gray day. I throw them out in the midst of the crowd around my existing wall, clustered three-deep now. The offices empty out and the furniture piles up outside.

Out on the street, standing in the semi-circle courtyard, I think about how to do this. It's tricky. There are too many zombies now to kill them all; I don't have enough bullets. If I try to push the desks back, they'll breach the gaps.

I delay that problem for later. For now I stack more desks to reinforce what I've got.

Back in the library I take out my USBs and bring up the prepper Bible on my laptop. While it gets dark outside I surf through screen after screen, advising me on guns, traps, pulleys and power. How to hot-wire a car intrigues me. How to filter and boil water. How to siphon gas, how to leech energy off a building's emergency power, how to jump current and voltage up and down to match appliances, where to find weapons and ammo in the city. I mark a few potential targets on my tourist map: the Police Academy a few blocks over, all major banks, certain police cars and vans, police officers themselves, obviously, even most bars and convenience stores.

My head blurs with it. There's a lot to take in. In woozy moments I remember the family I left behind; the guy with his broken collarbones, the daughter in the box, the mom and daughter tangled up in chairs and tables. I wonder what they're doing right now. Do zombies sleep?

I'm alone. I get cold. I bring up my phone and look at the battery, more than halfway down. I'll deal with that soon. I double-click it.

"Hello Amo," Io says.

"Do you think I'm the last human alive?" I ask her.

She thinks for a moment. She's noticing there's no Internet connection, no databank to scour answers from, and then scanning her own limited memory.

"I don't think I can answer that question, Amo."

I chuckle, but hearing the sound makes me aware of how foolish I sound. Talking to a phone.

I turn it off. It's not amusing, not really. Probably it's an early sign of madness. It's weakness and I can't afford to be weak.

I try to snuggle into the sofa deeper against the cold, pile more cushions on, but they don't do much. It's gone fully black outside, and now I hear the shushing breath of the zombies out there, like an ocean lapping away at my desk breakers. I feel ill and strange. There were a lot of things I meant to do today, but they stopped me. I couldn't even get a lighter, so now I can't have a fire.

Will tomorrow be the same? I don't know how I'm going to expand the semi-circle wider. Probably I need more signs, more widely spread. Lara, if she's alive and she even thinks to come to Sir Clowdesley, would barely get onto 23rd street for the horde that's gathering now.

The Last

There must be millions of them in Manhattan alone. That thought takes me to fitful sleep.

I wake to footfalls like thunder. It's pitch black and the darkness is churning. I roll up and snatch at my phone, scrolling for the flashlight. It blinks alight and I hold it out; the weak beam picks out chairs, tables, the balcony down to the bar below, and in the midst of it, zombies.

Sir Clowdesley is flooded with them. Their dead white eyes reflect the light and their gray faces look like ghouls reanimated to life. They shamble about the space knocking over furniture and sprawling awkwardly against the steps.

I dart to my feet, instantly flushed with adrenaline. At the top of the stairs I see they're crawling for me. Some are almost at the top.

I haven't got my guns, they're at the sofa and there's no time. I set the phone on a bookshelf, taking a second to aim the beam where it illuminates, then snatch up a wooden chair. I hold it ahead like a lion tamer, stride three steps down, and slam its feet into the shoulders and face of the nearest two zombies. A cheek buckles percussively, the impact jolts up my arms, and they both slither a step or two back.

Others crawl over them though, enlivened by the light, by the motion, by the sound.

"Shit," I curse, and throw the chair. It doesn't do a damn thing. One of them seems to have the stairs figured out and comes bounding up for me, bloody lips champing. There is no damn time.

I turn and run, grabbing my phone and pulling the rough wood bookshelf down behind me. I hit the emergency fire door, yank it open, and get through into the dark quiet of the stairwell a second before they hit. The catch clicks, I can't lock it from here, but I don't think they can turn a knob-handle.

I lean panting against the metal door while they thump on it, like an uncanny pulse, matching my erratic heartbeat. My breaths are ragged and I feel sick.

I just almost died. Not even Sir Clowdesley is safe. I don't know how they got through my desk wall, how they climbed through my window, but they did, and it's no safe place for Lara or me.

Shit.

It's cold in this drafty vertical corridor. My phone lights my feet in sterile white, picking out the spots and blots of blood and oil. Then that too is gone. I lift it up and thumb the button and screen, but the battery is dead. It's pitch black in here.

Something cold touches my back.

I freak the hell out, whirling and lashing out. My elbow hits something frail and sends it careening into the darkness. I run and grab for the railing and almost go over it. A body is shuffling behind me, and I take the railing with both hands and run as fast and hard as I can along it and up to the fourth floor.

I feel my way to the fire door and lurch through it terrified and gasping with a deep burn in my legs. I slam it behind me and turn the lock.

The office is lit by pale bluish moonlight. It is utterly barren but for the snaky coils of cables, the snail drag-marks of the mall cops I killed, the water cooler, the gray partitions, and me. I trail out into the cold pale light, and it hits me like a dumbbell bar in the eye, perhaps for the first time.

This isn't a game.

This isn't for fun, or a dream, or a chance to prove what a hero I can be. I'm cold and I'm scared and I'm tired. I'm alone. I don't have a blanket, bedding, or a gun. I don't have a damn thing. From below I can hear them, their bodies pushing, pattering and packing in to the coffee shop I named as my own. Now it's theirs.

I go to the window edge and look down. In the gray scale starlight the concrete below writhes with thousands of bodies pressed tightly together, more than in Mott Haven, more people than I've ever seen before except in stadiums or parades. They have flowed over and through my wall of desks like an incoming tide. They have poured in to Sir Clowdesley up a ramp of their own crushed bodies. Now they're looking up at me, so many white eyes like freakish stars in the sky.

I can't save Lara like this. I couldn't save Cerulean. I probably can't even save myself.

I retreat to the receptionist's desk. It is cold and barren, looking out on a bay of elevators from which a cold draft blows. The company name is Medisco. It's meaningless. I lay down the receptionist's chair on the gray carpet, use the padded backrest as a pillow, and try to convince my aching, freezing body that sleep is going to come.

10. FIRE

I wake from a Deepcraft dream. Cerulean and I are running the darkness, but we can never find the things we need. Each time the diviner tells us where to go, we arrive a second too late because some other picker has already come and taken it away.

"Sorry Amo," Cerulean says. "We just didn't make the grade."

He breaks apart into pieces that become Deepcraft resource blocks. With them I know I can build an excellent weapon, but I don't have the crafting pattern to do it.

I wake up with this thought in my head, afraid. I can't even use the things Cerulean did for me, moments before he died. I pat my pocket and find the comforting hard wodge of USBs still there. I pat the other pocket and find my phone and keys.

I take the keys out and walk to the office edge. I look down through the broken window and see the tide has started to bank up. There is a definite incline, bringing the heads of the zombie horde below me up to the second floor.

I laugh. It's just like my comic. They climb up each other.

I throw the keys out at them, like I'm dispensing free coffee to my constituents.

"Free latte," I shout. I get my phone ready to throw and shout, "Free espresso," but I hold back at the last minute. It still has all my music on, my apps, my mayorhood, if I can just get some power. They have battery chargers in any convenience store.

"No espresso," I shout down instead. "Make do with black coffee."

Their unblinking ice-white eyes show how intent they are on my every word.

I pocket my phone and hold out my hand. A few of them reach upward, like man reaching toward god in Michelangelo's painting. Suddenly I get angry.

"Do you want this?" I shout at them. I pat my head. "Do you want what's in here? You're not getting it! All of you listen up!"

I look over the throng bustling left and right on 23rd. It's an ocean wave carrying undead jetsam wherever I go. I'm like the moon, drawing them in with my gravitational waves.

"You're not getting one bite. And you don't get Sir Clowdesley! I am the mayor of this coffee shop, and I'll fight you to the death for it. Is that clear?"

Their stares tell me it is.

"Let's establish some ground rules," I go on. I don't know why I'm saying this, the words are just coming out, but the more noise I make the braver and more righteous I feel. "I'm waiting for Lara. You will not mess with Lara! Mess with her and you mess with me. Second, you will not climb up my building. You climb up my building, I'll do something about it. Third, you do not come into Sir Clowdesley again, ever, and certainly not at night. That is right out of line. You can have everything north of 24th street if you want, or south of 22nd, but this bit is mine. Do you understand?"

They shuffle to indicate that they do.

"Good! So get lost or suffer the consequences."

I walk away from the window. My stiff body is loosening up. I go to the water cooler, and like a civilized person I push the little tappet to pour myself a paper cupful. I drink it, then do it again. Three more cups and I'm stuffed. I notice my hands. They look like I'm wearing gloves, covered in old crusted blood and other fluids.

Ugh. I ate a sandwich with these things.

I pick up the cooler and carry it to the window, into the warming sunlight. I strip off my sweaty, filthy clothes and hand wash them with cups of 'Pure Spring Water'. I lay them out to dry. I take a shower using cups of cold water. Dirt and crud peels off me, staining the carpet. My skin emerges. I tousle my dark hair. I rub my eyes. I stand at the window naked and look down at them.

The Last

No words, now. This is a kind of dominion. This is how I'm going to go out, if I must. They have messed with the wrong hombre.

I scour the office for a weapon but I don't find anything, except for ballpoint pens, yellow legal pads, and a few old-fashioned telephone handles behind the reception desk. I don't like the idea of using any of them to fight off a zombie. I threw everything else out of the window.

OK, so I have another idea. I go to the fire door to the stairwell, open it, and lurch back. On the other side is a little old guy, wraith-thin, dressed in an oil-stained blue overall that says 'Janitor' on the lapel. He comes for me, and I jog him back through the office. I go stand at the open window, and at the last minute I spring to the side and push him on.

He tumbles out to join his fellows.

The stairwell is empty otherwise. I suppose he crawled up out of some nether zone to reach me. I head down.

On the Clowdesley floor I glance at the door to the library. They're probably packed in completely now, like my apartment, but it's a metal door in a concrete frame and I don't think they can get through.

I go out the other way, into the sunlight of the inner-block donut. I pick a brown stone building to the north, and smash a window through using a loose paving slab. I climb in and walk the corridor until it releases me into a spacious, empty lobby, decked out in dark mosaic tile and the old opulence of carved wooden arches. It's dim but light spills in from the street.

I smash through the revolving doors to get out. I stand on 24th street facing a 7-11. A few rags of newspaper scatter noisily before me, chased by a whirling plastic bag caught on a spring zephyr. There are no drifting zombies here, carried by the tide. I can smell them though, a ripe herd just one block south.

I cross the road, weaving between stalled vehicles: a bright yellow Humvee, a Yamaha motorbike on its kickstand, a silver BMW. The motorbike parked in the road intrigues me, another clue perhaps. Up in Mott Haven the cars were all crashed, as though the turn to zombies was instant. Here though, the traffic is frozen neatly. The people got out and turned off their engines before they turned into zombies.

I climb up into the hummer's cab and find the key still in the ignition. So thoughtful. I turn it and the engine revs to life. I imagine myself ramming into the mass of drifters with this tank. Not bad, but I can do better. I need to clear my whole street.

In the glove box there's nothing but papers, but in the trunk I find a tire iron. Good. I use it to smash out the 7-11's glass door and enter. It's empty and stale inside, smelling of wilting danishes and Big Red gum. I lean over the register and pluck up a sheaf of plastic bags, then I go shopping. I get candy bars first, then I add in bread, beef jerky, bottles of water, apples and oranges, a few chunks of cheese. I snatch up a bunch of newspapers and get two whole trays of New York-branded Zippo lighters. Beside the lighters there's a tray of noxious-smelling gas refill cans. I grab those.

There are New York-branded hats, shirts and towels, and I bag a bunch of them for bedding. On the back wall there's a range of kid's toys, including a Super Soaker water rifle, which I scoop up and bag. I find the phone chargers and batteries and get plenty, plus there are a row of nifty-looking solar-cell battery chargers. I get those, four stout-looking cheap flashlights, a bag of Skittles, and head out.

There are a few floaters out in the street now, rounding the corner of 24th. I set my new treasure down in front of the revolving door, then head over to the first drifter. It's a big guy dressed in black like a nightclub bouncer. I clothesline him with the tire iron, crunching his neck.

There are no gas cans in the hummer's trunk, but I keep on looking. I find one full two-gallon canister in the back of the BMW, and a little further down a black four-gallon drum in a Mercedes. It's probably enough. I carry them back along with my shopping through the revolving door to the lobby; it looks like the embassy for a third-world country. In two trips I get everything sealed inside the stairwell of my building, and in two more up to the fourth floor by the window.

I munch on the Skittles and sip water while looking out at the zombie ocean. Is what I'm about to do evil? Perhaps. I don't care. It's not exactly survival, because I've just proved I'm not trapped, but like I told the ocean out there, this is my coffee shop. I need it to have any chance of contacting Lara.

It'll be a bitch to clean up. I suppose it's a bit like napalm. I hope it'll reduce them all to slurry, which will drain down into the sewers when a good rain comes.

I open the four-gallon drum and breathe the heady stink of gas. The liquid sloshes as I heft it. I lean out, bracing myself with one thigh against the window, and tip the contents down into the mass of them. They soak it up like sun-dried kelp. Apart from those who've eaten dog brains, they haven't had a slurp to drink for three days.

I take the second can and pour it carefully into my Super Soaker, then spray it out over them all, repeating the process many times. I toss the lighter refill cans out amidst them, thinking they might blow like grenades if it gets hot enough.

That's all my fuel spent. I wash my hands off from the water cooler, spark the first Zippo, and think for a moment more about what I'm going to do. Then I dismiss any protest as irrelevant, and toss the lighter down. It bounces off a gas-drenched zombie shoulder and whuffs into ignition at once. Licks of vapory fire snap up at my eyebrows, singeing them, and then the bonfire catches properly, spreading rapidly to encompass the street. I can barely lean out for the heat.

The ocean is on fire.

I toss five more Zippos into the crowd. Some of them catch and others don't. The fire burns hot and smoky. They're tightly packed in like human tallow, and together they burn.

I gag on the BBQ stench of them. Chewy puffs of human smoke rise up, scalding me. I hear the crackle of their skin popping. At least they don't scream. One of the fuel cans bursts with a massive bang and the nearby bodies blow to the sides. The others burn and melt orange and yellow, though they don't scream at all. They continue to shuffle to the pile they've made against the wall throughout.

I watch for a few minutes, simultaneously fascinated and repelled by what I have done. On the one hand it seems like I had no choice. On the other it is a truly disgusting thing for a human being to do. I hope Lara isn't watching.

I can't stay, so I get in my Humvee and drive. It's easy to punch other vehicles out of the way. I go east on 24th to 3rd avenue, then south. I know the police academy is this way, and I'm in no big rush. At some points I can see the greasy black smoke rising from Sir Clowdesley over buildings like a bleak cloud, and look away. Probably that was a bad idea. If anything, it'll just draw more of them.

I go by a police car stuck in traffic, then stop and get out. I have the tire iron and the street is empty. The patrol car driver side door is open, and the keys are in the ignition. I pull them out and go to the trunk. I read in the prepper Bible that some of these cars have weapons lockers in the back, where I might find a shotgun or patrol rifle. The trunk opens, and there's a metal box built into the trunk that might be a locker, but the car key doesn't work to open. I give it a few desultory whacks with the iron, but it just clangs. I try to pick it up but it's built into the trunk. Probably the key is in the pocket of some floater cop roaming the streets.

Ah well.

The stink of greasy burning reaches me. It carries on the air. I look up 3rd avenue and see there's a thick fog of black smoke curdling closer. I get in the police car and start it up. I click buttons until I find the one that starts the siren.

The lights flash overhead, splashing reflections off the hummer, and the siren rings. I drive it back up to the fog, and there I wait.

The ocean comes, bringing the whole fire with them. They stagger on crisping legs while their bodies burn, their faces running like the Gestapo-guy in Raiders of the Lost Ark. It is horrific, but I'm in the middle now and I can't stop.

I wait until they're almost on me and the cloud of their black smoke is everywhere. Then I lead them away. I drive slowly north, with their burning bodies stumbling behind. None of them run now. I drive until they stop following and the trail of oily smoke gives out because they've all burned out. They lie behind me like a long black scar on the city.

Oh god, what have I done.

I find a bus facing west and I drive it back down 4th avenue. I don't want to see the slug trail of their bodies, but on 23rd I pull in and see them everywhere. There are myriad charred corpses on the floor and lying atop the scattered desks. There are deep black scorched carbon marks up all the buildings. The front of Sir Clowdesley has been obliterated with dark grease. You can't see my sign in the window for all the black. It's just a mess, and it reeks of half-cooked meat and gasoline.

I pull the bus in, and three-point turn it so it's blocking most of the western edge of 23rd where it borders on 4th. I get out and walk through the wreckage to the nearest car. The asphalt is hot underfoot, and my feet come away mired with black sludge, like I'm walking through treacle. A hand with most of the skin peeled away reaches out to me from a bubbly body.

I get in the car, so dark with tar I can't make out the model, and turn the key. My hands are black just from handling the door. The windscreen wipers work ineffectively to clear the mess from the glass. The engine turns and the wheels slip and skid in the human oil. I pull the car up and slot it lengthwise into the gap between the front of the bus and the nearby building. It's a near perfect fit.

Can they get past this?

I study the pattern of blackened desks. They've been pushed apart and backward, like broken levees where the mass was too much.

I drive the other cars on my road to back sidelong to the bus. They'll add their weight. In large numbers they could climb over, and even a few floaters could probably squeeze through the gaps, but I'll mortar those in with something. Maybe mortar. I flash on the prepper Bible, and where New York's construction equipment may be kept.

That would help.

I pull up about eight more cars to block 23rd to the east where it meets 3rd Avenue. These will serve as ballast for when I get another bus, backing it up. I notice I've left my patrol car inside the barricade, but it doesn't matter now. My lime green moped is still there too, though it's not green anymore, and it's been knocked on its side and crushed by countless feet. There are thick mucusy strands of something glistening around it, like organic padlock chains. Entrails?

This whole charnel pit stinks of barbeque and offal. This was a mistake.

I climb out of the cesspit over my barricade of cars, boost another car with its key in the ignition, and drive off looking for a bus. I see floating lost zombies and swerve to hit them. Doing this disgusts me, but I can't stop myself. They rattle up the hood, into the glass and over the roof. When the windscreen cracks so badly that I can't see, I get another car. I find a bus somewhere around 37th, and drive it back, crunching the crawlers beneath its ten-ton frame. All of these are mistakes but I can't stop making them. It's like I'm not myself, and all I can do is kill.

I pull the bus up flush along to the cars and handbrake it.

It's still not enough. Perhaps they can push them back. Perhaps they can climb over. I need more buses. I know where to find them.

The Port Authority bus terminal in Midtown feels like a dungeon, dark and dingy once I'm through the glass vestibule with its pop-red modern art. I use one of my stolen flashlights to illuminate my way. No floaters come for me, as it's empty inside. I walk through the massive dark interior, bigger even than the darkness, with only my footsteps as company. Right about now I'd talk to Io, if she still worked. What would I say?

Forgive me father for I have sinned.

I smash into a bus at stop C22, where I once took a trip up to summer camp in Boston. I was a camp counselor back then, working with at-risk kids from the inner city. I met a friend from Iowa State University by chance, sitting on a railing waiting for his Greyhound going west. It was bizarre. We talked about how easy it was to get lost in the bus terminal's dark nether halls, and what we both missed about college. We agreed to catch up online, but we never bothered. His bus came and we went our separate ways.

A different world, now.

There is no key in the bus. Of course not, that would be too easy. There are a few sleepy floaters though, rousing like this is finally their stop.

I leave them. I get out. I wander around the maze of buses for a while, feeling lost. Is this the nightmare, I wonder, or the reality? One of the ocean pops up around the edge of the bus alley I'm walking in, and I jab him hard in the throat with the sharp end of the iron. He falls to the ground. I notice as I step over him, he's wearing the gray uniform of a bus driver.

There must be a room where they keep all the keys. It would be an office for the drivers, probably protected by a pass card, some kind of electronic lock that would be fixed solid now, forever. I'll never find it before nightfall for sure.

I follow the buses to the exit. Light floods around me, shaping the mouth of this concrete nether-hall with black diesel smoke accretions. I feel sick at myself. I'm already tired of smashing my way into things.

I smash into a Greyhound bus sitting in the exit, which must've stopped on its way out. The keys are in it. I rev it up and drive. It bullies its way roughly down 8th Avenue, plowing other road users aside. On 23rd I turn left and pull it up across the gap where I slotted the car in. I work it back and forth until the flank grinds hard against the brick face of a Lush soap shop, knocking over a lamp-post and striking sparks off the other bus and car. This is my mortar. I get out and look up at my new wall.

It is impregnable. At first I'm not even sure how I'm going to climb it. Then I remember. I smash a few windows, clear the glass, and climb up them. Atop the bus I look back. My area is clear of floaters still, and grossly filthy still. A few more buses will do it.

I do the run to Port Authority on 41st and 8th three more times, swapping a stolen car nearby for a bus each time for the trip back. On the last trip back I stop off at the tech store on 44th street and pick twenty laptop batteries off the dark shelves, plus headphones and immersion goggles. I stop at a clothes store and pick up some clothes. I stop at a bed store and pick up sheets and a few duvets.

I don't have a gun. I don't want one now.

I climb back in over my bus-blockades, each two thick now. I have the whole street now, and it's disgusting. I traipse through the treacle of burnt bodies like an alien landscape, numb and barely in control of my legs. Across the street there's a liquor shop and I pick up a bottle of whiskey. I pick up another one. I carry all my stuff to Sir Clowdesley and look inside.

A few floaters mill in there. It stinks sourly, like old vomit and charcoal that's been pissed on. I see my new bedding has been trailing in the black and I let it drop. I drop all this shit except the batteries in their shopping basket and the whiskeys. I climb in.

The floaters come for me. I hit them in the brains. They must be dizzy, because they're slow. They let me come in, and up in the library I find my nest, and my cache of guns spread around the floor.

I shoot them in the throats. I go back to my shitty sofa and stuff tissue paper up my nose to block out the stink. A breeze carries it in from the street and circulates it.

I boot up my laptop from my pack. I get the spare batteries on standby. I get out the USBs and boot up the darkness. I plug in my goggles, my noise-canceling earphones, and escape.

If they come for me, I don't care. I can't do this anymore. What I've done today is already unforgivable, a kind of genocide. The fulfillment center peels open before me. Here everything is simple, there are shelves to walk like city blocks and there are goods I need to collect like guns and buses.

I laugh. It's all the same. I get a mouthful of the stench of what I've done. I run on through the darkness while tears run down my eyes and hang in the goggle-cups, obscuring the screen. I do what I'm told. I drink some whiskey and I do what I'm told.

11. THE DARKNESS

The fulfillment center is dark and calm. I go round and round in circles for hours, picking up junk and delivering junk, bringing some measure of reality and routine back to my existence. I could even imagine I'll bump into Cerulean soon. We'll run together. I'll go to bed in my Mott Haven flat, and the next day I'll wake up looking forward to my trip to Sir Clowdesley, because the barista called Lara's on shift.

It's a dream that makes me sound like a stalker. I'm in Sir Clowdesley now, waiting for her. It doesn't smell of lovely roasted coffee anymore.

I go to Blucy at the print-on-demand machines. She runs through her set script, talking about her books, selling me on Deepcraft, things like that. I watch as Hank and the others go by, endlessly grinding for loot in the darkness' monster-less dungeon.

Hours pass into the night. At some point I sleep with the goggles still on. When I wake up the laptop battery is dead. The goggles have dug sharp creases into the skin around my eyes. I don't want to take them off, but just for a few moments I must.

Sir Clowdesley's walls, ceiling and floor are streaked with black grime. Light creeps in around the tumbled blackboards and through cracked windows. Chairs and tables have been scattered everywhere. One of the floaters is actually lying dead near my feet. I didn't notice that.

I get up and drag it by the feet to the stairs, where I tip it down.

There are four other bodies there, each lying in a dark bloodstain in a pool of hot spring light, smeared with the ashy grease of their fellows.

I go to the toilet in the toilets off the stairwell. The water flushes for what I expect will be the last time. There'll be no water pressure any more to fill the cisterns. I open the door into the inner donut and look out. There's a deep blue sky, and the air here is so fresh it burns my lungs. I feel like a subterranean thing peering for the first time into the light.

It isn't for me.

I go back to my sofa. I unbox one of the batteries and slot it into place. I fish out my USB pack, wrapped in saran plastic, and unfold them. I plug the first in and peruse the files. It's all prepper stuff, but for the file labeled 'Cerulean'.

I take a long fortifying slug of whiskey, then I open the file. Hit me with it all. I find the code for a new non-player character in the mod file, and preview it. Of course it's Cerulean, his image and a coded text file. I find myself blinking back boozy tears. I boot up the center, slip my goggles back into their grooves in my face, and install him into the mod.

There he is, just as always, a green and blue parrot with a pirate on his shoulder. Immediately he starts walking away, down the long halls, and I follow him. I try to raise him with a text interaction, but he's not interested. He's got a program. He's not even looking at his diviner.

Just to see him brings home the reality. I'll never talk to my friend again.

He turns left at Blucy, walks straight by the supervisor who's making marks on his notepad, then stops at an aisle in the shelving. I see some new items there, they look like comics.

"Hey Amo," Cerulean says. The text bubble floats above his head. My hearts turns over in my chest.

"Hey Cerulean," I type back.

"I made this for you," he says. His parrot picks up one of the comics and holds it out. "It's good work. It means something."

I take the comic and bring it up across my screen, then laugh aloud, in the real world. It is a digital version of my own comic, Zombies of New York. It is completely fitting. I leaf through the pages, every single panel and cell I made in the last six months present and correct.

"I hope you don't mind," he says. "I just want you to know I'm proud. If anyone deserves to survive a real zombie apocalypse, it's you. You have the right kind of empathy."

I laugh again, this one more like a sob. Nothing I've done so far has been empathetic. I've only been brutal and cruel, and making excuses for the reason why doesn't mean shit. It is a weakness in me still.

"You might not believe that now," Cerulean says, as if he can hear me scoffing. "But you will. I've seen it, you know? I saw things in my coma too. If you're even alive, and you ever see this message, you'll understand, or you'll come to. Because these zombies are you and me, Amo. Did you know that? Yes/No?"

I recognize this question as the start of a simple decision tree. We programmed them into our non-player characters, to give them some diversity in their scripts. I type, "No."

"You don't? Think about it. Did you see any photos of yourself in your coma? Probably not. Did they tell you any of the weird stuff you did? Probably not. Do you know I went gray for a month, like a dead man? My eyes went white, like I had glaucoma. I was up and sleepwalking, following people. They probably didn't tell you any of that, because it's too damn freaky. My mother told me. It sounds like a zombie though, doesn't it?"

"Yes/No," he offers.

"No."

Cerulean flips me the bird. This is one of his jokes, a bird flipping the bird. I can't stop myself laughing again, through my tears.

"Use your head, Amo. Think things through. I'm here lying in my cripple bed, dreaming you're alive. Can you imagine what things will be like if you are? It's beautiful. It means I'm not alone, which means you're not either. I don't feel the twinges anymore. If it wasn't for my mom and her friends banging on the door upstairs, I could go out in the world and I'd be fine. I'm cured! Do you think that's a coincidence, the same day the zombie apocalypse hits the whole world? Yes/No?"

"Shut up, Cerulean," I type.

The parrot waits. His Yes/No dialog clicks up again. He'll have all the patience in the world, now. I wonder how far down the decision tree he planned this interaction, when he was lying in his bed listening to the Skype call to me ring out, with his mother thumping overhead. What did that feel like, to finally be free and know that it could only last for hours?

Now I'm crying again.

"Yes," I type. It's just a coincidence.

"Yes? Pull your shit together, Amo. You're being willfully blind. We started this thing, or it started with us, don't you see that? Whatever hit us a year ago primed us and the world. It's obvious, don't you think? We became the proto-zombies, even the incubators for this infection. We went gray, we got white eyes, we wandered. But we were cared for, because there were only a handful of us, and they brought us back. What if that's what's happening out there, now? We seeded this apocalypse. I don't have time to offer a Yes/No now, Amo. You've just got to be with me on this, because the next one is a big one."

He goes quiet.

"What?" I type.

Thirty infuriating seconds pass.

"Are you ready?" he asks.

"For shit's sake, Cerulean!" I shout in Sir Clowdesley. "Tell me."

"Then consider this. Your doctor warned you never to have sex. He said it might cause something worse. Do you remember that? I don't know for sure, but I'm guessing that is what happened with you and Lara. You are a charming bastard. You had your date, you took her home, and the earth moved forever. Whatever chemical buttons that act pushed in you, it also triggered the world's zombification. The infection began in New York, Amo, I gathered that much from the first blush of its spread. It went everywhere after that in hours, across the globe faster than any wind vector could carry it. People were primed to a wavelength, it has to have been something like that, because they were all pre-infected, and you were the trigger. You and Lara got down, and you birthed this new race."

He goes quiet. I lie on my filthy grime-smeared sofa and stare at an image on two goggle-vision screens, while the last cold hard chunk of text bobs above his parrot head.

What the?

"Amo," he types. "Are you listening, Yes/No?"

I stare. I caused this, he's saying? I caused this by having sex? It's true the doctor told me to masturbate clinically, to never indulge in romance, and I did exactly as he asked until Lara, and then...

Then I killed the whole shitting world?

"Amo," he types again. "Are you listening, Yes/No?"

I want to punch his stupid bird face. I want to burn myself to the ground.

"No," I type.

"Are you listening, Yes/No?"

"No!"

"Are you listening, Yes/No?"

"Yes, goddammit, yes Cerulean you bastard!"

"Yes, so get over yourself. Get over yourself Amo. You cannot for one second feel guilt over this. You died multiple times in a coma. You spent a miserable year running around in a fake dark cave with a cripple. That it was you who first reached out of your confinement means not a damn thing. If it hadn't been you, it would have been one of the others. There must be others, Amo; it can't only be you and me. The chances of only us finding each other are infinitesimal. There must be hundreds like us, out there somewhere. Perhaps some of them have been in comas this whole time, and now they just woke up. Have you thought about that? Think about that.

"And of those hundreds, any one of them might have recovered sufficiently to have sex, and thus trigger the end. But none of them did, because none of them are as defiant as you. Do you understand that? You were brave, Amo! That's human. You were willing to risk dying just to live a little, you chose man not mouse, and that's nothing to be ashamed of. There is no guilt here; you had no conception of this godforsaken outcome.

"Now, your duty is clear. Your people are out there, all the lost ones who never found each other and have no idea what's going on. They're going to need guidance. They'll need a leader. They'll be lonely and broken, like I was when I found your center. You have to do what you did for me, for all of them. Do you understand? Yes/No?"

I stare at the block of text. The Yes/No tag repeats insistently, refreshing once a minute. Steadily it pushes his speech off the screen. This was Cerulean. He isn't here, but that doesn't change anything. He was my friend, and I won't disrespect that even if I don't believe or agree with him.

"Yes," I type eventually.

"Good. I'm glad. I can die happily, knowing you're out there doing what you can, in the full light of the truth. You're a good man, Amo,

Michael John Grist

you'll be a great man, and if there's any way to save these infected millions, or to alleviate their suffering, I know you'll find it, just like you did for me. I know you'll die trying if you have to, and no one could ask for more than that."

I look at his damn bird. It looks glassily at me.

"Goodbye Amo. Good luck."

The parrot doesn't disappear or fade, it just stops talking. Its diviner blinks, and it starts walking away. I watch it go.

Now it's just a non-player character like the others, a true ghost in the darkness. It passed along its message, one it carried across the vast distances between this broken world and the world when it was still on the cusp, and now it's for me to carry onward.

It bows me. I crumple beneath it.

I tear off the goggles and drink.

I rouse in the evening looking out over 4th avenue, sitting atop one of my Greyhound barricades with my legs dangling like a child's over the side. The ocean spreads gray and white before me, its arms reaching up like the fins of fish, its eyes glowing white like the lantern-antennae on those hideous deep-sea fishes that lure other fish in.

Cannibals.

I swig the whiskey, which I hate. I pour a little out for the floaters to enjoy, on their faces and heads.

"I'm not going to burn you," I slur at them. "Don't worry."

They wave and drift like fronds of seaweed in the water, like groupies holding up their lighters at a stage. Their fingers sometimes plink against my shoes, tickling me gently.

I drink and think about Cerulean and Lara. I wonder how my parents died. I think about the cosmic sex that sent a signal out that somehow caused this.

"Did you know?" I ask the bodies below. "Did you feel it? Do you feel it now?"

They grope and waggle like anemone fronds. I pour the rest of the bottle on the head of an obese man wearing a sodden brown velour training top. As the liquor splashes he lifts his face and I get it in his mouth.

This makes me laugh hysterically. He blows bubbles with it.

The Last

I get to my feet and throw the bottle as far as I can. It hits the darkening asphalt across the intersection but disappointingly doesn't smash. Rather it chips and skitters away, like a flat rock skimmed over calm waters, receding underneath a resting car.

I laugh. I look out west along 23rd and north and south on 4th. The sun is going down, a nice burnt sienna, and it's really just me. There's no sign of Lara, and if she was here, would she even want to come within a mile of this disgusting charnel fiefdom?

I laugh. I have screwed myself, by surviving.

Down amongst the midst of my crop of floaters there is a cop. His uniform is easy to pick out. I pull one of my guns, strapped like bandoliers now across my chest, and shoot at him.

His shoulder blows out, and a floater behind him takes the slug and his dark blood in the chest. It's quite hilarious. I shoot again and the top of his head comes off, the face behind him explodes, and still no holy retribution rains down.

I get these for free. I shoot until the gun clicks out, but he still hasn't gone down. There's blood all over him, his head is in half, there are pockmarks torn into his chest and flesh, but still he sways his glowing eyes at me like lanterns in the depths.

I throw the gun and it disappears beneath their mumbling feet. I pull all my guns and shoot them blank at him. This is the way to fish. I get about five rounds before all my guns are blank, and I throw them.

He's still standing. He looks like a stick of pulped meat.

I drop back inside my blackened block as the sun goes down. I head for the liquor shop, through the darkness as night comes on, with his one burning eye still foremost in my mind.

12. RV

Lara isn't coming.

I figure that out the next afternoon, looking over the ruin of my domain from the fourth-floor office. She isn't and she won't, because she's surely dead like everybody else.

I just had to have sex and screw everything up. It's like those horror movies where sex damns the heroes, but my sex has damned the whole world. It's a sick kind of vanity that allows me to feel responsibility for this, to feel guilt for 'what I did', but still I do.

I need to find other survivors.

There have to be some. Cerulean promised.

I go out the embassy back door, still drunk in the clean morning light, with a whiskey bottle in my hand. I hate the taste but it's starting to grow on me. I wander up the street, tapping out silly rhythms on deserted car frames with the bottle and shouting at any floaters that come near. I hit one with the tire iron and fall into an ugly embrace with him.

He grabs for my brains, and I get on top where I can press the tire iron in through his eye. Of course that does nothing. I have to pull it out again, fascinated and grossed out by the black blood welling up from the ruined socket, and press it into his throat. Getting it through the skin is hard, but with enough weight it punctures.

He doesn't die until I sever his spine. So I learned something.

I wander on. Somewhere around 26th and 5th I see a horde

gathering in the distance. What are they so interested in? I wander over. There are hundreds grouping near Times Square. I round a corner stacked high with blank digital screens and see.

It's a dog, standing somehow atop a city bus in the middle of the road. I laugh. He's skinny and barking, some kind of brown/white terrier breed, and he's probably a few hours from dying. He keeps on barking like somebody's going to come save him.

Poor little guy. He's meat for the ocean, now.

Some of the horde peel off and come for me. I move like I'm in a dream, climbing into a nearby SUV. The keys are there in the ignition and I rev the engine. More of them flow toward the sound. I put my seatbelt on, press the pedal down and drive right at them.

I hit the first with a thump, the second with a thwack, then it's a barrage of thwack, thump, crack for a hundred yards, running over bodies and sending them flinging to the side like Moses parting the Red Sea, until the windshield is fractured so badly I can barely see and my forward momentum is halted by their sheer mass.

A breaking wave of gray and white faces stares at me through the white-webbed glass less than two yards away. Dryness has pulled their lips back from their bloody teeth in a series of rictus grins, shriveling their cheeks into dark hollows. Death is really changing them.

The dog is still somewhere ahead, barking frantically. He sees me, he knows I'm one of the good guys.

"Just a second," I call, and twist to look through the rear window. I shift the stick to reverse and rev backward.

Thump, bang, crack, smack. Bodies impact and go smearing across the asphalt, bodies crush beneath my wheels. I rev back until my tire marks run dry of blood and I've dinged off a dozen cars, clearing something of a path.

They're charging again. I slam the horn down and charge right back.

It's like ten-pin bowling for people. They go flying in all crazy directions; off to the side, over the top, bouncing back into the crowd. Bits of them start to get tangled up in the windshield's fractured web, here a scrap of tongue, an earlobe, a gobbet of dry gray skin.

"Come on!" I yell into the fury of the stampeding storm. I hit the solid depths again and rev backward. The poor dog won't shut up. I ram backward and forward like a steam piston. When the windshield breaks inward it takes me totally by surprise, showering me with crystal glass and zombie bits. Hands grope inward from bodies suspended on the hood.

I race back and friction pulls them off. I stop an intersection down, spy out a better machine, an RV, and get in. The keys are in the dash, it revs up nicely, and I bring it to bear like a battering ram.

The dog barks. I crush dozens of them. I splatter dozens. I probably grind hundreds under my wheels. In all, it doesn't do a damn thing. I can't get closer. Hot tears splash off my hands. One damn dog! I couldn't save Cerulean but maybe I can do this.

"I'm coming!" I shout to him. "Buddy, I'm coming." I hammer at the ocean but the ocean is an ocean and it swells to encompass me. Rather than getting closer, each time I get driven further away, carried on the surging tide. I can't think for the dog's crazed barking.

"Hold on, I'm coming."

Then the barking stops. I don't see the moment he gets pulled down. It's a wholly unremarked death, like every other death in this new age, and it makes me seethe. I beat the crap out of the steering wheel with my fists. Ramming them with an RV is not enough for this. Burning them won't cut it. I need something more.

The RV punches through the glass entrance hall of the Police Academy with ease. I drive it on into the lobby until it cracks to a halt against the elevator shaft.

HOOOONK.

I ply the horn, drawing the floodwaters out. The lobby is low and wide; more of a space to line up and wait, like the DMV, than a place to be awed and impressed by.

HOOOONK.

Some of the ocean come, trickling out of their hidey-holes. There's a few regular cops amongst them, plus some more civilians. They bang against the RV's sheet-metal sides. I feel like a turkey in tinfoil packing, waiting for the heat to turn on.

HOOOONK.

Maybe there are fifteen. Many have blood on them, masked around their lipless mouths like gory lipstick. I pull the RV back and ram them.

It works well for this many. It breaks necks and crushes limbs. It only takes one more go before they're all down. I get out and run over the glass-sprayed, blood-smeared lobby floor, to one of the cops. He's burst like a bloody piñata. I crunch the tire iron through his neck and pluck out his gun.

I have some familiarity with this now. I flick the slide to check the clip, full. I toggle the safety off. I stride the remnants of this horror show and put them out of their misery.

Looking back at my RV is disgusting. It is not white any more, but a maroon-brown the color of guts and shit. It looks like a hairball made of blood and sinew, with hundreds of scraggly tufts of skin and meat caught on tears in the metal and cracks in the glass.

I collect three more guns and put them in my pockets. I collect two flashlights from utility belts. I look for the stairs. There's bound to be a shooting range in the basement. Near to that there's bound to be a munitions cabinet, and a key.

I rummage in the darkness, deep into the building. I shoot a few. I find pitch-black stairs and descend. In the mad, cold dark I advance, until I hit a long alley leading through swing double doors and onto a deep low-ceilinged range.

HANDGUNS ONLY

The sign is very helpful. It tells me this is not the shooting range for me. I keep on going until I find another one, with a mixture of long and short-range targets. My flashlight can't pick out the furthest ones.

I scavenge around. I shoot bits of kelp that come jogging out of the shadows, leaving them gurgling. I find a room with long metal roll-cupboards, and I shoot at the locks until it becomes clear that won't open them. I search in nearby desks and ranks of keys hung on hooks on a wall in an office somewhere until finally I find the one I need.

The cupboards roll open and they are not bare. They are full of sleek black shotguns, AK-47-like rifles, and what look like sniper rifles.

Beneath them are banks of ammo in nice bright cardboard boxes, orange and green and purple. I find a gear-bag and stuff it with boxes, then throw in two of each gun type on top.

I make five trips or thereabouts to the surface, filling up the RV with munitions. I go back to Times Square. I stop a block away from the throng, where the marks of my passage are clear in blood and broken bodies.

I bolt the RV's door closed. I pop the skylight and push my gear bags through to the roof. Already they're coming for me. I settle on top with one of the sniper rifles. I work the new slide, line my eye up to the scope, and shoot.

The kick punches the scope back into my head, and blood springs out of my face. I gawp in shock at the fountain spurting out from above my eyes.

"Shit!"

I slap a hand over the wound and drop the rifle. I drop back into the RV and rummage through the cupboard until I find sticky bandages and a mirror. The wound is a half-moon just above my right eye, cut by the scope's sharp edge. I laugh and bandage it up. Blood seeps through but not much, and the first wave hits the RV hood.

I climb back up, fetch a shotgun, and shoot down into them.

The butt slams up into my armpit painfully, but three of them evaporate in gray mist. Brilliant.

More are coming. I get down on one knee above the windshield, take aim vaguely, and let rip.

It takes hours. Stragglers still come, drawn on strange tides.

I've killed them all. My trigger finger burns with blisters. Shooting the AK-47s was the most godlike. I sprayed wave after wave and they went down. I got better at shooting them in the throats at a distance, like scything down a row of corn.

SPAT SPAT SPAT DROP DROP DROP

Reload. They came on and I shotgunned them to brain-shells and dust. At one point they cleared far enough back that I popped out the sniper rifle again and set to work.

SMACK SMACK SMACK

They went down. They went down all day long.

Now I'm standing surrounded by the strange coral creations of their bodies, a landscape of the heaped-up dead like a full-color image of the holocaust, and it's too much. I can't take this, I don't want to kill them anymore, so I take the path I ought to, which is really the only decent thing to do, having come this far.

I hold a handgun to my head and pull the trigger.

13. AARON

When I was younger I had a brother. His name was Aaron and he was four years older than me, and he specialized in riding his Schwinn bike, playing WWF wrestling games, and calling out the endings to movies we watched as a family.

"Stop spoiling it!" I'd complain. "Mom, tell him."

"I haven't even seen it," he'd laugh, spreading his hands. "How's it a spoiler if I'm just guessing?"

We used to ride our Schwinn bikes up and down the street outside our house, jousting with fallen corn stalks picked from the fields. The stalks usually bent on impact, but they hit hard enough to hurt. That was part of the excitement though. The harder the hit the more we'd laugh.

Afterward we'd compare welts and bruises on our chests and shoulders, and guess at how mom would shout down the house if she ever saw them.

"For that one she'd shit a house," I'd say, pointing at a good bloomer I'd landed across Aaron's sternum.

"She'd shit a whole farm," he'd answer. "Even the barn!"

When I was fourteen Aaron died. It was a hit and run, he was in a rented Oldsmobile with his date for the prom, and whoever did it totaled them. We never found the guy. Just out of the darkness, my brother was stolen away.

I stole my first zombie comic a month after the wake. In the mall, it was easy to do. I lingered for ages, fingering all the copies, leafing through them, hoping I'd become invisible to the clerk on duty down at the checkouts.

I knocked the comics over. I picked them up. I straightened them out. I luxuriated in the raspy touch of them, the wrapping paper feel of them, the vibrant colors; all that blood and gore.

I asked myself, is this what Aaron looked like when he shot through the front windshield and they found bits of him spread all across the corn? I thought knowing might help. I hated the zombies because they were like the guy who killed Aaron, but at the same time you had to forgive them, because they didn't know did they?

We don't hate tigers or sharks or bears, though they kill and eat people sometimes. We don't hate cows or buffalo in the fields, but they can trample people to death. A horse can kick the jaw clean off a man's face. A camel can bite off your nose. Maybe some people hated camels, I wasn't sure.

The point was, I couldn't really hate the zombies. They fascinated me too much.

I started stealing a copy a day. I'd slide it up my shirt or down my pants. Always I did it a different way, like each time it was a different crime and they could only get me for one, because there was never a pattern. On the way home I'd always do something good, like help an old lady carry some bags, even just a little way. They thought I was such a little saint. I'd help a little kid find his lost bit of green glass. I'd smile at a baby in a stroller instead of scowling, while all along the comic would be burning its secret message into my skin, trapped against my belly or round my back.

Hot, sweet shame. It was something to feel, something to be.

I'd never been into art before that. I was a sports junkie like Aaron, but every time I took to the field after the crash, all I could see was his burst-out eyeballs on the road, his guts piling out while he panted a few last hot breaths, wondering why nobody was coming to help him.

I got good at art by studying the comics. I started doing them myself. It wasn't always zombies, but it was always monsters of some kind; strong monsters that made everything seem hopeless, who could wring every bit of life out of heroes and leave them desiccated and weak. It had to be that way, so I could make myself stronger. Shit happened in reality, and true strength lay in knowing and accepting that, so you wouldn't be surprised when it hit you in the face like a clothesline out of the black on a weaving county road.

You saw it coming, like Aaron and the end of the movies. It didn't surprise you so it couldn't hurt you, not more than physically. You were the one left smiling, no matter how badly bruised, no matter how physically broken, because you'd seen it coming and kept on driving, kept on riding, kept on stealing anyway.

It was your decision. It meant something that way.

One day my dad caught me reading the comics up in the tree Aaron and I had once shared. He played it cool. Six months had gone by, and I had a stash of hundreds tucked away wrapped in plastic beneath a loose board on the porch. Maybe he'd known about it for a while.

"Sport, what have you got there?"

I told him. I admitted I'd stolen it. He climbed up the tree and put his arm round me and we sat like that for a while.

"We need these things," he said eventually. "I understand, we all need to heal, and god knows healing isn't pretty, but there comes a time you have to start back, Amo. You can't stay in your hole forever, you've got to come out. It's never too late to stand up and be a good man. Do you understand what I'm saying? Aaron's gone, I know that's a bitch, it's a bitch for me and your mom, I won't lie. But we pick up and we act right just as soon as we're able, and not a minute delayed. I think you know that."

I started to cry quietly.

"You'll take those comics back to the store. You'll explain what you've done, and I'll come in and explain what it means. You'll pay them back Amo, whatever they ask. It's what a good man does. He doesn't take the things he doesn't need, and you don't need to be taking these. What even are they?"

"Zombies," I snuffled.

He looked at the one in my hand and made a squinty face. "Rather you than me."

I laughed. We laughed.

I miss my dad. I miss my brother. I miss Cerulean and everything that's gone.

I wake with a burning headache.

The skies above are gray with cold, thick clouds. It must be a whole other day.

I have really screwed this up. I lie there in Times Square and watch the clouds churn, because I can't move. I've become a paraplegic like Cerulean. I try to tilt my head to the side but it doesn't move. My arms and legs are a foreign country I can't even see.

The clouds morph into faces, just like Zombies of New York. Here goes Lara. There goes Cerulean, or Robert, his silly parrot bobbling by. I try to wipe my eyes but of course I can't. Worst of all I can hear the ocean. I can't tilt my head to see but I know they're below me still, lapping at the RV's sides with the sighing breath of the ocean.

The RV starts to move. They're pushing it with their mass. I feel like a fallen Viking warrior, sent out to sea in his funeral ship, caught on the tide.

The tops of buildings pass through my vision. They're bringing me into Times Square. Perhaps we'll go see a movie.

I laugh.

It starts to rain. It comes down hard and sleeting, it gets black overhead, and bright flashes of lightning fork the sky like Odin's wrath. Whoosh! My cheeks and forehead get peppered in a cold military drumbeat, driving in and out the pain. I open up my mouth and drink the water down. I'm dead but I'm not dead.

The ocean patters happily below me, slapping and slipping in the slick water. It's filling up the streets and the sewers, it covers me and gathers me up, dribbling in and out of the holes in my brain, getting ice cold and slushy into my thoughts.

A dog called Buddy comes to mind, and a little boy running up and down jousting with his older brother. He always let me hit him too. He was such a good brother and I loved him so much, until a faceless monster rubbed him out forever.

I never think about this. I want it back. I want to see my brother again.

"Can you show me that?" I shout into the rain. "Can you give me that?"

We never talked about him. It got so bad that if I even saw his name I'd go into a migraine that lasted for days.

"My dear boy, coming back to the world of the living."

My mother flashes before me, standing at the top of the steps with a tray in her hands, smiling down with misery-filled eyes. I see the misery now, and the fear. We were all so afraid, we've all been so afraid for so long.

"Aaron!" I cry into the rain, out to the floaters and the kelp and the ocean all around, because I don't have the words to say whatever it is I really mean. "Aaron!"

My brother smiles in my face, so mischievous, and I remember we were planning to firecracker the school's mailbox to celebrate after prom. BOOM. Such fun. We would run away laughing, with the janitor on our tails and a security alarm going off from a nearby car.

What have we done? What have I done? Oh my brother, what have I become?

When I next wake it is silent and still. Overhead the sky is a beautiful and clear black, graffiti-sprayed with stars. I shot a hole in my head, but I can still appreciate this.

I think of Sir Clowdesley. He was a great British navy admiral, whose death prompted the rush to uncover the secret of longitude, which allowed European ships to traverse the great gulf of the Pacific Ocean to the Americas.

He prompted the rush by failing. His ship foundered on rocks in the British channel scarcely fifty miles from land, because he didn't know where he was. All of his men perished, or so the legend goes. So progress was born from loss, and humanity advanced.

I lift my arm to stroke the stars' patterns. My fingers are red and angry from trigger-work, but they paint the sky like delicate brushes in the most complex dot-to-dot.

The air is chill and eats into me. The RV's roof is frigid under my back, but I can't complain. The ocean have fallen quiet and I'm at peace.

My head lolls to the side. I see them, all lying down on the ground. Their bodies are entwined, and by moonlight they don't look so monstrous. They look like brothers and sisters holding close to each other through the night, waiting for the warmth of the sun. Despite their filth and raw wounds and tight gray skin, they seem content.

I realize I can move.

I lift my arms. They are my actual, real arms. I lift my legs and the

RV roof flexes with a tinny clang.

I lift my hands to my head. I feel the dry scab where I put the muzzle just above my ear. I probe it gently; it's tender and springy, because surely the bone is gone. I probe the other side, and find a large and ragged scab.

The bullet blew out and took a good chunk of bone with it, but somehow it still sealed. Somehow I'm still alive, and thinking.

It's impossible. I've heard of people surviving gunshots, but not like this.

I push myself to my knees. The roof crumples and rolls. I'm unsteady, my balance is shot and the world whirls, but here I am on my knees. I pat my body down. All here. I look slowly around me.

The ocean is on all sides, white and gray in the moonlight. Their eyes are closed and they all lie still, wrapped in each other's embrace, asleep.

I've been spared.

A shudder passes through me. I run my hand through my hair, down my neck to my spine, and make my guesses. This is what kills the zombies. Perhaps this is what kills me too?

It reframes the infection. I imagine data shunting from my brain into my spinal column like gigabytes transferring to USB, changing the way I think, the way I eat, the way I live.

I don't need my brain anymore.

It's a bizarre and meaningless revelation, the purpose of which I am lost to explain, but it is a revelation still. It means the ocean are like me, and I am like them. After all, I made them.

Kneeling in the dark, I make my vow. I will not treat them like this again. I will not exact revenge. They are what they are, an ocean, and there is world enough for us all.

I leave most of my guns on the roof behind. I climb down the ladder on the RV's back, then dizzily weave my way through their sleeping bodies.

They let me pass. I don't understand it. I accept it for the forgiveness it is.

14. PIED PIPER

It's a new world. I climb to the top of the Sir Clowdesley building for the first time and look out. Eight stories high everything looks different, smaller and more manageable, like I'm viewing it through a tilt-shift lens. Buildings look like Deepcraft blocks, and everything is a resource I can mine.

The ocean are inconsequential. They are the trucks and cars going back and forth in a huge game of Frogger, part of the natural environment now, and it's not worth the cost to my soul to destroy them en masse. It wouldn't even be right.

I bring up my phone, holding a nice charge now since I plugged in the battery packs, and double-click it.

"This city is a grave," I tell Io.

"New York, New York," she says. I nod along. I realize I have that track in my library somewhere.

"Play Frank Sinatra, New York New York."

"Playing," Io says.

Frank comes in. What a crooner. He sings an elegy for the lost city. His rich voice rings out over the rooftops and down the building sides, swooping like Spiderman. I get shivers down my skin. I look over the grand towers of the Big Apple, these monuments proclaiming all the amazing things we did, and feel pride. We did good things, and maybe, just maybe, we still can.

The idea comes to me full of cheek and irreverence, and I embrace it.

I need to make something of this. I look across the skyline to the skyscraper that was always my favorite: the Empire State.

Cerulean could be right, there may be other survivors. Lara could still be alive. I need to give them a sign big enough to see, a lighthouse of sorts for this transformed world, guiding my people safely in.

I start to smile. I am an artist after all, and a Deepcraft adept. I'm going to remake the world.

I start small, sourcing cleaning equipment: stout wooden brushes, chemical scourers, bleach, a hundred water cooler tanks, from hardware stores up and down the streets outside. I find a few gallon drums in the back-end of a pizza shop. I roll them to my truck and stack them with all the rest.

As long as I avoid the throng developing outside my slice of 23rd street, I can move with relative freedom. It takes them time to notice me, and I don't give them that. I sometimes stumble upon a few by accident, but I feel no qualms to shoot them like this, to save myself. I do it clinically, as neatly as I can, clipped through the necks. They drop. I finger the scabbed holes in either side of my head. It isn't revenge, it's just getting along.

I get along.

On the street of 23rd I pour the bleach into the drums and splash in chemicals. The liquids fizz. I dip the first of my brooms in and wonder if it's going to come up with the head comically dissolved. It only steams faintly in the air.

I put on safety goggles and long gloves, and I get to work scrubbing down the black grease stains covering the walls, caused by the firestorm.

It's worse in certain areas, I suppose where they were gathered densest, but it comes away fairly easily, like soot, and runs down to the sidewalk in gloopy dark trails. I splash water to push it on to the sewer grates and move on.

In a day I clear the ground level of a few walls. The painted bricks, store windows, and doors look brighter than they probably have for years. I stand back and admire my work. It feels like I'm polishing a toy train set to a fine buff, before I show it off to my friends.

The Last

I won't whitewash though. I'm not trying to undo the past. I'm going to leave a clear record of what happened here, so if I'm to be judged, let me judged for the things I truly did.

In Sir Clowdesley the stink remains, like the stale tang of cigarette smoke that lingers in your hair all day. The fresh food in the bar is now wilted, rotting and brown. I dump it in a bucket and toss it down a sewer. In the pokey office I dig out a spare key and open up the front door for the first time.

It feels good to walk in and out like a human, no longer crawling through the broken window. I drag the dead floaters out by the heels, to the bus-wall. They're rotting quickly, their gray skin falling in on itself. I can already see bone. I wonder if touching them can infect me. I avoid it.

If they continue to rot at this pace they'll dissolve in a few weeks, and I can inter them in the sewer.

Into that first new night I clean Sir Clowdesley. I scrub the living bejeezus out of it. I clean every book's spine lovingly with a toothbrush. I degrease the floors and walls and set all the tables right. I tidy up the bar display, clean the windows, and set my chalkboard L A R A back in position.

I made that less than a week ago. It feels like a lifetime.

I sponge clean the sofa and set it up with fresh bedding. I polish the floors. As a final touch, I make some coffee. I set a big pan of beans percolating over a generator I dug out of the building's cellar. Ah, roast coffee. I drink a slug of my first brew and it is delicious; dark, bitter, and life-giving.

I clean for the whole week. I barely need to think.

When I finish at ground level I drive one of the cars around as a movable scaffold. I get blisters from scrubbing which pop and heal. My back hurts and gets stronger. It rains and that helps clean the mess away. For the stains that reach especially high I use a ladder.

My cleaning stocks deplete. The street gets clean. I line up the cars just so. It is a wonderful day in my neighborhood. I whistle along to Mr. Rogers as I stride upon my bus battlements, looking down on the ocean. They're piling up again, climbing over their own desperately to reach me. I'm causing this too, which is a kind of needless suffering.

I move to the next stage of my plan. First though, I must leave behind a record.

I find tools in a trophy-maker's shop on 47th off Madison. Learning how to etch a bronze plate is tricky business, lit by a gas lantern picked up at the Army Surplus on 17th, but I get it slowly. It's rather like developing a photo. The laser etcher is too high-powered, but I can still use the old stencil-cups and acid.

I set them out and leave the metal to score, while looking out of the window at a batch of posters on the building opposite, for a movie. I remember how hotly anticipated this movie was: Ragnarok III. It makes me feel warm to think about it, the memento of a world gone by. What comic artist doesn't love and identify with superheroes?

It takes a few trial efforts to get a plaque which looks moderately professional. It comes with holes pre-drilled, so I don't need to do that. I set it up over the door to Sir Clowdesley.

RIP

Here I committed a genocide of some thousand of the ocean (zombies).

I burned them alive with gas and lighter fluid.

I will not do it again.

Come find me at the Empire State Building.

I hesitated for a long time over how to sign it. I could use my name, of course, but that seemed too simple. Banksy was Banksy, like a legend. There was JR and Space Invader and others.

It comes to me on a dime, and I use it. It is, after all, what I am, and the mantle I am assuming. Arrogance be damned. Plus it's fun, and I get to decide.

Last Mayor of America (LMA)

The lighthouse is coming. First I have to make the streets safe.

I go to Yankee Stadium and survey the task ahead. Members of the ocean drift here and there and I avoid them with care.

I ram into the stadium through the glass doors of Gate 1, just like I did in the Police Academy. A few floaters come running and I race ahead, driving my RV around inside with the headlights on, through the broad circular shopping esplanade, until I find the access stairs to the field.

I climb up and emerge. It's gorgeous, a beautiful diamond marked onto the earth like Nazca lines, though already the grass down there is starting to look a bit unkempt. It is wide open though, and empty. It will make a beautiful home. I count the banks of seating, well over a hundred. I make notes on my phone. I know the capacity is 50,000, of course that's for the seats. It doesn't include the ground itself, or all the shops inside. I wager I can get about 100,000 inside, maybe more.

I mark out hospitals on my tourist map; New York Presbyterian on 68th, Mount Sinai on 57th, New York Hospital in Queens, Bellevue on 1st Avenue. I only need to hit one though to get over a hundred generators, Bellevue. They are tucked away in a huge dusty storeroom in the basement. I load them up in the back of a construction truck I find at the building site down at Coney Island, where they were redeveloping the amusement park. I tip out its sand and fill it up with gas drums siphoned from a tanker parked by the Shell station at the east end of 23rd. I raid two electric shops to pick up all the stereos and CDs I'll need.

It takes a few days to get them all in position, spread out throughout the Yankee Stadium stands, the shopping area, and a few down on the field. I stand on the pitcher's mound and look around at this stadium I've only been to once before, when it was alive, and pick out all my little black hi-fi installations. Banksy never did anything like this.

I drive my RV down to 23rd. The throng clamoring for my brains has only grown more massive, spreading over multiple blocks. It's getting quite difficult even to get in through the embassy backdoor. They're starting to pile up in siege mounds of the fallen everywhere.

I turn up the music. For this part of the journey, I've selected a long-loop of the Beatles discography: Let It Be, Abbey Road, Help, Revolver, Sgt. Pepper, the White Album, and so on. It's over two hundred tracks on my phone, feeding the system via Bluetooth. Modern technology is beautiful.

I've got a pretty good idea where the main clumps of the ocean are. Now I just need to go pick them all up.

The music kicks in and I crank it to maximum. The ocean turn. More than ever, they look like zombies now. It's been nearly a month and they're wholly gray. Their skin is gray, their hair is gray, even what ragged clothes they still wear are faded almost completely gray after constant exposure to the sun. They are a gray tide, slowly emaciating, with tight rictus skin and those glowing white eyes.

If anything though, the loss in weight has made them faster. The first few come off after me like whippets. Great. I pull away.

Weaving a path through New York now is like a massive game of Centipede. I can't double back on my own trail because I'll run into them, and there's not enough ammo in the world to spray them all down. I can't stop because they'll catch up to me. I can only go on and on, and pray this whole thing is going to work.

It is exhilarating. My heart yammers like a drum and bass line. Fresh air blasts in through the RV's open windows, and the Beatles pulse out from the generator-fired speakers mounted on the top. John Lennon sings about peace and imagining a new world, and those crazy bastards rise up from their floating haunts around the downtown quaysides to follow me. Ringo does his Yellow Submarine bit and they shuffle away from the killing fields of Times Square, where they have since regrown.

The music calls to them like the Pied Piper, and they follow. These brilliant, hideous, kelp-like floaters float my way, and I lead them in their tens of thousands. At times when I switch from eastward to westward, a few blocks north of my earlier track, I can see the centipede trail of them stretching behind.

They go on and on. It is the conga line of the century. It's one for the Guinness Book, surely.

"Come on!" I shout out at them. "Lots of candy at grandma's house, come on!"

They come on. Some of them peel off the pack and come straight for me, cutting up 7th or 8th Avenue.

"The more the merrier, bring it on!"

I lead us onward and they follow. I weave the gridiron streets of Manhattan like I'm darning a sock, east to west and west to east, always heading north. When I come across a horde I circle round it to the north and add it to my centipede's mass.

Twenty thousand now? Fifty? I have no way of knowing. It's a goddamn ocean of bobbing gray heads back there, stretching to infinity.

I pull up to Yankee Stadium. I park the RV round the side, near the bank of three buses I have set up to seal the doors, and turn the music off. I'll need this baby to escape.

The Last

I stand in the entrance of Gate 1 and watch the leaders of the pack sprinting for me. Good. I wave. I reach up to the spot where I've mounted the speakers overhead and fire up the generator. It gutters to life, and one hundred decibels of Taylor Swift boom out at the entranceway.

I duck under it and head in, stopping at each of the wall-mounted generators in this trail of crumbs through the lobby to punch them all on. They gurgle, spit smoke, and the music dials up.

I run on, circling the shopping mall that runs the whole stadium's periphery, flicking on switches as I go. Gap streams by on my left, a McDonalds, a Burger King, a TGI Fridays. My feet clap on the marble floor and the interior echoes with the raucous yawling of dozens of simultaneous pop tracks.

At two hundred and seventy degrees I stop, not daring to look back, and ascend up the Gate 12 steps into the open air of the stands. There I do the same thing in another grand clockwise circuit, switching generators and stereo systems on behind me, blaring out discordant, mismatching music. I had to take whatever CDs I could find: vintage Kanye, The Sound of Music soundtrack, Prince. I'm just glad it isn't raining.

Halfway round the stadium I spot the first of the ocean emerging tentatively, like woodlice, back into the light. They turn left and follow the trail of sound. Pretty soon they're a flood. They halt to hammer at the first machine making the noise, but that only forces them to bunch up. They fill up the rows and ranks of seating beautifully around it as they all try to get closer.

Finally it goes down, even the generator stops chugging, and they spread on past it. I couldn't have planned this any better. They follow my trail round, slaves to the music, and crumb by crumb the stadium fills. At the two-seventy degree point I stop again, and now I climb down from the stands and onto the diamond.

I run out to the middle and fire up the clutch of speakers on the pitcher's mound, which I've locked inside a steel equipment cage used for holding computer servers. The Beatles blare out on endless repeat, one of my favorite tracks: Here Comes the Sun.

I turn giddily and watch the stadium fill up with gray ocean matter like lines of blood in a drip tube, inexorably leading to a vein. It is beautiful, rhythmic, and masterful. It is a zombie mandala, emblazoned on the earth. You could see this shit from space.

They fill it all up. They fill it up doubly, driven now by the impetus of their own sound and movement. They prowl like animals, looking for a way to get down to me. How long will it take, I wonder, for the whole thing to fill? How far back does my centipede trail go?

It's like watching a sand egg timer. More of them flood in until they're so crammed that they start to fall, popping over the edge of the stands like firing popcorn. They bounce off the sponsorship boards around the diamond, then get up, awkward-limbed and twisted, and start for me and the Beatles in the middle, performing in the park.

I run. I dodge smartly between their grasping arms, shoot the ones who get too close, then duck down and in through the player's tunnel. I crash out through the changing rooms, locking doors behind me, until I come upon the owner's area and private corridors. From there I ascend to the viewing box I've laid on for just this purpose.

The beer from the generator-driven fridge is cool. I crack Bud Lite and drink. I eat some Cheetos, and treat myself to a burger I rustle up on an electric grille. It is a perfect viewing point to see the stadium fill far beyond capacity.

It turns gray. I have kegged the ocean, and it is filling still.

I let an hour or two go by. I watch the center grass fill out like an inflating balloon. The stands are packed now, it hardly matters that most of the stereos and generators have died. A few of them even blow up and start minor fires, but without gas to drive them on the flames soon die out.

The speakers in the middle are still playing. It drives the ones nearest crazy, and they thrash like rockers in a mosh pit. To be honest, it looks like they're having a great time. In time they pack in too tight to move at all, squeezing up against the railings. It'll buckle under the pressure at some point, like the tenement door, and the Beatles will be forever stilled.

It's getting late. Five o'clock, and dusk is coming. I take the trail back through the building, walking on a private owner's access route above the outer skin, filled with hot dogs stalls and shops. I look down and see this layer of the circle is utterly packed too, like gray cream in a donut. Happily though the thread of stragglers pushing their way in through Gate 1 seems to have diminished.

I exit through the owner's door. It's empty round there. I pad round to Gate 1, and the few who are coming in are making so much noise themselves, they don't notice as I get into the bus. I drive it slow and steady across the smashed-open entrance, crushing hardly any of them, shouldering the vehicle up against the walls.

The few stragglers whack against the glass windshield, and I leave through the back emergency exit, as planned. I pull two more buses round, sealing the stadium up like a powder keg.

That's for them, now.

That can be their new home.

I get in my RV and drive away. I'm grinning like an insufferable fool. I hardly killed any, and now the streets are far emptier than before. The hordes are just not there. They can wander and moan and just get on with their lives, maybe even do some shopping.

I start to sing Yellow Submarine at the top of my lungs, feeling irrepressible. This is how it should be done. Now I just need to put up a bat signal for the living.

15. ONE MONTH LATER

A month passes while I work, until my lighthouse is finished and I'm ready to say farewell to the zombies of New York, because I'm not meant to stay here forever.

The horde is waiting for me in the stairwells of the Empire State Building, as ever. I rappel down past them like a ninja, nudging the occasional one with the muzzle of my AK47 when they lean a little too close. Boom, I imagine. The report would ring out and the recoil would sway me like a pendulum, right into their waiting arms. Zombie brains splatter somewhere that no one will ever see or care about, and my brains quickly follow.

It's all a kind of art. But I don't need to, so I don't.

I hit the ground floor and glance around at all the supplies lying on the tarpaulin sheet: another twenty cans of industrial-strength paint, both blue and white, the fumes of which I've been faintly high on for weeks, plus ammo, weapons, ropes and harnesses, a few generators, gas barrels, and lots of window-cleaning equipment.

I don't need them now. Maybe I'll come back for them in years to come, like my own private geocache, but I doubt that. I don't think I'll ever come back to New York again, there are just too many shitty memories.

Zombies lean over the railings above, reaching down through the gaps and out of the security gate I've locked across the stairway base. They're so easy now. I don't kill them if I can avoid it; it'd be like shooting fish in a barrel.

I kick through the ammo and pick up a few rockets for my RPG. I found that in a military bunker inside city hall. If I come across a horde they may be useful as a distraction. Blowing gouts out of the horde itself would only smash up the road and make it impassable for me, but I can shoot out a nearby hilltop or gas station, and they'll go busy themselves with that.

I check my belt for gear and find a few paint rollers still slotted in there. I was using those for the upper floors, where I last finished up. It was nice to use the graffiti cans in the early days, like following in the footsteps of my heroes, but they were really just a marker. To really ensure my cairn stays visible for the longest time possible I had to paint the exterior, in the same kind of thick industrial paint they use to make traffic markings on the road.

It's been a hectic month. It took two days just to get the window-cleaner's carriage to work, providing power and figuring out my safety protocol if it cut out. It took the rest of that week to spray on the outline, with me getting a deep appreciation for how hard any large-scale art must have been for the ancients, like the Nazca lines. It's been the best part of a month since, coloring it all in.

I read about cairns in a book on how the social media layer has changed our world. It talked about how the augmented reality of geo-locked bulletin boards and systems like Jeo's mayoral system made for a new kind of cairn; a way of leaving information, supplies and advice behind for those to follow.

Cairns were used primarily in the Arctic, back when those icy wastes were unexplored and the men who adventured there had to fight for every mile they took, where having a Snickers bar in your back pocket, or laid up and waiting for you in a little stone pile ahead, could mean the difference between life and death.

Shackleton, Scott, Amundsen, all the greatest Arctic and Antarctic explorers used them. They were tiny finger-holds of civilization in the desolate white wastes, crammed as the world's first geocaches with maps, logs, coordinates, food and water, whatever could imaginably be useful; enough to allow those earliest souls to drag themselves out to the poles and back, thus mastering another facet of our world.

We don't master anything now. The cities and the oceans and the airwaves and even our own bodies and minds are lost to us. We are divided and scattered, if any people yet survive. We badly need cairns again, to help us claw something back.

So I've built one. I'm going to build a trail of them, like a dragnet belt across the country. If there's anyone left alive in America, in this whole northern continent, I'm going to dredge them up and give them a place to go.

I bid the echoey stairwell hall a silent farewell. For over a month it's been my workplace and these zombies have been my colleagues. I bow in the center. They applaud with their feet, always desperate to get close enough to touch, to kiss, to caress.

Farewell and be merry.

I roll out through the Empire State gift shop, snatching up a token key ring at the dim register, in the shape of the building itself. I'm thinking I'll collect these at every city on the way out West, then make a collage out of them; a museum to mankind's greatest achievements in bric-a-brac miniature. Cerulean would get a kick out of that. I'm still providing fulfillment with the best.

I step into the daylight of the cleared street and blink in the hot sun. Funny how the smell of baking asphalt brings me right back to reality every time, and I think of days long gone by, when becoming mayor of a tiny New York coffee shop was about the limit of fame my poor little mind could take.

Now I'm the self-proclaimed mayor of all America.

I stride east along West 34th street, kept company only by the rustling of old newsprint trapped in doorways and gutters. It still impresses me how much paper remains from our old life, carrying headlines two months out of date, reporting on a world long dead. I imagine them blowing west across the country like flyers announcing my coming tour.

At the intersection with 5th Avenue, surrounded by huge video screens suspended on the buildings, all blank now, and the bright splashes of color from giant bill-boards advertising Coca-Cola, Apple, some new fragrance called J'Habite, I stop by my JCB construction vehicle. It is bright yellow and zombie-proofed with welded grille plating around the cab, sourced also from the Coney Island construction park.

Beside it I climb onto the roof of a Subaru SUV, one link in a perimeter chain of parked cars I created a month ago in advance of this endeavor. Back then I just wanted a clear stretch of road to walk along without needing to shoot out straggler zombies all the time.

Now it's my own rat-run maze across the city. I've cleared about a mile of streets all in, from Sir Clowdesley to here, the culmination of so many plans. After filling up Yankee Stadium it was easy, just driving and parking, like moving blocks around in Deepcraft. It was advanced valet work. I herded away any zombies trapped inside, killing only a few recalcitrant loiterers.

Now they bumble up against the flanks of the car-walls, unable to figure out how to climb over, at most gathering two or three deep. There aren't enough of them anymore, and I've given them no clear space to mass. Rather they line my route and wave to me as I come and wave to me as I go between here and my base in Sir Clowdesley. I've grown to quite like it, like my own ticker tape parade every day.

In all there are probably tens of thousands of them still, but they're spread all over. There must be millions in Manhattan, but most of them will be in tenement buildings, locked into boxes of their own making. For that I can only be thankful that the switch happened around midnight, with the streets devoid of the daily crush of tourists and workers.

From the dust-marked roof of the Subaru I look over the heads of the nearest floaters to one of the wandering herds, up on 5th Avenue somewhere near Bryant Park. Some of them do this too, endlessly wandering like the ghosts in a game of Pac-Man. I suppose whatever adaptive behavior has evolved into their funky brainstems, it rewards a hunting approach of both nesters and roaming hunters.

At first I watched these developing packs carefully, but they rarely massed at a barricade. The most I've had to contend with for a month is the odd one or two somehow finding their way onto my parade route, like lost sheep.

None of them have died yet. I look down at their sun-bleached gray faces and ice-white eyes, and they look back up at me like groupies to a rock star, as ever. A few feet closer and I'd be torn apart, like the cat or the dog, but standing here all they can do is strain, like blind Venus fly traps. Their hair is coming out now and they're very thin, many of them are sporting old wounds that don't heal; bites and broken bones. They're draped in ragged clothes crusty with old blood and bleached gray by the sun, but still, they're looking remarkably well. Not one of them can have eaten in months.

I wonder, as I often do, if they will eventually die, or if this is some kind of holding position they're capable of maintaining forever, perhaps metabolizing carbon directly from the air like plants. For all I know they could be cannibalizing each other at night, or eating moss, or anything. I know I eat far less now too. We're linked in that, at least, perhaps having a brain in the spine is a more efficient way to run things.

I climb down from the wall and get into the JCB cab, firing up the engine. I make a pointed effort to not look up at my work on the Empire State Building. I've got a spot all picked out for that.

The JCB rumbles over the asphalt on its caterpillar tracks, and I lean my hand against the lever taking us south toward Madison Park. This has been my daily commute for a month now. As the streets amble by, accompanied by the grind of my vehicle's heavy metal treads, I go over my checklist another time. There are two vehicles in the convoy pulled by this earth-mover, one a battle-tank filled with weapons, water and supplies plus my living space, and one a delivery truck full of gas and all the painting supplies and other stuff I'll need to stock up my cairns.

I'm not worried. I've cleared my route out of the city already, a few days work pushing cars to either side on 34th street and through the Lincoln Tunnel. It was like grinding out experience points in World of Warcraft, a game I used to play when I was a kid; little reward but a sense of hard work done. I'm certain there are plenty of supplies out there across the country though; enough to feed me for a thousand years, but it's better to be prepared.

I haven't spoken to another living soul since Cerulean died. It's just been me and Io and the ocean.

The streets ramble by, each of them blocked off by cars I cleared ages ago. Shuffling zombies track me as I go by. I pull up to Madison Square and take the JCB right over the curb and down the walkway of the Park, toward the Admiral David Farragut monument in the middle.

My convoy is waiting beside him, already linked up and bristling with weapons. I climb to the battle-tank's roof, actually a yellow school bus I fitted with howitzers and multiple mounted AK47s pointing out the windows, plus a Bluetooth relay hub. I settle myself on a bright orange beanbag I liberated from a Tommy Hilfiger window display. The sun is starting to set over the city and country, leading the way to the west.

I pop a beer and lie back with snacks at my side. I hardly need to eat or drink anything these days, just like the zombies, but these things still taste good. I've already chainsawed down the trees that might block my view. At last I look up at the Empire State building's south face, and see my art.

f

LMA

This is my work, a gigantic white 'f' on a blue field, blazoned across each face of New York's most iconic tower, covering the windows and the outer walls. It is ten stories high and nearly as wide as the building itself: a symbol for our modern times more potent than a cross or flag or sickle moon.

We are all one, it says. We are all friends under Zuckerburg. I chuckle, because while it's ridiculous it is also patently real. No one will see that symbol and be scared, because no one thinks evil cannibal-survivors have that kind of sense of humor.

It's given me a purpose, and perhaps, if there's anyone else alive out there, it will give them a purpose too. It's my lighthouse to guide the others safely in, to the ground floors of the Empire State building where they'll find my social media supply cairn: a mayor giving out free coffee, transposed to the real world.

I hung a billboard on the front wall of the grand central lobby, where anyone can post their name and date of arrival on, with my new LMA tag and date at the top. I wrote my map and directions of where I will go across the floor; a plan of the entire journey and every step that I will take, with coordinates of all the cairns I plan to leave behind like giant geocaches along the way, so they can follow. I left a big tray full of USBs with every point of the map marked out inside too. There's no shortage of laptops now, so I left plenty of them to read the USBs by, laid out like display units in an Apple store. I left GPS units too, and solar panel chargers, and in the basement below are a dozen RVs with enough gas and supplies stacked in their backs to take anyone clear across the country.

Of course there's coffee too. Down one wall there are ten Nespresso machines, in case there's a crowd, each stacked with its own brightly colored pile of refills, packaged in neat little boxes like shotgun shells.

If there's anyone left behind they will see this trail I've left for them. Perhaps they'll follow, and find me, and then I won't be alone anymore and neither will they.

I sip my beer, a craft brew I rescued straight off its microbrewery production line in Yonkers, and admire the giant 'f'. My work looks crisp and neat hanging in the sky above this abandoned and overgrown city, visible for miles, the graffiti tag to eclipse all other tags. I can relax, the first step is done.

It feels especially meaningful seen from this viewing point beside the Admiral David Farragut. I read about him in an encyclopedia in a book store; a lot less convenient than Wikipedia, but just as useful. Like Clowdesley he was a naval officer, the first full admiral in the US fleet. He distinguished himself in the civil war amongst numerous other naval campaigns, though he was most famous for his quote: "Damn the torpedoes, full speed ahead!"

I have adopted that catchphrase now, in light of modern events, and adapted it. It's the sweltering summer of 2018 and no one uses torpedoes anymore.

Damn the zombies, full speed to the West!

I wrote it on the floor of the Empire State Building foyer in the same thick paint I used for the 'f'. I wrote it here at this ancient hero's feet and signed it with my new tag in full, Last Mayor of America, LMA for short. These words will last for decades, maybe centuries, long after I'm gone. All these marks I'm leaving will be a symbol for others until the Empire State Building comes crumbling down and New York is left as rubble and dust for the zombies to frolic in.

That makes me feel better, and helps still the gnawing loneliness that bites at me every day. I lie back and wait for dark, listening to the comforting sound of the ocean lapping against the barricade. Tomorrow my odyssey begins. It might take a week, it might take a year, but at the end I'll settle down to watch our last great movies in LA's Chinese Theater, beside the Wall of Fame on Hollywood Boulevard, and wait for the others to come, because I can't truly be the last in all of America, in all of the world, left alive.

INTERLUDE 1

The street was quiet when Lara slipped out of the redbrick tenement in Mott Haven, two months earlier. It was just past dawn, a fresh spring morning in New York, and the wet dew-smell from the scrubby park across the road filled her nostrils.

She smiled at the memory of the night before. It had felt like falling into a movie, a cushiony velvet script that carried them along quickly, full of wit and promise. The sex that followed was like a bomb going off. Her whole body tingled in ways it never had before.

She shivered, walking down the street. Willis Street, she saw. She knew roughly where that was, though she'd rarely ventured into the Bronx. Her parents would disapprove. She chuckled and ran her tongue around her fuzzy teeth.

Wine-mouth. She was probably still a little drunk. She felt like simultaneously shouting out and giggling.

"It was so weird!" she expected to tell Alejandro in their shared apartment in Queens later on. "He rolled out this ancient pick-up move, reading my palm for color, and I was ready to get up and walk out, but I don't know. There was something magnetic about him."

"So you screwed him," Alejandro would say, poking her in the belly with a banana. "All the best magnets screw each other."

She'd laugh and he'd tease and they'd relive the whole delicious, bizarre thing together.

She chewed on a bit of her dark hair pensively. It was a good note she left. Good to keep the mystery.

At the bodega she turned the corner and started south. There had to be a Subway line somewhere along here, or a bus stop, probably the 25 would take her at least to the bridge to Queens.

She brought up her phone and clicked through a few text messages. There was one from Alejandro, time-stamped around midnight, just after she'd sent him a frenzied misspelled message that she wasn't coming home.

> Look out, y'all!

was all it said. He was trying it out as his catchphrase. She slid it by and brought up her email, full of the usual garbage; junk mail, notices from the Sir Clowdesley Jeo list, and something from her mother.

> We love you dear. Come home if you can.

That was strange. She clicked to bring up the number and called. The phone on the other end rang and rang but no one picked up. They were probably asleep, especially if they'd been up at, what? Lara laughed. The time-stamp on that message was 2am. She imagined her white-haired old French mother fussing up in the middle of the night to go to the toilet, then settling in for some ancient black and white movie on TV, probably with a glass of warm milk and cognac.

Lara looked up from the phone at the intersection, and saw a bloody torso and head crawling toward her. Beside it lay a smoking upturned car chassis, and between the two lay a trail of bloody organs, linking them together like yoyo string.

Her brain melted for a few seconds. The head stared back at her with bright white eyes. She blinked and tried to fathom what on earth this apparition really was, some weird kind of cat hit by a car, a pig fallen out of a crashed meat van, or a...

BANG

The explosion rocked her awake, a huge blast that she felt through the curb. A cloud of black smoke rose up from further down Willis, and she understood.

New York was under attack. She glanced once more at the grotesque creature in the road. Was this what nuclear fallout looked like? She clamped her hand over her mouth, turned and ran. After five strides she stopped, pulled off her high heels, then ran on barefoot in her stockings. What the hell? She fumbled in her bag and got her phone out again, dialing 911 on the trot.

She got a busy signal. She dialed again as she jogged back past the bodega. Her feet were cold and her heels hurt where they thumped on the paving slabs.

Still a busy signal; 911 was down or inundated. How many people were calling in the same emergency at once? She looked to the sky, expecting to see the contrails of more incoming planes, or, what, missiles, but there were none. The streets were silent.

Where was everybody?

She bolted past 143rd with Amo furthermost from her mind. In the middle of the road lay a car with the engine ticking over and the door open. She plunged into the driver's seat and slamming the door behind her.

The unnatural quiet of the city receded, replaced by the white shush of the air conditioner. The keys were in the ignition and she twisted them a click over to kick the engine in. It coughed to full life. Out of habit she checked the rearview mirror, and saw another one of the victims coming for her.

It was a girl wearing a white dress covered in blood. Half of her face had melted away, replaced by mottled purple underskin. Her eyes shone like radioactive cesium.

Lara punched her bare foot hard on the accelerator, lifted the handbrake, and burnt rubber the hell out of there. For the first twenty or so blocks she could barely think, too busy weaving in and out of a constant stream of stalled traffic.

There were more badly wounded people wandering around the streets, but they didn't hail her for help. They started running after her, and though she knew she ought to stop and help, there seemed something very wrong about them, like they were infected. She kept the windows rolled up and raced on.

Somewhere at the top of the Bronx she saw a heaving tideline up ahead; a mass of people filling out the street, gathered like they were walking in a parade. She stopped half a block down from them and rolled down the window to shout.

"What the hell's going on?"

They started running. Their eyes were white and many were dappled with blood. She didn't hang around to find out what they wanted, sending the car back and racing off to the left. After that she drove manically, not stopping for anything, just weaving her way north.

She flew out of New York along the Sprain Brook Parkway, dodging constantly around the abandoned vehicles, here pulled neatly to the sides. There were people here too, and they came with their eyes blazing and their arms out, some running directly at the car. One boy ran right into the bumper like he wanted to go under the wheels. He did.

Lara drove on, until the frozen traffic thinned out and the detritus of the city fell away and she switched lanes automatically to the 684, the 84, the 87 headed north. Soon she was in amongst the bright spring greenery of lower New England. Red oaks proliferated, and the highway swept in over them on a raised plane, like the rings around Saturn. Every now and then one of the infected people was there in the middle of the road, wandering near a stopped car or truck, like they were lying in waiting for her.

She didn't now what it was anymore. Nuclear didn't make people turn crazy. She flipped on the radio and scrolled all the stations, but got only static. She called home again and again, tried Alejandro and anyone she could think, but none of them answered and her phone stopped working altogether fifty miles out of New York. The signal cut out and it wouldn't even attempt to dial, so she flew on alone in furious silence, her jaw working silently under the skin, bound for one place: her parents' home in Utica. If anybody knew what was going on, and what to do, it would be them.

Lara pulled up to the outer gate of their community, Oakwood Briar, a little before midday. Barefoot she got out of the car and went up to the wrought iron metal gate.

"Hey," she called through, hoping to snag the attention of the security guy in his little booth, but no one was there. She shook on the metal but it didn't budge. She backed out onto the road, a safe bet now with no other cars in sight, and ran her stolen Toyota around the circumference. The wall from the gate continued for about fifty yards, then ran down into an intermittent screen of Douglas firs.

She bustled out of the car door and into the heady brown matting of pine needles that lay beyond the grass verge, still damp. The needles pricked her feet softly, and sent up the hickory smell of Christmas. She pushed the damp branches aside and emerged into the Oakwood Briar community, on a looping one-way road that encircled the community.

She ran along the grass of people's front yards, glancing into windows as she went by. There was no one around at all. Cars were in driveways, doors were closed and curtains were drawn, though it was noon.

"Hello!" Lara called. "Anybody home?"

No answer came. She heard barking as she rounded the first cul-de-sac and followed it. Round the corner of a Georgian-style retirement bungalow a crowd of people was gathered, circling the chain-link fence on a backyard. They were pressed so tightly Lara could only see glimpses of the backyard, within which were a pair of full-grown German Shepherds, now racing back and forth and barking frantically at the crowd.

In the crowd were old guys in pajamas pressed hip to hip with grannies in floral nighties, kids in bright superhero romper suits, a few security guys in reassuring dark blue, and one or two young men in bright boxers.

Lara didn't run over to them or shout out. She crept carefully away. When one of the dogs abruptly yelped, and she saw its body swing up over the fence in the arms of the crowd, who dropped it to the ground, tore at its face and belly, and ducked their faces into the gore to eat as though bobbing for apples, she understood.

Zombies?

She covered the distance to her parent's place not expecting anything good, muttering, "Get your shit together Lara," under her breath. She went round the back and opened the basement door with the slim-jim her father, a hobbyist mechanic, kept hidden in the drainpipe.

The basement was quiet but for the low hum of the dehumidifier, working to counteract the natural damp of the surrounding clay soil. The light clicked on and illuminated a familiar square space. Shelves circled the bare concrete walls, laden down with old rolls of carpet, her mom's doll house and her workshop. Along one wall hung all the tools for making her dad's kit cars, and of course their computer, banished to a little faux lounge where a TV and Lazy boy had been set up.

This was the Lara cave, where she spent most of her time whenever she visited.

"Mom," she said, so quietly there was no chance anyone would hear her. "Dad."

She padded over to the tool wall, and trailed her fingers over the chipboard-backing full of pinholes. Adaptable shelving spokes jutted out to hold her father's tools. She settled on a heavy metal mallet, which he used along with a lug wrench to knock the screws off wheels.

Was she going to brain her zombie parents? She snorted at the thought. This was all some crazy, revolting dream. But maybe a little bit?

The air was cold and the concrete colder. She started up the carpeted stairs, which led up into the kitchen. She reached the top and her hand on the door trembled. She opened it tentatively and entered the corridor, enjoying the familiar flex and the warmth of the cedar boards underfoot, and looked around.

"Mom?" she whispered.

She heard a creak from the kitchen. Two steps further and she'd see. Lara lifted the mallet back with both hands.

"Mom, I'm holding a mallet."

Her mother burst round the side of the kitchen and bounced off the refrigerator so hard she set it rocking. There was blood round her mouth and the same furious white in her eyes, and she came grasping hungrily for more.

The mallet dropped from her hand and Lara leapt back, at the last moment grabbing the basement door and yanking it fully open. It caught her mother on the shoulder and rolled her, and Lara leaned in to that roll, pushing the door and her mother with it closed.

The back of her mother's head hit the door jamb with a solid thunk, Lara gave her a shove, and she tottered through and fell. Lara slammed the door and jammed her back to it, while from the other side came the thump thump thump of her mother tumbling down the stairs.

"Oh my god," Lara said.

She looked to her left. Her father was standing there. The strangest thing was, he was wearing a plain white T-shirt with words sprayed across it in purple car-body paint.

We love you Lara.

He came for her. She pulled the same trick on him, more smoothly this time, though his weight as the door caught him across the face almost knocked her back. She kicked off the wall and rolled round, shoving him off-balance as she'd always learned in Wing Chun classes, and kept the door closing. It felt like forcing a crab into a hot pot, but he went down.

She slammed the door. Thump thump thump he went all the way down. She opened the door and looked. He was OK, he was getting up already. Her mom was already up, though her leg seemed to be twisted at a nasty angle.

Lara closed the door, locked it, then ran to the sink to puke.

So this was the zombie apocalypse, then.

Nothing much happened for a long time after that.

Lara laid low. Zombies came up to the door in dribs and drabs, like Mormons, but they were often distracted away by dogs or cats. There was a cat living on the roof of the folks across the street, and every now and then it came down for long enough to run down a mouse. There were dogs barking constantly, though their number steadily diminished as they were rousted out, or died of starvation.

Lara stayed mostly on the second floor, looking out of the windows, far enough away from the basement that she didn't have to hear her parents rattling around down there. She'd been down to look at them once, and had surprised herself by not crying.

It wasn't that she didn't care about them. She did. But this was so emphatically not them. The message of her father's shirt had told her all she needed to know. They'd known, they'd had enough warning to send her a text and write her a farewell, and wasn't that nice and tidy?

She was in shock, true enough. She sat on her chair by her old roll-top desk, where she'd blitzed out on learning drugs to help her study for law school, and looked out through the lacy windows like Mama Bates, waiting, but nobody came.

No army, no navy, no CIA. She had the radio on but nothing played but a lonely hiss. The electric went out and then the water, but she was hardly hungry or thirsty. She stopped eating almost altogether, just little bites once a day. She watched the old zombies flow up and down the street, stopping at her door only to be lured away. She watched them go gray, watched as more splatters of blood appeared on their clothes from the dogs they'd managed to pry out of their yards.

After a week of lolling, waiting, watching and reading her old books and diaries, she tooled up. Her father kept a shotgun, a pump-action Remington with forty shells worth of ammunition. She took one of his fishing jackets and stuffed the pockets full of shells. She hooked a knife through her belt. She put on two pairs of jeans and two thick jackets, then duct-taped glossy magazines round her arms and legs, round her midriff and chest. She found an old football helmet and fitted it to her head.

She loaded the shotgun. She went down to the basement.

It was easy. Boom, boom.

She emerged through the basement door into the yard. This was hunting.

She took out two near nice Mrs. Batcher's hot tub. One of them tumbled into the water and sank like a turd. She reloaded and continued on. She patrolled the community, finding them in strange pockets; some gathered around the last few emaciated dogs, some at water sources, others wandering aimlessly.

She blew them all away. One almost got her when it ran up silently from behind, over grass. It smacked hard against her back, one area she hadn't been able to armor well, and she felt the hard crunch of its nose bone against her spine.

She hacked its chest to shreds with the kitchen knife, then blew off its head, digging a gout into the patch of yard with the point-blank shotgun blast.

She patrolled until it grew dark. Many of the neighbors still remained inside their houses, hitting against blood-smeared glass, but she left them where they were.

Other than it growing quieter and more still, nothing changed. Back in her house it was too quiet. It got dark and she was alone. She got out lipstick and wrote on the dresser mirror.

What now?

The words stared back at her.

She loaded up on food from neighbor's houses, clearing out the zombies as she went. She found more guns and more ammo; hunting rifles, handguns, a few more shotguns. She piled them up in her munitions area in the kitchen. She buried her parents in the back yard.

She made rotas of her sweeps around the community. She set up shop in the security guard's room, and found his stash of secret porn in the desk.

At times she thought of Amo, and their strange and wondrous night together. She thought of the message she'd left him.

        Good luck with the zombies.

She was too tired to laugh.

Weeks went by. She tried going out of the community again, but the streets outside terrified her now. She found the car that had brought her from New York where she'd left it, spattered with bird shit and gummy seedpods from the fir trees. There was enough fuel for a run round the block, so she made it.

Nothing. In the distance, down by the strip mall on Chesapeake, she thought she saw a gang of zombies breaking into the gas station.

It was getting hotter out. Of course the AC wouldn't run. She took to sitting in people's cars, running the engine just to keep the air on. She played on an old Gameboy she found, running her score on Tetris high enough to get the spaceship to launch. When the gas ran out she just paused her game and moved to another car.

She swam in the neighbor's pool. She read an old John LeCarré book. She talked to her parents' graves about all the things she had hoped to achieve in her life. She stayed calm, like a lawyer, and waited for someone to come.

Two months went by, and still nobody came. The radio hissed. She stood at the top of the basement stairs looking down, and wondered how long she could last like this before she put a noose round her neck and joined her parents.

Over several days she packed her father's car; the latest model was a Hyundai. She put her guns and her Gameboy and some food in. Could Amo be alive? If anybody was alive, it would surely be in the city. Maybe he was. Maybe somebody was.

She thought of his comic, the last few panels he'd shown her. Sitting at the wheel in her parent's driveway, decked out in her clammy magazine armor, she wondered if his tower of straining zombies was what she'd find in Times Square, reaching for the sky

At least that would be something. Anything would be better than this.

ROAD TRIP

16. FAREWELL

Lincoln Tunnel is empty of the ocean, and the road out of New York is a peaceful affair, bar the rumbling of the JCB's treads thrown back at me by the dark tunnel walls. I flip the hinged window out and enjoy watching the dot of light up ahead getting closer, like a distant vision of the world at the end of an impossibly long birth canal.

It has been a nightmare. I have done things I never thought possible. I have been so evil I had to kill myself, and I've been so good I'm still on a high.

I burst up into the light. A toll bay tells me to stop but screw it, I go straight through. Some rules, like road tolls and parking violations, just exist to be broken. The metal barrier rail bends backward then snaps off its hinge, clattering to the side. The JCB is so wide it strikes sparks off either side of the gate.

Booya!

We rumble on. There are more cars here, where the tunnel bleeds into Weehawken and up to the 495. I circle the on-ramp loop, keeping an eye on the convoy behind, but they're well tethered and none as wide as the JCB.

I put on my music. I've set it up remotely from my phone, wireless with a Bluetooth signal booster taped to the battle-tank's roof. I click for the art mix I used to paint to, shuffle, and the first song kicks in from speakers strapped to the back window of the delivery truck: Katy Perry's Roar from 2014. Fitting.

A few floaters bob by and I wave at them. This is a big day for them, to see living prey. They'll probably follow me until their socks come off. Most of them have lost their shoes, at least the soles of them, a long time ago. They trudge around on raw skin.

We loop up round a Port Authority loading yard, then we're on top, on the highway as it begins. A few other vehicles lie scattered around, beginning to sag on their tires and rust round their light fittings.

I pull the JCB to a stop on the corner, open the slot in the roof, and climb up to stand on the cab top. I walk along the tail fin I welded to the back, which bridges me neatly over to the top of the battle-tank, and from there I take in the panoramic view of New York back across the Hudson river.

Ah. This is New York as I remember it, from movies and the imagination, sparkling like the fabulous city on a hill. From this far away the rot and decay already setting in at street level is invisible. The buildings glisten and shine like crystal shards. The Chrysler building galumphs like layers on a frosted pudding. Above a block of red and white modern tenements to the right rears the spike of the Freedom Tower. Right in the middle, iconic and towering, stands the Empire State Building.

It is nearly ninety years old and cost millions to build, equal to almost a billion dollars now. It is the pyramids of its age, dream and nightmare both, and now it has been rebranded.

f

This work brings a tear to my eye. The lines are crisp and sharp. For all the world it looks like I'm wearing my immersion goggles and seeing an overlay placed atop reality. The Facebook website was never a place or a real thing, it was never something you could reach out and touch.

Now it is. I'm making the digital spaces that connected us, across thousands of miles of oceans and deserts and forests and tundra, real.

Community of the people, by the people, for the people. Now I'm making myself emotional. I take out my phone and snap photos. I've already got ones from Madison Park and hundreds of the painting process. They're in my blog, actually a log now because there is no web, saved in the USBs I left behind in the cairn.

I also left entertainment for the journey: a copy of Zombies of New

York in pdf format. It's the one Cerulean put together, right there in the root directory, along with a note explaining the contents and the cairn and everything, kind of a mission statement.

I smile. I wanted it to be a treasure trove and it is. It is a geocache and a cairn, perhaps the biggest ever devised, and a way forward for me and maybe others. Entertainment is a huge part of that. To overcome, we have to show that we're capable of overcoming. To laugh at our losses and our failings is the best way I know of doing that.

Farewell, zombies of New York.

I get back in the cab and I rumble out, heading west.

The city steadily recedes out the window, and the convoy maxes out at about 20 miles per hour. A warm summer wind blows stickily through the open window, and since the JCB has no air conditioner I strip down to my boxer shorts. Out the window I see urban gray resolve into bright green foliage, old forests that would have stood back when the Indians hunted the land.

I smell cedar and apple wood on the air, mixing with fresh grass pollen and the comfortable tang of baking asphalt. There are weeds beginning to shoot up in the cracks at the highway's verge, amongst the off-cast strips of tire rubber and desiccated chip packets. Moss grows on a low surface coating of windblown dust.

I rumble on. Forest gives way to farms interspersed between little towns, bound northwest on I-80 that will carry me clear across the country, through Pennsylvania and Ohio, Indiana and Illinois into Iowa, right near to my parents' house. I think I'll stop in, though I'm not sure what I'll do if I find them there.

Maybe I'll open the door, if they're trapped inside their house, and let them wander free like gazelle. They shouldn't be cooped up, like the girl I left in the box. They should be able to feel the sun and go naturally to the earth when their time comes.

Through a little settlement swallowed up in woods, Allamuchy Township, I rumble by. My music draws the ocean on like a tide, following behind. It'll also send out a flare to anyone surviving here. If they come in numbers, if they're cannibals or murderous Satanists, I'll deal with that. The battle-tank is well-equipped.

But I don't think that's what I'll find. As I roll through this little town, bypassing only a few Jeeps and Chevy Impalas pulled over to the roadside, past cute New England townhouses and a sagging banner above Main Street declaiming it is the second most beautiful town in New Jersey, I can't imagine that'll happen.

Resources are not scarce, so there's nothing pushing good people to fight. In all of New York city I didn't see a single other person, so I don't expect to see any more than one or two out here. They would pose little threat to me.

There are a few crowds of ragged floaters at the edge of Allamuchy, gathering in the parking lot of a Walgreens. It looks like they're picking over the remnants of a shopping trolley. I turn off my music, pull up past the mall, and idle the JCB. It winds down and I'm left in silence but for the lapping of the ocean up against the back of my convoy.

I climb up and stand on the top of the battle-tank. I do a rough count, some five hundred maybe? I lie down on the orange beanbag and look up at the blue sky. Hopefully they'll all trail away, when the sound and the heat from my engines fades. There's food out there, probably wildlife in these woods, and maybe they'll go for that.

The air tastes good, fresh and clean. The ocean don't have a scent anymore, they're not rotting like we think of in the movies. Now they're kind of dry and sterile, like old lichen creeping over a grave. I've theorized about it plenty. Their skin has taken on the texture of smooth bark, withered but tough. Whatever food they had in their bellies has passed out of them, and they're left like desiccated little corpuscles, creaking around on leathery legs.

I look at the ones on the parking lot. A few peeled away to come check me out when I rolled past, but most of them are still picking through heaps of trash. I wonder if there were survivors here once, to get all those trolleys out and fill them with food. Anything exposed and organic will have turned to dust a long time ago, in the sun and the rain. The ocean will be left with packaged Lays and Twinkies. Can they open them?

Nearly three months have passed now since Cerulean died. I pick idly at a cuticle. I wonder about Lara.

Some of my crowd drift away but not all. It's fine, I'll outstrip them on the highway anyway. It's nice to give them a chance to be with their own kind.

I roll on. Hours go by, and I hum my way into them. The road twists contentedly, unfolding the vistas and trees of New Jersey. I have a bite of a Hershey bar, swilling the chocolate round in my mouth before swallowing. I chase it with fresh spring water from a bottle, purportedly from the French Alps. I could never really taste the difference.

I exit New Jersey through a clutch of red maples in Worthington State Forest, where a sign tells me:

> You are now entering Pennsylvania.

In the road ahead a semi-truck with a long white trailer rests diagonally, punched through the central concrete dividers to block most of the four lanes. It lies peacefully in an opening in the evergreen forest, on a low bridge running over a shallow creek, the Delaware Water Gap a sign tells me. At first I think it must be an accident caused by the infection, but then I notice the letters graffitied across its side in thick red letters, and my heart stops.

SORRY

I stop the JCB short of it and read the letters again. They are slightly faded, dim as though they've been there for a few weeks, drizzled by rain, but they can't be something from before. They must be fresh.

I scan the road. A smattering of cars have pulled neatly to the sides, up to the low concrete barriers running either side of the bridge. I peek in through their dust-frosted windows, and there I see some markings, not entirely clear, but they look man-made, nothing the ocean would have done.

I climb out of the cab, still in my boxers with the hot sun tanging at my skin, and run back along the battle-tank to get a better look. The marks are written in the dust of the BMW's passenger side window, faint and already covered over with more dust, but undeniably there.

:)

Oh my god. My heart is racing. A smiley? In the cab I struggle into pants and a T-shirt. I strap on my boots, two handguns, and un-slot my shotgun from the rack behind the cab seat, pumping a shell into the breach.

I climb up through the roof and run back along the top of my convoy to the truck, where I take out the floaters below, listening to the music. It's only a few. Of course the sound will draw more, but I don't care, they're already coming for the music and at least here on this bridge there's something of a bottleneck. I slide down the ladder bolted to the tank's side and hit the hot asphalt running.

"Hey!" I shout. Desperation comes off me in waves and I don't care. "Hey, anybody!"

I run round the front of the semi, squeezing between the engine grill and the highway fender. There's nothing on the other side though, just the same landscape of snaking road populated by a few cars and a few floaters, pinging back and forth on the fenders either side of the road like ball bearings in a pinball machine.

"Hello!" I shout.

A floater, maybe once a buff young guy, wearing a Harvard sweater so faded I can barely make out the lettering, draws near and I blow out his throat and head with the shotgun. He makes a cracking sound, like I've felled a tree, and powder spumes out of him. It's not mist anymore, its dust like a seedpod bursting.

I run down the semi's far side, yelling. The back doors are open, hanging wide out from the flank like wings. My heart thuds. Could this be a trap? It's a roadblock in an exposed spot, overlooking a lovely view of deep green forest, the brook down below, cackling away with floaters wandering up it like salmon. There's a small industrial-looking station down on the water, maybe refuse or recycling, and I scan it hurriedly. Are snipers waiting inside, or hiding in the trees around me, waiting to pick me off? Are they under the bridge like trolls?

I don't care, and keep running and shooting.

Almost at the back doors and swinging wide, another floater comes bobbing out from behind the open door. I shoot it in the throat at a run. Another peels out and another, and I stop. They were obscured before by the angle of the truck, hidden at the open back end like they were helping to unload it. I open the shotgun and pump shells into the breech from my vest while backpedalling.

There are five six, seven, and they're all running.

Shit. I shoot one, then my lead-time is too low to risk anymore. I back up more and jump over the verge, vaulting the fender to balance on the edge of the bridge. From here the drop is directly into the shallow water below, a fall of maybe twenty feet. Shit.

A second later the ocean hit the low fender and reach across for me, and it's all I can do to bat them away and keep my balance, leaning back at a perilous angle. I certainly can't shoot this close without the recoil sending me over.

"Shit," I say to the seven of them, up close and personal. Their faces have really degraded. They look more like gray nuts or withered old flowers than anything that used to be human. "Shit, Jesus, give me a break."

They give me no break. I start running along the narrow lip between the fender and the fall below, hoping I can outrun them, hop back over, and take them out at my leisure. But they run damn fast now, and pace me every step of the way. They've got a clearer go of it than me.

I run until the bridge hits the steep bank, where the road dips sharply down a grass slope. I stop on a dime and almost go over, tumbling end over end down the thick grass to a line of scrubby bushes on a brown patch of coarse soil by the brook's stony bank. The fender ends in about fifty yards.

Shit!

I spin, and see one of them is crawling up the embankment on hands and knees, freshly delivered from the water. I'm cornered, and it's time to stop messing around. I pluck one of my handguns, set my feet as best I can, and start pinging the seven in their throats.

POP POP POP

A few go down. A few don't. The bullets don't seem to have the percussive power they used to. Whatever has withered the floater's necks must have toughened them too, making the spinal cord incredibly resilient. I shoot one of them pointblank so many times his head only holds in position with a few wriggly threads, stretching taut as he bobs and moves, but he doesn't go down.

"Jesus," I breathe. I haven't tried to cap them with a handgun for months, I suppose. I empty another clip but it does no good, and none of them drop. They're invincible and I'm trapped.

One of them flumps over the fender and lunges for me with his jaw gaping black. A shotgun blast blows his head to dust, and I get driven back by the recoil, falling down the steep slope and into a breakneck tumble.

I come to sprawled at the bottom against the bushes, what can only be seconds later. The shotgun is gone and I don't know where my handguns are, torn away in the fall. I look up the steep bank and see the one who was crawling for me is now rolling down, only about ten yards away, joined by two others. One of them is slithering down through the grass like a gray snake, while the other two get to their feet either side of me, pulling clear of the bushes and getting ready to dive.

Oh shit.

17. SOPHIA

I bolt to my feet and hurl myself backward over the scraggy brown bushes, with no time to see where I'm going. My jeans catch on a tough stalk going over and I come down awkwardly, cracking my left shoulder with a sharp knock on a hard root. My body pile-drives after it, pain and a sharp nausea grip me, then the ocean surges over the bushes to land snapping at my side.

I lash out, punching the nearest one in its knurled gray peanut head, then two more flop over belly first, like damn salmon skipping upstream. I scamper backwards on my butt like they do in horror movies, utterly ineffectual, and cold wet clay shuffles down my belt line and into the seat of my pants. Already the one with most of his neck gone is on his feet, so I get to mine too and break into a desperate run. My left arm whelps in pain as it swings but I can't do a damn thing about that now.

It's a rooty, scrubby brown clearance area, and it dashes by underfoot. It looks like they've been digging here, maybe preparing to build another damn fast food outlet, but it's early days and the ground is still lumpy with a creek-bed and twisted gnarls of root, so my legs tire out fast running in and out of dips and craters.

I chance a look back and cry out, because the no-neck guy is right on me, literally inches away from snagging my hoodie, with revenge burning brightly in his cue ball white eyes.

On a dime I stop dead and drop to all fours. His calf kicks into my butt hard, his falling knee thumps into my back, and then he's flying past me to roll hard in the dirt.

The next races on and it's all I can do to kick a leg up to meet him, catching him in the balls. It doesn't do a thing to make him cry out, his balls must be more withered than his peanut of a face, but it holds him off; only now he's holding onto my leg and leering his yellow teeth closer, while the two others lope round the side, pincering me like raptors. What am I supposed to do? Think Amo, you bastard.

I lurch hopping to one foot as the guy holding my leg pushes closer. No-neck is behind me and I manage to grab him by the mangled few shreds of throat with my right hand. The purple-gray skin of his inner windpipe feels as cold, stiff and dry as sun-cracked leather. His jaws smack and he paws at my hand and we hop backward over the scrub together, a strange kind of lurching train, me sandwiched between them while the third circles toward my belly. I don't have any more limbs left to hold him off so I just hop.

Three hops, four, five, all the time wriggling my fingers deeper into No-neck's torn throat, striving for something to snap. I close on a springy tendon at the back, surrounded by chunks of shrunken, rock-hard bone. These are spinal discs, then. I give the tendon a sharp twist.

He spasms, his head lurches to the side and his legs go out from under him.

I follow, falling heavily on his chest and cracking his ribs, while the one holding my leg falls toward my back. I manage to roll away so the two of them smack chests. I spy a rock nearby, grab it, and bring it down on the second one's head just as he's getting his arms under him again and coming for me. His shrunken skull cracks, my arm reverberates, and I hit him again, then the third is on me.

I drop the rock and fall to my back, barely able to hold him off with a palm flat on his sunken chest. The second grabs my leg again and I twist to get my other foot in his face, holding him off. No-neck paws feebly at my chest, and now I am truly screwed, with all my legs locked and my one good arm engaged. Their loose jaws snap and they lunge in toward my belly. I'm tiring fast and they're not. Any second I'll be dead.

My feeble left hand snags into my pocket. I manage to get my numb thumb to double-click the button, and I shout.

"Io play the Beatles!"

"Playing the Beatles," comes her muffled voice from my pocket.

The Last

The signal goes out by Bluetooth, boosted by the battle-tank transmitter, and just as the third guy is nudging round my arm and his head is about to plunge into my soft belly, out comes the roar of the speakers from the rear of the delivery truck, back on the road, fittingly the first line of 'Help!'

His dive stops, and I play dead in the hands of the ocean. They look up and tune into the sound. The third one considers for a moment, looking at me lying there perfectly still, then up at the road. I can only hope their AI really sucks.

He goes with it. He gets up and runs away. The second lets go of my leg finally, and runs off. Even No-neck tries to follow them, but he's gone all weird now, jerking like he's having a fit.

I lie there and listen to the Beatles save my life, while No-neck thrashes about. Dammit, I do need somebody.

"Good job, Io," I whisper.

"My pleasure, Amo."

I laugh. No-neck reaches for me again and I high-five him. Then I get up, put one foot on his shriveled chest, and using both hands get a firm grip under his chin. My left hand is weak and shaky still, but it can do this.

I strain back and pull his head off. It comes with a snap, as the tendon of his brain-stem ruptures. The light goes out of his eyes. It feels like holding a Terminator skull, but only as heavy as a coconut husk. Alas poor Yorick. I drop it beside his motionless body.

Screw these zombies. I hobble back to the bushes and climb over. There's a cut on my leg where it caught on a thorny branch going over, torn through my pants, and blood is dribbling down. I feel sick and wobbly in my shoulder. I barely make it on hands and knees up the embankment, pulling at clumps of grass and digging my toes into tufts.

Over the fender, onto the road I go. There's no sign of my shotgun. Screw it, I've got others. I squeeze back down past the semi's grill. The ocean are congregating at the rear of my convoy, enchanted by the sound of the Beatles. They pay no attention to me. I climb up the cab, pull another shotgun from the rack, and ascend to the roof of the battle-tank, then walk the roofs to the delivery truck.

At the edge I brace myself and shoot down. One, two, three, to eleven, I dissolve them in powdery puffs of gray, like Tinkerbell's magic dust. It's better now they're so dry, less grotesque. It doesn't feel quite so much like murder, though I don't like it. I made a promise.

I double-click. The Beatles are thunderous back here. "Turn the music off Io."

"Turning off."

It cuts out over her last syllable. I'm left in noisy panting silence, cursing myself.

I thought I was ready, but here I got lucky. I would probably go into debilitating shock now, if I didn't already know enough about how to deal with that. I drop into the battle-tank and pour two bottles of cool water over my head. It chills my brain and gives me something else to think on, something emphatically not fight or flight.

Stupid.

In the silence afterward I pour medicinal alcohol over the ragged cut in my thigh, dabbing away the crunchy bits of thorn. I put a bandage over the top then reload my shotgun. My shoulder throbs but it doesn't seem to be broken. I just need to be more careful. Io as a wingman is also pretty handy.

I put the music back on. That can be my standard operating procedure now. It pulls the floaters safely away from me. So, to the twerking majesty of Nicki Minaj, I pad back round the semi's grille. I walk down its side, past the powdered body of the first one I shot, and take a wide berth around the hanging open rear door, to peer into the interior.

It's not a good sight. It's a girl, hanging. For a moment I think she's about to open her eyes and talk, but she's too pale for that, and her feet are not even touching the floor, and she doesn't have any eyes at all.

I feel myself begin to come apart. Electrical cable has been worked around the metal light fixture of the storage cab's interior, dangling tautly down to bite into her throat. Her head is at a sharp angle, bloated and starting to rot, with the eyes already pecked away and long trails of bloody tears down her cheeks.

The smell is strong. She smells like the dead, before they became the dry and crusty things they are now.

"No," I say. I envision myself running forward and grabbing hold of her legs, trying to lift her up to take off the pressure while crying out frantically, 'Somebody cut her loose, somebody call an ambulance!'

The Last

I don't do it. I take a step back. The fight goes out of me and tears come to my eyes. She's a survivor, not one of the ocean, and she did this to herself. She broke her own neck to make it permanent.

"Wait," I say feebly. "Wait a second."

She doesn't answer. Her dead eye sockets, eyeless now and squirming with fat white maggots, stare back at me.

I am too late. I can't look at her. I run away from the rear of the semi and drop gasping to my knees on the asphalt. Now the shock really hits.

The knots are too tight, so I use a pair of bolt-cutters to snip the wire. I wear a kerchief for the smell. She falls with a ringing thump to the metal floor of the trailer's interior. It's hot in here, baking in the sun, making her rot faster surely. I wonder how long she's been hanging here.

I wrap her in her own bed sheet, like a mummy. I can't take her accusing face anymore.

I lower her to the asphalt, then turn and study the trailer's inner gloom. It is sweltering and buzzing with flies. It is plainly her home. I look around. She's got a sofa at the back, a generator of her own with a few gasoline tanks nearby and an ad hoc chimney to carry the fumes out the back. There are lots of wires and fat blocky transformers plugged into cable extenders, leading to a music system, a huge flat screen TV, a bed, a fridge. I pad inside and open the fridge door. Bottles of clotting milk stare back at me in the dark. I wonder if she actually milked a cow, or this is reconstituted stuff from powder.

There are about twenty bright red boxes of a sugary kid's cereal stacked by the wall. It's little details that this that hurt the worst. On the rug there are reefer papers. I suppose she'd been lighting up a few spliffs. Why not? I find a stash of her tobacco and dry fine-grain weed in a pouch by the coffee table. I haven't rolled a fat one since college, but I do it anyway. I light it up and smoke it down. It tastes like shit, but it helps with lifting her body onto my good shoulder, while some ridiculous pop jingle plays out from my speakers.

I have to roll her down the embankment. I follow carefully. In the scrub, I dig her a grave. The dirt here is loose, bar the tangles of slim roots, but the shovel blade cuts through them brightly. It doesn't take long.

Sophia, her name is. I find it on ID in her pocket. She was a pretty blonde girl, maybe twenty-three. There's a student ID in her purse, and some change, odd pennies and dimes. It feels sour to hold them. What did she think she was going to spend these on? Alive this would have been a funny thing I could have teased her about, and maybe she'd make the point that they might still work in a vending machine, or perhaps they remind her of the past, and our best presidents.

Like this they feel like unfinished stories, so thin and vulnerable, her whimsy remaining as a pathetic reminder of her failure.

I drink some whiskey to help the high buzz on.

Sorry, she wrote on the side of the semi. That's what gets me worst. She said sorry, though she'd seen no one for months, known no one for all that time. She killed herself surely with the ocean at her feet, looking out over them and the glorious view, hanging there with her feet kicking and...

I throw dirt on her gently, feeling the guilt descend. I didn't do enough. I should have been out here a month ago, two months ago, instead of playing my silly games with the Stadium and the Empire State. Maybe if I'd found her then we could have helped each other, even saved each other, but I didn't do that. I didn't lift a finger to save Cerulean either.

I haven't done a damn thing.

I revel in the sorrow, to feel something. I smoke another doobie in her hot home. When the music cuts out, because the generator has run down or the battery's gone out in the Bluetooth booster, I don't care. I sit on her sofa, where she must have sat a thousand times chewing vaguely on food packed by hands long-taken by the ocean, and look at the TV. She's got great choice in DVDs, a lot of Bill Murray. Groundhog Day is one of my all-time favorites.

I read her journal. It is a litany of hope dashed. She went to her parents but they were dead. She went to her boyfriend but he was dead. He attacked her and she had to kill him with a frying pan and a skewer through the throat. She went to town and everyone was dead. She tried to press on. She even brought her medical books; she was studying to become a doctor, and tried to make some headway. She dissected the dead, studying their brains and brain stems as best she could.

The brain stems were engorged, thicker than normal, and pressed sharply against the windpipe, which caused their characteristic breathing sound. The brain itself was alien, the normal structures altered with thick nerve fibers running from the eyes, the nose, the ears, the mouth, and a new squarish shape suspended right in the middle. Everything in-between was turning to mush.

I sit back and laugh. I suppose they have come for our brains.

'Transmitter?' she has written next to her diagrams of the new structure. To me it looks like a circuit board of flesh. Her notes ramble on in bizarre theorizing, about the purpose of this new organ. She too was aware of how quickly the infection spread, faster than any disease we've ever seen before.

'Receiver?' it says on another diagram. If I'm reading her ideas correctly, it seems she's suggesting the brain has been completely repurposed as a two-way signal box. Signals go out, signals come in. It could explain some things, I suppose; how they work so closely together, how they know I'm there even when I'm silent and invisible, and how the infection started.

It came out of my brain. It leapt out like an Electro-Magnetic Pulse, and it fried everybody nearby. Their brains had already been primed, and they transmitted the signal on in seconds.

I wonder if there are still survivors, up in the Arctic somewhere, living on isolated islands where the signal never reached. They must be really confused about now. Anyone they send to go find out what happened, won't come back.

I read on. Her journals get darker. She had glimpses of hope, though it doesn't seem she really believed them. She was headed for Lewington, the next big city over, where she thought maybe they would have an electron microscope. She was hoping to study the spinal tissue in more detail, perhaps with some hope that the condition could be reversed, despite the massive changes to the brain. She outfitted the semi truck for survival, just like my convoy.

But she couldn't kid herself enough. She didn't even make it very far. The looming road defeated her and the loneliness tore her up. All these brains around her were lost, along with personalities and everything that ever made them human. She wasn't going to be able to help them, and watching Bill Murray on the TV screen alone in a nightmarish world of the dead just wasn't enough for her.

Sorry,

she wrote in her final journal entry, addressed to other survivors she couldn't know even existed.

> I wish I could do this. I feel like I'm letting you down. But I can't do it anymore.

She left everything neat. She parked the semi across the road because she couldn't bear to go completely un-noticed, even in death. She craved to be seen to the last, to be witnessed, to be held and remembered.

I held her dead body. I will remember her for as long as I live, because I know exactly how she feels. I feel I have let her down too. I want to tell her that, tell her I'm sorry too, but I can't. I have come too late, and there is nothing I can do.

I fire up her generator and I watch her movies. The part where Bill Murray kills himself again and again hits home hard. I can't stop crying when he finally makes a meaningful connection with Andi McDowell. He's earned it, by this point. For everything he's done and all the changes he's made, he's earned it.

I lie in her bed in the darkness after, listening to the lapping wheeze of the gathering ocean outside, and think about the comas. She'd survived them too. She'd come so far, and built this semi-life with ingenuity and luxuries I never considered, so resourceful, but at this final stage she fell. Her dream wasn't strong enough, the propellant in her jetpack not potent enough, and she just couldn't push through the emptiness in those empty skulls.

It is somber and sobering. I go to sleep and dream of Cerulean's phone call, and the seconds after when the line went dead, when I knew I'd never talk to him again.

Robert. Sophia. Lara. I've left them behind like they were nothing, always moving on. I have no meaningful connections left, and any moves toward that have been kidding myself. Signs left behind mean nothing if there's no one there to see them. The world is empty, it's lonely, and it's going to stay that way for the rest of my life.

18. IOWA

I drive in a daze, only half-watching the road. Miles go by, this JCB has no odometer, and we rumble on. I play my music half-heartedly through forests and over hills, through little towns and past a million strip-malls, running by flag-pole signs for various fast food burger joints, pancake huts, ice cream stands, all of which would have once spun and flashed to catch my attention.

They look so foolish. They don't mean a damn thing.

I stop to fill the JCB's tank from my barrels. Floaters run toward me but I have time. I eat a cold hotdog on the battle-tank roof. I could cook it but why bother. It's bland and slippery. I bring up my phone and scroll through past messages; to and from Cerulean, my mom, my other older friends. The record goes back years, all my mail. I eke myself forward with these pathetic memories.

I look at my photos. There's my work on the giant 'f', happy deluded selfies, like what I was doing was actually worth a shit, like posting on the side of the Empire State was anything like posting on a digital wall.

No one will see it. If they're anything like Sophia they'll already be dead. I see her loss eating into me, I can feel it crushing my spirit, but there's nothing I can do to stop it. I don't have the resources anymore to buoy myself along. I need outside intervention, but there is none. It's a real boulder crushing me down, and I can't fight it alone.

I double-click my phone just to hear Io's voice, but she only talks when I ask her questions, and half the time she can't understand what I say anyway. She's just programming, imperfect code made by people who are all dead now.

Shit bits, Cerulean would say. It's all shit bits, one step away from glitching through a shelf.

I put the phone away because it's a fantasy. I turn the music off too, because I'm kidding myself. I've been kidding myself since the massacres. That was the reality. There is only kill to live now, kill the ocean every day to live, and I don't know if that's enough.

I rub my eyes. My head aches from thinking these same things. Sophia has done a real number on me.

I drive on. Rain comes at me over a hill, a drumming wall of gray passing across the land and I plunge into it. I bull through the wreckage of a bus torn in half. Torn bits of the ocean reach out to me, from the twists of melted slag and rubber.

I pass through towns that are empty bar the ocean. The old guilt surfaces now and then, that I did this. If I'd just kept my dick in my pants Jeo would still be a real thing. I would see Lara every day in Sir Clowdesley, from afar but at least she'd still be alive, then I remember how shitty that felt too, for how long.

I feel the whole weight of the country pressing down on me. Three thousand miles is such a long, long way, and what's even waiting for me at the end?

I remember as a kid I'd wake up to hear the night freight train pass by on the tracks a few miles distant, past Meller Creek. There was something so lonely about lying awake in the small hours listening to that long high whistle calling out its passage.

Now I'm the last train, roaming the barren world and playing my music like a whistle that nobody will hear. I'm so hungry for contact; I'm just as bad as Sophia. I'm leaving my sad little cairns with such miserable hope it makes me sick.

They'll find me dead too, and they'll see my pathetic record of events, photos of what I did, my zombie comic, my vainglorious strain for a connection, and it'll only make this feeling worse. I can't win.

I am too alone. I am going crazy with it. Shit shit shit, I can't take it away. I can't do anything.

I drive on.

The Last

Hazleton, Danville, Lewisburg. I pass through and I don't stop. There are corpses upright and staggering about everywhere. There are baby carriages left standing idly on street corners, spatters of dry bone strewn across the gutters, cars lying like strange colorful mushrooms in the road, sprouting round with veiny ivy. The ocean get thinner and grayer, but still they rumble on.

More of them are naked now; their clothes have slid or worn right off their skinny frames. They are walking skeletons, rasping at the air.

I shoot one with the sniper rifle, then get down and saw off its skull top. The inside is hollow but for the fibrous nerve-bands Sophia described, just like a cored coconut. I could cut it in half and use it like maracas, clacking my way through town like Don Quixote tilting at windmills.

I cut out the squarish block of matter in the center, the transmitter/receiver. It is shrunk and as hard as a Brazil nut. I wonder that there must be one of these in my head too. If I shake my head, can I hear it rattle off the coconut walls?

I pass from Pennsylvania to Ohio, watching the landscape change. I see a few Boston Markets interspersed amongst the Burger Kings and McDonalds. There are more Kroger's, for some reason. I find myself wandering through a J. C. Penny, I don't know why. I blast the dust out of floaters that lap near. I pick out a new pair of jeans and put them on. No rips, they feel good.

There are signs for Pittsburgh, signs for Akron. Somewhere in the distance Cleveland, Toledo, and Chicago pass me by. I'm through Ohio to Indiana, bound for Illinois.

I'm in a daze. I follow the road like a train track, my music off now. I don't leave any of the cairns I'd planned to. I just can't, it seems so pointless. Nobody will see. At times at photos of the giant 'f' I left in New York, trying to decide if this is a good thing or if it just puts me in the same category as poor wilted Sophia.

I keep her student ID to torture myself with. She is pinned to the JCB cab. I start to masturbate to her image at night, lying in my battle-tank and staring into her eyes and dreaming of her touch, her voice, of teasing her about her kiddie's cereal while she moans for me, for me.

Each time I finish I feel pathetic. I am pathetic. I push her picture far away, like I've sinned against her and myself. I go to sleep mired in guilt, and when I wake I have to climb through it just to breathe. I see my failure everywhere.

I get out my RPG and start to blow things up; billboards at first, then chain restaurants. They crunch and explode, sending bin doors, deep fat fryers and bright plastic chairs flying out in beautiful sprays. These can be my cairns. Let them read like Braille across the country, a story of loneliness and loss. I can only be honest.

I make slow progress, so much it feels like a crawl. I am constantly nudging other vehicles out of the way, stopping to shoot floaters or clear the backlog behind the delivery truck. I stop too much. I can only drive at the speed of the convoy. Once I come upon a herd of the ocean near South Bend, tramping across the landscape from north to south like a river, and I wonder where they're going. Then I rev the earthmover and drive through them.

I kill hundreds, probably. They are like a bad storm raging around me, hammering at every inch of my convoy, beating for a way in. I turn the music up to make them go crazy. I consider getting to the top of the battle-tank and letting rip into their ranks with the howitzer, but I'm beyond that now. I'm not in this to get revenge or cause pain.

I just need to get through. I won't give up like Sophia, but I can't promise what I'll do when I reach the West Coast. Maybe I'll swing there too, last mayor of America taking in the view.

I rumble over bridges and down a hundred Main Streets, through little towns cored by the move to Yangtze same-day delivery drones. As I swing through Indiana, I remember why my country is so religious. The vast empty expanses of flat overgrown cornfields spread to either side like endless yellow skies, and the loneliness here is palpable. Maybe I too can sense god, in these fields and this growth.

I enter Iowa on a Thursday, at 9:56 in the morning. I keep my phone charged with batteries and solar rechargers. Without it I would have no idea of the date, but Io remembers. This is my land, my home state. The mega-church thirty miles past the border is still there, sprawling like a holiday resort; the mass capitalization of faith and loneliness. I consider going in and alternately praying or shooting up the place.

I do neither. I'm like flat soda left out in the sun. I eat sugary cereal and don't taste it. I drive. After Des Moines I pull off I-80, bound for the little town I come from, where my parents may be even now;

The Last

Creston. I pull in a day later, wondering if this experience will defeat me, like Sophia.

The neighborhood is unchanged, bar nature growing out of control. I pull up to the house, typical Americana; a swing on the sheltered porch, mosquito nets on the doors and windows, woodwork painted pale lime and white. My folks don't actually have a white picket fence, but the neighbor Mr. Connors does.

The grass is out of control in the front lawn. Dad loved his John Deere and would never have abided that. Just seeing this makes me start to cry. Of course I know they're both dead already, but seeing this damn grass makes it real. Maybe coming here was a mistake.

I start up the music and get out, drawing a few floaters to the truck. I trail the shotgun barrel noisily behind me, scraping a line up the concrete path, then stop at the door. I actually have a key. It feels so strange in my hand, like a piece of magic to access this world, so far away.

It slides into the lock, I turn it, and the door opens.

Inside it smells of slowly baking mahogany and cedar. It's a timber-framed house and they've got dark wood furniture throughout.

"Mom," I call, into the musty corridor. Plenty of light radiates in through the windows. "Dad."

To either side are chests of drawers, one adorned with a few petite Chinese-style vases. Mom loved these, and would often boast of them to friends and neighbors, though they were plainly reproductions probably cast a few miles down the road at the hippy commune near Shenandoah.

I go down the hall, past the neat kitchen, to the den. Nothing is touched or has been changed. Wooden ducks fly across the wall above the TV, still a thick old CRT model. I'd been meaning to buy them a new one before the coma hit. I run my fingers through the dust on the kitchen table. We used to play games of Rook here when I was little, me on my Mom's side, Aaron on Dad's, and it doesn't hurt to remember that, though it feels like ancient history.

I wander through the living room, where the coffee table is still piled neatly with mom's women's magazines. In the back room the piano rests silently. I play a few notes.

"Mom," I call again, but no answer comes.

Up the beige-carpeted stairs, I look in on each of our bedrooms one by one. Theirs is plain and unadorned; large cupboards, a dresser, a full-length mirror, veils on the windows.

The guest room, which used to be Aaron's room, is barren, with nothing of him left here now. My room is empty too, though it still bears many of my teenaged decorations, like a time capsule. I stand in the middle and look at this hollow space in the air, thinking there must be millions of rooms just like it across America, emptied out.

I open my drawers, looking at my collection of old Transformers. I run my fingers over their plastic shells, their holographic stickers, so colorful and bright. Perhaps if I cared about these things now, I'd be like Sophia. They would be my flimsy roots, too easily plucked up and exposed to the air, wriggling weakly. Loss of them might break me, seeing them like this could hurt me, like she brought her movies and her kid's cereal along for the ride.

I don't need them. They don't mean anything to who I am now. I've died so many times between then and now I can hardly remember. This room is a shell I've grown out of.

The basement is the same. It was my prison for a time. I sit on my old bed and look up at the door, imagining Cerulean in a place just like this while his mother hammered her way in. She brought him into the world, and she took him out of it.

I go out into the yard and wander through the long grass. A few thick hotdog reeds have sprung up at the edges, where the rainwater always collects and tries to make a pond. Bulrushes? I can't remember. Io can't tell me.

They're not here. I could go to the back of the delivery truck where the locals are gathering and study shriveled peanut faces looking for them, but even if I found them they still wouldn't be here.

I put Sophia's ID card reverently in my desk, along with my Transformers. That's enough of that, now. All of this is a farewell, and I've felt guilty abusing her poor, lost image for so long. I am a seed of a long-dead plant, caught on a wind and untethered by any trailing, unmet desires, and that's fine.

I get in my cab and drive off, to the west, with my comet trail trudging behind.

19. ENDLESS

In an endless landscape of corn, I run out of gasoline.

The battle-tank is empty of supplies. It's not that I planned it wrong, or I forgot to fill them up. There were countless opportunities to fill up, I could have siphoned any of the tankers I've passed, I could even have rigged a pump to bring it up from the depths beneath a gas station. I have those kinds of skills now.

But I didn't do any of that. It is a clear-headed and clear-eyed choice. I rumble the convoy on until it stops, the engine gutters, and goes silent.

Hot sun bakes down. I leave my phone behind on the seat. I contemplate taking all my clothes off and going out naked, but there's no need for that. It will happen itself, when time has thinned me down like the rest of them, and the sun has baked and worn them so much they slough off.

I'll wander free like the herds that fill out this land. I'll finally belong again. I want to face it, the same fate that I gave to them all.

I climb out of the cab. I don't need guns or music now. It's all right.

I start walking. The sun is hot and the corn is indescribably beautiful. I've never seen it grow so out of control before. The stalks get thick and tangled, interweaving like unkempt threads in a greater organism.

We are all like this. I take step after step and feel lighter with every one. I am walking into my freedom. If Sophia had been brave enough she would have done this too. Yes there will be pain, but then it will be over. Like my parents there'll be nothing left to find because I'll be gone.

I leave no message, no 'Sorry' scrawled hastily over the battle-tank's side, because I am not sorry. This is reality and I'm not ashamed. I am not willing to kill a single floater more to survive, for this. My life is not worth it. I'd rather run with the herd, hunting down buffalo in the wild and bringing them down, feeling the hot blood gush down my neck and chest, swallowing, swaying together like kelp on the tides.

I get misty-eyed thinking of it. It seems like a beautiful life, and I am proud that I finally see that. Life is nothing lived alone. I don't want to be in my basement anymore, I don't want to hide away in my cab afraid and clinging to the past. My eyes are open.

A member of the ocean peels out of the corn. Just one, and I wonder at his long and winding pilgrimage, a bit of jetsam tossed upon the golden waves, like me.

His leg is twisted and he can't run. So much the better. We can dance together one last time. I walk and he walks behind me. We walk together, and I slow my pace to let him keep up. It can even be beautiful, a harmony of kinds. I turn once at a rise and see my convoy so far behind, so small.

We are all so small. Like Aaron always taught me, the key lies in seeing that smallness and knowing it. You have to see the reality or you are lying to yourself, and I can't be Sophia. I want to be like my parents, absorbed by the flow, to go forward unafraid and as boldly as I can.

We walk together, him or her and me. Its body is so shrunken I can't tell the gender anymore; any hint of genitalia has shriveled up into the body. I start to cry, and now it is a release. Tears flood down my face. I'll walk until I run out of strength, then I'll turn this body over to the flood. That at least is honest. It's facing death down and accepting it with open arms, hiding no more, man not mouse.

I reach out and stroke the ears of corn, fat and yellow. I pluck one and eat it as I walk. The natural sugars are ripe and rich, sweeter down my throat than any of the processed, canned shit I've been on for months. The air is so clean. I look back to make sure my friend is still coming.

He's been joined by another. They both hobble along, neither of them running. I don't know why this is, he doesn't look injured, but I'm grateful. They will run me down, but with respect. I will give myself up in the same way. I duck them a low bow and we walk on.

I toss the corn back into the field. Dust to dust, ashes to ashes. It was a grand dream, really. I no longer feel bad about my New York cairn. Perhaps others will come, in time, and it will help them. They'll take strength in what I've left for them, and they may even make it to the West Coast alive. It won't matter that I'm not there when they arrive, if they've already made it that far. They can build their own destination. I just made a starting point.

I'm smiling as I walk. Joy rises up in me like a flood, withheld for so long. Now I feel proud again, and it doesn't matter that no one will witness my death, because I'm here. I don't need the others for this moment, I don't need to apologize or to be witnessed, because which one of us goes into death with others by our side?

We all go alone. Cerulean went alone, Aaron went alone, my parents went alone, but we all go the same way. We come into the world and we go out of it the same, so perhaps we are never truly alone. This is a path so well trodden it is worn into stone, and finally, I feel the company of all these ghosts in the air around me.

I'll run with Cerulean and my parents, with Aaron and Lara and them all.

I walk through the day, until there is a crowd of dozens behind me. Not a one of them runs, and with each one added to the slow trudge my heart fills a little more. This is my audience. They will leap upon me and tear out my guts, and we're going to do it together. I am giving them my body for their sustenance, and in turn they are making me one with them.

Who ever said birth was pain-free? Life is hard and it hurts. The first thing a baby feels is a slap to make it breathe, and the indignities just keep on coming. Lost love, lost friends, broken bones, all of it part of the tapestry of life. I am part of it too. I started this thing and finally it's caught up to me.

The cornfields don't end. At some point nearing dusk, when my feet are growing weary and my vision blurs with the heat and exhaustion, so tired I can barely take another step, I stop and I turn. There are hundreds of them now, all my brothers and sisters, and now I am sorry.

I'm sorry for the family I locked within their home in Mott Haven, and for the mall cops I killed with monitors above Sir Clowdesley, and for the thousands I burned and the thousands I mowed down with bullets and the tens of thousands I locked into the stadium. I would take them all back if I could. Why should I have any more right to the world than them? Why should I be the one to go on, clinging to a past that is no longer real?

I spread my arms to them. The gray tide draws in, folds around me, and I am encompassed. Their limbs and their skins find mine, tenderness reigns, and we are all rolled into one in the blackness together.

INTERLUDE 2

Lara saw the giant 'f' on the Empire State Building, and at once she understood.

Amo. It had to be Amo.

The streets of the city were near deserted. She drove through Manhattan with a sense of burgeoning hope in her chest. He was alive. He was alive and he'd done all this. Somehow the city was clear; somehow he'd put up a sign she could recognize at once.

He was alive.

She raced to the lobby of that great building, and in. She found within a cairn that surpassed any of her expectations. There was a plan, and supplies. There was a wall laid out with a bulletin board, and upon it at the top was his name and a date.

```
Amo - Last Mayor of America 06/08/2018
```

She laughed and cried. She took up the spray can and filled in her name beneath his, through her tears.

```
Lara - Last Barista in America 06/30/2018
```

She read his log and his comic. She fired up his generators and drank his Nespresso. She reveled in the map, cutting a path west across the country, to Los Angeles where the Chinese theater awaited.

It was beautiful. It was proud, and it filled her up in a way she couldn't express. She loved him for it. She loved his will for doing it. It was a good thing, with no doubt in her mind.

She wasn't alone any more. Amo who she knew, who had been through the worst of it just as badly as her, who had been through even worse things, was alive. He was out there. He could be found and known, and she would not be alone anymore.

She gathered up one of his laptops and a USB with his map, she picked up one of the RV keys and ran down the stairs like an excited child at Christmas, to find the vehicle stocked and ready. The gas tank was full.

She revved it to life, set the map on the passenger seat before her, and pulled out onto the first stretch of the route he'd marked out in blue felt pen, leading from the basement of the Empire State and through the Lincoln Tunnel, all the way across the country.

She found the gravesite of the suicide girl outside Stroudsburg. Amo had shifted the semi-trailer to the side, but painted his brand across the road in the same thick yellow paint he'd used in New York, along with a message:

Sophia - RIP

06 / 11 / 2018

I should have reached you in time

LMA

Lara found the grave he'd dug. She cleared a few roaming zombies with one of the shotguns from Amo's RV, then climbed into Sophia's trailer.

It was peaceful inside, and cool in the still afternoon. She sat on the sofa and leafed through a journal, which Amo must have read too. He left it there for her to read.

There was a line of three spliffs lying on the glass coffee table.

"You idiot," Lara said, and laughed. Emotion flushed up in her. God, it was Amo. He'd been here, how long ago? She brought up her phone. It was July 4th, Independence Day. She hadn't even realized. All that mattered was she was a little over three weeks behind him. The thought stunned her.

He was really out there. He was out there clearing the way, like some self-appointed janitor for the world, like the mayor of America, clearing a path through the brush and tidying up the dead en route.

Lara lifted one of the spliffs to her mouth. Her hand was shaking. She hadn't smoked since college, before law school. Her fingers remembered though, and using the Zippo she lit up. Mellow smoke filled her mouth, filled her lungs, filled her up. Amo's hands had rolled this, had prepared this like a party favor at some crazy wedding, where the guests would come one at a time if at all, spread out over the years, to pay their respects at the grave of a dead girl and get high.

She almost coughed but held it down until her lungs burned, then exhaled. Bluish smoke wreathed out and up, spiraling and twisting like drops of oil in water. A buzz hit her quickly from the tobacco, followed by the cushioning descent of the marijuana. She snuggled back into the sofa, imagining Amo was outside with Sophia, getting some milk or something, and they were all going to get high and party down together.

She read Sophia's journal. It was miserable and ecstatic by turns, a record of ups as miniscule as spotting three zombies in red jackets in a row, of lows so deep she scrawled in a rabid scratchy hand, repeating the same words over and over again:

What can I do? What can I do? What can I do?

Poor Sophia. Lara smoked the spliff down to the quick, then left it there in the ashtray, another signal to others. She rooted out a ball pen from her pack and started writing in answers to Sophia's long-silent entreaties.

You're all right now, Sophia. We're taking care of you. You are an important trailhead on the way out West. Your death was not for nothing. You will not be forgotten. I wish I'd known you, you sound like a lovely girl.

Thank you.

She wrote answers in Sophia's journal to her every moment of loss and misery. It did nothing, but it seemed to do something. These words were an unanswered plea that remained, and now they were answered. Sophia would never know, but that didn't make it any less real.

The others would know.

Lara signed it, Lara, Last Barista in America. LBA. She added the

169

date.

Then she started a new entry, on a clean page. She kept it short, but described how seeing Sophia's grave made her feel, and how it excited her, that others could be alive.

```
I hope to meet you, at the Chinese theater. You,
   me and Amo will watch movies together. And
whatever else we like too. Plant radishes and
         suchlike. We're going to be OK.
```

She put the journal down where she'd found it. She hunted out the spliff papers; there was no more weed but there was some tobacco left. She rolled a fresh cigarette, to replace the one she'd smoked. She laid it up neatly in line with the others. It felt like a kind of offering.

Poor Sophia. What a sad shrine, but strangely full of hope too. Amo's passage had made it that way. Her passage would make it even more so.

A waypoint on their pilgrimage.

She left.

There were no signs of Amo for a long time after that. She saw evidence of destruction at the roadside, passing through Indiana; a destroyed burger joint, its ragged outer walls blackened and splintered; elevated billboards that were burnt and had chunks missing.

That couldn't have been him, could it?

She reached the rolling cornfields of Iowa. In the summer blaze, the golden spread looked like the fields of Elysium, stretching into forever. She drove on over flatlands that went on and on, wondering if she was gaining on Amo, wondering if others were coming up behind her even now.

Were they in New York, at the first cairn? Were they at Sophia's shrine, the second? What would be the third?

In the midst of the corn, on a long and lonely road in the middle of nowhere, she found it. It was immense, and it changed everything.

20. REBIRTH

I remember my coma.

It was terrifying; I was a child again surrounded by colors I couldn't recognize and shapes I couldn't distinguish, shifting constantly like warping reflections on a soap bubble.

Have you ever seen a coma victim blanche so completely? I mean, they always lose their color in a week or two, it drains out of them, but this?

It was overnight.

I've never seen the like.

I 'hear' the words, coming to me through a gust of color like a digital brush-stroke, 130-point font and meaningless.

His brain activity is off the chart too. Something is happening in there.

But what?

But what.

I rumble and roll on an ocean of bald heads, so many shades like a million disconnected eggs. These are all heads and their thoughts twist together like twine in a bungee cord, conjoining from a flat weave to a tubular extrusion, like intestines curling themselves from to existence, like sausages bulging into life.

He may hear us. He may not. The eyes are the thing that get me though.

It looks like they're lit from behind. How is that possible?

Some simple phosphorescence, like a jellyfish. Whatever he's got inside him, it's changing his metabolism.

Are we talking an infection?

Not any infection we can see. It's a disorder of the entire nervous system. If I had to hazard a guess, I'd say something is remaking him.

His DNA shows no change. We checked that.

Not at the genetic level, then. Structurally. Look at the alterations in his brain pattern over time. It's been remapped completely.

The voices distend and balloon into curious clouds, into animals folded out of meat and bone. They bend in and out of time around me, drifting on a breeze of scent.

My mother's perfume, I'd recognize it anywhere. It stumps up and pats me on the head. It speaks.

My dear boy. My darling boy.

Later, much later with time as a food I chew on and excrete, she speaks again.

Not again, please. Not him too.

I breathe in my body and breathe it out again, flapping like a sail on the ocean of bald heads. There are great canyon-walls all around me made of bodies which are zombies, people lost and reanimated, reaching up for me.

Father.

They say.

Mother.

I reach out to them. I want to help them. I scoop their bodies up on my tongue, listen to them etching words across my skin, I see them growing older and changing by the minute. I reach out and feel the barrier between of this maddening reality flex and twist, like an image trying to bend its way out of a television screen.

Whatever this thing is, it's beyond our control. It's not a virus like any we've seen before, not bacteria, it's something physical that's rewriting him.

Like nanobots?

Ha. If that technology existed out of a Crichton novel, I'd say yes, but it doesn't. This seems to be natural. It may even be evolutionary, a key that was always waiting in the brain to be turned.

You said his brain-

I said his brain looked like an infant in the womb's. It does. Have you compared the stills I showed you? The telomerase counts are all getting reset at a mitochondrial level for brief periods, so for each of those brief periods it lasts, he isn't aging. That's undeniable.

He's the fountain of youth. Your paper argues-

I can't publish that paper, not yet. I need more.

But he's waking up.

Put him under again! Put him under and we'll see.

I am pushed back under, lost to the world beneath a layer of forget-me-nots, when all I want is to rise. They put me down again and again, until I'm scrabbling up a tower of a thousand bodies of the dead, fighting for breath.

It's stopped. Whatever it was, it isn't working any more. If anything it's starting to stunt him in ways that look necrotic. It's eating him alive. If we keep him under any longer he'll die.

Then let him die. This is research that could change the whole world.

This is a man whose parents are kicking up a mighty media storm. We can't just keep him. We'll never keep his records to ourselves if anyone

suspects. We need these records if we're ever
going to-

So let him wake up. We'll lose the greatest
scientific breakthrough in the history of our
race.

I think that's a bit-

What? Histrionic? Do you not see we're making
history here? His brain was resetting itself! He
was getting younger before our eyes!

And now it's stopped. Whatever it was, it was
wonderful, but it's over now and it's starting to
curdle. We have to let him go.

So wake him up. Screw you, and wake him up.

I rise. Everything hurts, from the back of my tongue down to the
sound of my own pulse. I am inside out and upside down. I don't know
where I'm thinking, what taste I'm seeing, everything is a jumble.

"It will be hard for a time," a voice said. How long had I been
unconscious? There was cotton wool in my mind, fogging me up.
"You've been in a coma for two weeks. We have no idea what
happened. How do you feel?"

The first of the twinges got me then, that new and persistent
companion. It got me good and hard and it laid me out. I didn't know,
but I know now. They used me. Something was happening to me and
they broke it. I was a butterfly emerging from my chrysalis, and they
kept me in too long.

My thoughts chuttered and jolted like a faulty boiler, sweating like
burnt toast. I reached out against the glare and the movement tore new
sinews in my mind.

My mother was there. My father was there, and I grew calmer. My
doctor came and went, a new voice, an Indian with red glasses. I liked
him, I trusted him, because the red and brown chimed perfectly
together, though they did look a bit ridiculous.

"Think of it like diabetes," he said. "Once you've got it you can't go
back, and one lapse can lead to serious complications."

Now I remember my lapse. I remember Lara. I remember reaching
out to reality, and what it became, and what I am now, surrounded by

the dead.

I wake surrounded by the dead. They are everywhere, pressed up against me skin to skin, their gray faces in the still repose of sleep, their white eyes closed, lying beside me like family, like lovers, like breakers in some almighty, unknowable weave.

I am alive. I jolt and start up. I look down on my chest and belly, study my arms and my legs, pat my face and my neck and my shoulders urgently, but there are no bites. There is no blood, there are no wounds at all.

I am alive.

The deep wheeze of their breath is everywhere. It is dark but starlight shines over us. I am sitting on the road where I stopped, the corn swaying in a warm wind on either side like walls of water waiting to descend, and all around me are the ocean.

There must be thousands of them. Their bodies stretch from me into the distance, on the road and into the corn, all lying down, all skin-to-skin, all asleep, and in that moment I understand a truth that changes everything.

They don't want to kill me. They never even tried.

Guilt, sickness and joy fall within me like stones plummeting down a deep well, each chasing the other and hammering off my heart on the way down, pulling me in and out of balance. The ocean's breath wheezes like a great placid ocean in time to the clanging bell of my heart, lapping at my sides, ringing in the change.

They are touching me. They have their arms across my body. They have oriented themselves with their heads closest to me, like a thousand sunflower seeds pointing little dry peanut heads seed-first at me, so I am the center of their mandala, and this is all they ever wanted.

Tears spring from my dry eyes. The touch of those closest to me is cold but tender. Here I am adrift, but for the first time in days I no longer feel lost. I am finally reaching through to the truth, and seeing it with open eyes.

I killed so many of them. I burned them, I trapped them, I taunted and slaughtered them, I laughed while they died, and I never once waited to see what they wanted. I never even tried.

Waves of shame pulse through me. Waves of joy chase them,

tsunamis that cleanse all my sins away, because they are here now, with me. They are around me still, my brothers and sisters, my children all, and all they want is the very thing I have wanted for so long, and fought for, and killed for.

Belonging. Acceptance. Forgiveness.

More memories slot into place, that I never saw them kill a single person, that though I fought them many times, and their bodies clashed with mine and their mouths grazed against my chest, they never once bit down. They never tried to infect me.

Because I had already infected them.

"Oh god," I whisper, the sound escaping me like it has been torn free.

I was the first. My body began this evolution or devolution or whatever it is, and in doing so rewrote them all. I incubated them, I made them, and then I killed them.

I rise to my knees. There are so many it's like Times Square again, only then I couldn't see it. I should have. I look over the expanse and silently give thanks. I have done such terrible things.

Now I will do better. I will help them in any way I can, and I will bring all those left alive with me.

"Thank you," I tell them. They are asleep and dreaming whatever strange dreams zombies see, but I hope they can hear, as I heard every word uttered by my bedside in the days of my coma. They are in the wilderness, and maybe I can help guide them home.

I walk, and like sleepwalkers in the midst if a shared dream, they rise and walk with me. They buoy me on. At some point I wander through a barn, and fish out a keg of fuel. I carry it until I reach the convoy. Returning to it is like seeing a long-lost friend.

"I'm sorry," I say to it. I pat the JCB's flank. I pour the gas in.

I drive the convoy slowly with the dawn, and they part before me, following behind. I leave the music on endlessly. Stimulation hurt me, it made my brain twinge, but I got better. No baby wants to be slapped to breathe. Life is cold and hard, but there are such joys too. It is worth it.

I drive the convoy with the JCB door open. It has become a sunny day and the road is clear ahead for miles. I take selfie photos of the endless swarm in the road. I can't stop grinning. At times I get out of the cab and walk amongst them, reveling in the touch of something alive that doesn't want to kill me.

I film my passage, to show this is real.

"Here I am," I tell some future audience, touching the ocean's shoulders and backs as I pass. "They're harmless. They don't want to hurt us. Look at this!"

I hold my phone's lens up to take in the panorama. It records them reaching their withered arms across my chest, pressing their heads to my arms, like affectionate cats. I smile and they breathe as one. I laugh.

"Hey, not there!" I crow, as one of them pokes me in the nuts. He backs up. A child takes his place and pats at my hand.

"What do you want, buddy?" I ask.

He doesn't want anything. He wants to pat at my hand, so I let him. I let them groom my hair and stroke my skin. I look into their wizened peanut faces and see not killers, but lost, sleepwalking souls. They may be in there still.

"You can hear me, can't you?" I ask a pucker-faced old man. "You're in there still."

His eyes glow. His mouth is a rictus grin, the skin pulled so tightly back. I touch his cheek, the tenderest expression I can think of.

Before I would have blown him to dust.

"What do you think of this?" I ask the phone's lens. I show my posse, many thousand strong, with me in the picture. "Can you believe this? Could you have ever imagined this? Would you like an entourage like this too?"

I wink playfully. I nudge them and they nudge me back. I pour water on their heads and they lap at it wildly, like those memes of cats drinking from the faucet by dipping their heads under.

We drive slowly through the day, moving to be moving. They circulate amongst themselves, so the ones closest to me are always new. They gather near, suck in their fill of my presence, like blood cells oxygenating, then radiate away. The ocean is breathing in whatever signal my brain is transmitting.

We walk and we drive and we listen to music. I hand out snacks for them to eat. They drop them from hands that have become useless claws. I imagine shooting out T-shirts from a T-shirt cannon. "And if you look under your seats…"

"It's a zombie armada," I tell Io that night, after my first full day as just another piece of jetsam on the ocean. It was wondrous. "They're all boats on the waves, not the ocean itself."

"What waves are those, Amo?" she asks.

I shrug. I'm lying atop the battle-tank, weary but feeling more alive than ever before. My whole body thrills to the sound of their breath below, and the despair is gone.

"Waves of thought? I don't know honestly. I don't know if they'll ever come back as people, or if they're too far-gone now, but it isn't pain, is it? They're together with each other. They're roaming together, they're following a pattern that I can't understand, and they might still wake up."

Io contemplates this for a time. "I hope it makes you happy, Amo."

I smile, and click her off. It's another misleading response the geeks thought up for her, so she wouldn't have to say something disappointing and banal like, 'I'm sorry, I don't understand.'

I don't care. It does make me happy. I climb down so I can lie amongst them. I lie down on the still-warm asphalt, and they lie down beside me.

In the morning they are gone entirely. I stand atop the tank and look out.

"Hello!" I call. "Where are you all?"

No reply comes from the tangled corn.

"Have you all gone for a pee?"

No reply. I turn and scan every direction but there is truly no sign of them. It is amazing. It touches me in a new way, like when I first saw a flock of sparrows massing and changing direction in the air, driven by the deep imperatives in their tiny sparrow brains, forming something beautiful, chaotic and amorphous, but at once ordered and logical and driven by an invisible calling.

They've had their fill of me. What I denied them in New York, with barriers and walls and locked doors, they've now gorged on, and are moving on. Will it save them? Will proximity to me, to my mind and my body and the patterns buried in my immune brain, somehow bring them from their long hibernation?

I hope so. I really hope so.

It feels empty now with them gone, here on this barren stretch of road, but not lonely. My body remembers their presence, and my hands remember the dry rasp of their skin. They're out there now, wandering the wilds, heading for god only knows what, perhaps the very thing that can save them.

The sun is coming up on a new day. It's July 7th, 2018, and I know exactly what I need to do. I know what the contents of the next cairn will be, and what I need to put in every cairn after that, because I can't let anyone else kill any more of them, not when contact and time is all they want.

I know where to go. It isn't even that far from here. I get in my cab and I roll back along the way I came.

21. INDIANOLA

The building is immense, a warehouse without any windows, and I pull the convoy up in the staff parking lot just outside Indianola, where my mother used to drop me off. I wasn't allowed to drive, back then. She'd hand me my lunch, sandwiches in plastic wrap, and kiss me on the cheek.

"You're doing so good," she'd say.

Perhaps there is hope for my mother and father. They could have been in the horde that came to me yesterday. Perhaps I touched them fleetingly as I walked amongst their ranks. I wouldn't know, but I think they would remember. That makes me feel good.

The JCB engine winds down as I turn the key, and I reach behind me for a shotgun from the rack in the cab, then stop and chuckle. I don't need that now.

I climb down from the cab without it and look around. There are none of the ocean here; I haven't seen any all day. There are just trees circling the parking lot, and cars parked in it, already fading in the sun. Their windows have the white hoar of sun-warp in the glass. Weeds have grown up in the dust accumulated against their tire rims.

There's a pink Cadillac, maybe Hank's. I think he used to work a night shift. And that has to be Blucy's little VW Bug over there. I laugh. When I went to her house to play Deepcraft for the first time, we drove in that.

I walk over and rub at the rain-dust on the side window, holding my eyes to my cupped hands to look in. The glass is hot to the touch on my nose. In the back bucket seat are two plastic cartons filled with books.

Vampires of the Amish Plain

I laugh out loud. "No way."

It's one of the covers I did for her. There must be two hundred books branded with my image stacked in the crates. That is crazy. They've been sitting here for months, slow-roasting.

I peel back and look up at the fulfillment center. There is only the smallest of signs to let me know it is Yangtze. This is not a customer-facing location. It is an immense cairn, filled with all the stuff we humans ever needed to survive, and the staff who used to man it.

It is a supply depot for me, now. It holds resources I can mine and craft into something better, if I can just get through the zombies alive.

I start across the parking lot. The staff door is metal and red, and the knob is hot in the mid-day heat. Summer has come, and it's a scorcher.

It opens. Of course, these places never close. They serviced our needs 24/7.

Inside is the corridor through the admin offices; a kind of smaller intestine, snaking with a little canteen, toilets, changing room, staff room, meeting room, supervisor's room, and center manager's office. All of us passed through this system the same way, before passing beyond into the greater intestine that is the darkness itself.

It's dim and hot in the corridor. I fire up my head-mounted flashlight. It feels strange to not have a shotgun and bandoliers of ammo across my chest, or the familiar weight of my handgun at my hip, but I couldn't bring any of them. I'm too afraid that, in the rush of a zombie charge, I'll use them.

In my pack I have my laptop and my USBs. That's the only heat I'm packing.

The air smells of linoleum and plastic-wrap. The center was only built a few years back, another of the changes sweeping our country. The supervisor told me all about it in the induction, but I was too busy staving off the twinges.

I advance. I peer in to the staff room, centered round a circular table where we used to sit, and the others would laugh and tease each other. I'd always try to get in and out fast. There's a soda machine in the corner, I never noticed that before, and a good-sized window onto a square plot of parched yellow grass.

I go by the offices and the changing rooms.

"Anybody here?" I call softly as I go. "Blucy, Hank?"

They don't answer, and nobody comes out to meet me. Perhaps they all found their way out. I hope that, but I expect it's not true. They couldn't open that metal door, and I've seen no broken windows yet.

They're still inside.

I advance to the entrance to the darkness; a single swing-door watched overhead by a very obvious CCTV camera. I give the non-functioning lens a thumbs-up, then push the door open.

Inside the heat dissipates at once, swallowed up in the cavern that is the warehouse, and a cool breeze meets me that smells of dust and packing material. My headlamp illuminates the nearest shelves, flanking the central aisle, but does nothing for the depths. Beyond the faint halo of light lies pitch black.

Something is moving out there, a rustle that becomes a slapping footfall. I flinch as months of defensive habits kick in. My heart begins to race and a cold sweat breaks on my forehead. I'm still clutching the door, and I want nothing more right now than to put myself back through it and run for the convoy.

Instead I close it behind me. I step out into the center aisle, 'Main Street' we used to call it, and wait.

"I'm here," I say, more loudly than I meant to. "It's Amo." I pause while the slapping of footsteps gets louder, then add slackly. "I'm back."

I catch a glimpse of the figure running, briefly visible as he goes by a slit of reflected light cast off a silvery edge halfway down the warehouse, then he's in the dark again. It was Hank, tall and skinnier than ever, his footfalls slapping more loudly each second. Others join him, a stampede of bodies running in the darkness, maybe Blucy, North Korean Bobby, travelling Linda. I stand there waiting for them, with plenty of time to question everything I've seen and think I've learned.

Are they really friendly?

Hank pops into view again, no more than twenty yards off and charging like an emaciated hipster bull. I take an involuntary step back, because he'll be on me in seconds flat. My fists are itching to fight or run or hold a gun, my nerves are firing like an AK-47, and it takes everything I have to take a step forward.

His eyes glow like halogen lamps, his feet slap the floor, and I manage a hasty, "Easy big guy," before he hits. His body crashes wholly into mine and we go down hard, rolling and slapping, until his face is against my head, and his hands claw at my back and his shoulder punches my chest, and I think that at any minute the first bite will come that will finally make me part of the in-crowd.

It doesn't come. We roll and tussle and I manage to push him off me, though he clings close, and he doesn't bite.

I look at him and he looks at me. We're lying there on the cold floor like he's just done a really good football tackle, and we're about to start laughing. My butt and side hurt where he took me down, but that is all the pain I feel. He didn't attack. More than anything he reminds of a really over-eager dog. I half expect him to start panting and wagging his tail.

"Good to see you Hank," I manage. "You're looking well, considering."

He stares at me. I nod to inspire confidence.

"I know, yeah, this is weird. Hang in there. Where are the others?"

A second later one of them hits us, connecting like a ground tackle in the small of my back.

"Shit!" I cry out, and turn, recognizing the cannonball behind me by her eponymous blue hair.

"Jesus Blucy, you could have killed me!"

She cozies up. Hank cozies up on the other side, so I'm like a human sandwich. The next three or four that come pelting out of the darkness hit into them and not me directly, so that's better because I don't think broken ribs will bother them the way they would me.

"It's good to see you guys," I say, as we all lie there in an orgiastic heap. I feel warm and ridiculous though their bodies are cold. "I never thought we'd all be lying like this in the middle of Main Street. But yeah, it's good."

My wit is lost on them. I pat at them, trying my best not to be condescending. I stop short of saying, 'Good Blucy, there's a good girl.' Instead we just lie silently for a while, breathing together. It's amazing, and despite myself I start to cry. These are the first people I've seen that I actually know since the world ended.

They look bad.

"You look good," I say to Hank's wrinkled peanut head. "It's a good look on you."

Somehow he's managed to get his scarf, an affectation he used to use to 'attract the ladies', since it has little silly kittens on it and was a good talking point, caught in his hair like a turban. I untangle it. He watches me with unblinking eyes.

"OK, cool."

After a while of that I get up. They get up with me. They follow me down the aisles, as I head for the place I've really come for. I explain to them a little what my plans are, and what I've been through. I tell Hank the play I used to 'reel' Lara in, color reading her palm. I tell Blucy how my book cover career was going, and about the big 'f' on the Empire State Building.

She is suitably impressed. I take her hand as we walk. It is a wrinkled bony thing, like a witch's, but it reacts, curling around my fingers like a baby's grip. We walk hand in hand toward the print-on-demand book machines.

This is my plan. Listen closely children, because I'm going to drop some art. It's called-

Zombies of America

And I'm uniquely placed to make it. First though I need power, and light, and paper and ink, and to understand the book machines, and to make the art and the words, but all that will come. This is a fulfillment center after all, where all your dreams come true.

The layout comes back to me quickly, and I prowl the aisles of the darkness following the invisible diviner in my head. I find the generators in no time, a whole section devoted to them, and my group follows on behind, touching my arms and back when they can. I pick up the first generator, a C-540 model, at least 80 pounds, and think 'Damn that is heavy'. I offer it to Hank.

"You want to help?"

Did he shake his head? I can't tell. He doesn't take it though. It's too heavy to be carrying. I go find a trolley and collect five generators. I drop them at the book machines then take the trolley out to the convoy and gather a drum of gas from the battle-tank.

The staff of the center look strange in the outdoor light, trickling along behind me like a line of baby ducks. I suppose this is the first time they've been outside in nearly four months. Their skin is still a light gray, but their clothes are oddly bright, like new. They wait patiently while I roll the gas drum out and get it on the trolley, then they walk alongside me like little kids gone shopping with their mom, holding on to the drum's sides.

I patrol the darkness looking for gear. I get cables and transformers and lamps and socket extenders. I get paper and card and glue and ink and toner, mustn't forget toner, and everything else I think I might need. I start the first generator burning beside the book machines and plug in the lamps.

Let there be light. It warms the place right up, and the generator's thrum gives the darkness a pulse. I pull up the old sofa Blucy installed back here, take a comfortable seat with my peeps lying down around me, and dig into the book machine operating manual.

Hours later, I'm ready to try a sample run. I've got everything in the right position, probably; ink in the trays, paper in the loading bay, glue topped up, toner roll inserted, and power running into the machine through a triple-decker transformer tangle of cables and plug combinations.

The machine operates off pdf files, and there are several in the RAM already, one of them being Blucy's latest masterwork, 'Werewolves in the Pliocene'. The cover is shockingly bad, not one of mine.

I press print. The machine starts to kick and flash like it's bottling a storm, rocking itself back and forth. Ah, the book machines. I settle back on the sofa like we used to all those months ago, almost a year now. It's so strange to have Blucy right here beside me, in withered body if not in spirit. Hank too, and some other new ones I don't know. It makes me sad that they're probably dead, but happy that they're here still, to keep me company for this.

"Sit down," I tell them. I pat the seat by my side. None of them sit though. They either stand nearby or lie on the floor watching me, while I watch the machine.

After five minutes the bucking and fizzing stops, and out spits a book onto the conveyor belt. I pick it up and study it. It is fine work. It is digital bits, words and numbers and a little bit of art which until now were floating in electromagnetic storage cells in a steadily decaying hard drive, now converted to a real, tangible thing.

Brilliant.

I shut the machine down. I flick off the lamps and power, then cart another generator with me back to the outer offices, to the canteen, where there's a window and a desk, and a fridge I can maybe get to work. It's hot as hell though, so I open all the doors and set them with jams, from the outside through to the darkness. I even open up one of the loading bay doors in the warehouse, by jumping the circuit from one of my generators.

Light floods in, and a delicious cool breeze blows by, clearing out the dry and stale air. I smell grass seeds and undergrowth, and they are sublime. Now I just need a corn dog and some Bud to watch the big game.

Back in my new office I feed coins pilfered from petty cash in the supervisor's room into the vending machine until it spits out 7UP cans, which I then put in the little fridge, plugged in to the generator. It tastes great going down cold. Sophia had the right idea with her little luxuries.

The heat clears out and the breeze keeps on coming. The staff wander around their transformed world, seeing portions of the darkness in light for the first time. At times they come to stand by me while I get to work.

I rig my workspace with a top of the line iMac, stylus and graphical pad, hooked up through Photoshop. They watch and listen with interest as the machine boots up. I feel like a conductor with them as the orchestra, so I tap the pad with the stylus like I'm signaling for attention. I start music playing through my phone. I open a new pane, the right size for the maximum pdf the machines take, and put my pen to the tablet.

I begin.

It takes five days. I take breaks but they are light, because I'm that focused. I love it, throwing myself into the work again with renewed vigor. Every panel I complete feels like a new kind of victory, more than the big 'f' in New York, more than I can really describe.

The Last

I tell my story. I tell it from my coma all the way to now, about brave Cerulean and Lara, about my massacres and forgiveness, about Sophia on the way and the big 'f' and my empty family home, all with as much honesty as I can. I put myself into comic book art: lying down in the road to die, and waking up alive.

It is a hell of a story. I draw over a hundred panels, full color, high resolution. I outline and colorize, I add in text and narration. I try to resist the urge to give myself cooler reaction lines, and fail. I am the mayor, after all.

Of course I sleep, and eat and drink soda, and take breaks when my back or my wrist hurt. Somewhere along the way, on one of my walks to and from the convoy or around the silent, peaceful center, my audience leaves. They don't say goodbye, they just melt away into the world, gone wherever the others have gone, with their quota of Amo-time filled.

I salute them, standing at the door, as the last of them traipse off into the woods. We're all moving on.

I sleep on the roof of the battle-tank, except when it rains and I sleep inside surrounded by my cairn supplies, listening to the steady thump of raindrops on the metal roof. I dream of Lara bounding through fields to meet me, like Hank, but she's properly alive. I wake feeling good, that I'm doing something worthwhile and maybe even saving lives.

After five days all the work is done, with my hand aching and blistered from working with the stylus. I format the pages into a single pdf, I trim the edges and manage the bleed on the front and back covers. The front is an image of me borne aloft by the zombie ocean, one living man amongst a sea of thousands of the dead.

I run it through the machines, all of them hammering and clattering at once, like a barnyard of oinking pigs. I run it and run it, printing copy after copy. When the machines jam I unjam them. When they need paper or ink I feed them. When the generators start to fade I fill them to their gurgling lips.

I stand on the top of the center in the middle of the print run, so high up I can't even hear the machines thumping, and look out at the sky. It's silent and unblemished. The air smells ripe and dusty, like a storm is coming. This is a full-throated Iowa summer. It's so silent, and as the sun goes down it gets beautiful; the sky lights up in burnt sienna and ochre shades, like firing clay.

I can hear the sound of jackdaws in the forest. The traffic on nearby I-80, my road, is absent. There are no co-workers below, bustling in and out of the office, gossiping while smoking up at the loading bays. There is none of the constant supply of semis coming to unload goods or to pick up goods for delivery.

It's just me, mayor of everything I survey in this empty and barren land, but it doesn't feel barren. There's life growing everywhere I look; green overtaking the parking lot, trees rustling in the wind, the birds, the drone of bees going by, the buzz of cicadas in the bushes living out their short lifespans.

I'm not alone, and this truly is a beautiful land.

I cart the stacks of my comics, let's call them graphic novels, to the battle-tank. There are several thousand, filling six plastic cartons. I throw out most of my weaponry to make room, leaving it in a bonfire-like pile in the middle of the parking lot. There it can rust away to nothing, and that's OK by me.

I get back into the cab, and look one final time at the Yangtze center. It's empty now, but I imagine Cerulean's digital ghost rolling through its halls, though he never once went there in life. It was his favorite place, still, and where for a time we both belonged.

I rev the JCB and pull away. I return to the spot on the road where the revelation first happened, flanked on both sides by corn, a nondescript locale but for the geo-tag I placed in my phone.

There I build my third cairn out of Blucy's bug and Hank's Cadillac, dragged along at the back of the convoy. I array them either side of the road and draw a thick checkered bar between them in white and black, just like the start and finish line of a race. I tag it LMA, and draw arrows pointing to the two vehicles.

In the bug I put my books, some two hundred of them. It's ambitious, but I've always been that way. I set up a nice bit of custom shelving inside, so the books are handsomely arrayed. There's even a sign that says:

```
The zombies won't hurt you. Pass it on please.
```

I want to make it completely plain. In the Cadillac I leave a digital cache, dozens of laptops, batteries, and USBs all with the same stuff I put in the Empire State, but with my video of the friendly zombies foremost in the filing system. It's a short highlight reel showing me walking in their midst, lying beside them, laughing with them, moving freely and unhurt while surrounded by an ocean of the dead.

"Don't you want an entourage like this?" I've titled it. I've drawn a picture of a zombie modeled on the famous Banksy image of a guy throwing a bunch of flowers, and used that as the cover image. I even draw that onto the hood of the car itself. The zombie isn't throwing flowers though, he's throwing a nice pink brain.

You've got to laugh.

I stand back and look at my work. It's the starting point of a new journey, one that will catapult me and any who follow to the West, and what we might find there. The destination takes on mystical power in my mind. It's a brave new world with such dreams in it.

I get in my convoy and I rumble over the start line. It's only as I'm falling back into the monotony of the drive, watching the yellow fields slough by on either side, that I realize something vast and unavoidable.

Cerulean is alive.

It hits me like a punch. He had the coma like me. He remained uninfected like me. His mother was hammering at the basement door to get down, but I don't think she wanted to kill him, not if she was anything like these others. She would have knelt at his side until she was ready to go on, leaving him there in his basement, waking from his methadone dose.

Oh my god. Cerulean is alive.

The epiphany dizzies me and I have to pull to a stop. If Cerulean is alive then perhaps Lara is too. For whatever reason, she didn't become a zombie in the middle of the night like the rest. She left a sly note behind. Maybe the act of sex immunized her, present at ground zero for the infection's spread.

The ocean will lap against them both, but it will not kill them. I feel that for certain.

God damn.

WEST

22. UTAH, ARIZONA, NEVADA

I press on, feeling the race biting at my heels, like blazing this trail is the most important thing I'll ever do. Day chases night and I chase after them both, always following the sun and the moon over my head and off to the west, always west.

At night I dream of Cerulean and Lara, out there somewhere, perhaps together and united by the New York cairn, rolling and walking hand in hand with the ocean. Gray bodies lurch around them like emperor penguins in the Arctic, too damn docile to fight back, because they've never seen humans before and don't know that they should fear us.

I drive and I sleep and time burns away behind me in dropped cairns. I place them in all the bigger towns, getting the process down to a fine art. In Nebraska I hit up Omaha and North Platte; in Colorado I drop them in Brighton and Frisco, tagging each one LMA. I leave my books and my digital footprint, I add large blackboards sourced from nearby coffee shops for a a register, with my name at the top.

I drive on through the endless waves of corn, alternating at times with the leafy green soy plants sprung up from rich brown soil. On stretches there are hay bales lining the road that have been there for months, steadily mulching down. The high sweet smell of their fermentation carries in the air, along with the cloying scent of sugar-beet plantations in the distance. Water towers mark my progress, and by the names written across their bulbous flanks I chart a path from tiny town to tiny town.

I walk with the ocean and I ride with them. When I sleep I sleep amongst them and we breathe together. Come the morning they are always gone, and I follow.

In Denver I ricochet through streets clogged with emergency vehicles and milling floaters. I hazard a guess that out here they had longer to react to the infection as it spread. People had time to call for help.

It didn't help. I don't see a single living soul, or any sign that anyone survived.

I bulldoze my path gently.

I smash my way into the Wells Fargo Center, fifty floors tall and laid out like a gridiron of perfect square windows with a wavy curve for a rooftop haircut. I rig a pulley in the stairwell then haul my gear up: drums full of bright yellow street paint, rollers, rope, generators, gas, food. Hiking fifty floors is an insane workout.

I wander through bank offices around the fortieth floor. The view is epic, of course. Here I pass amongst desks and chairs, along static-rustling gray carpet looking into cubicles and offices. Nothing has changed since the world flipped on its axis, bar the people and the power. It wouldn't look any different from now. At one point a worn-looking security guard comes pelting for me.

I sidestep at the last moment and he goes by, then I step up close so he can't charge me again. I pat him on the burly shoulder. "There we go."

He puts his wrinkly hand on my shoulder too. No problem. We conga that way back to the stairs.

The roof of Wells Fargo is a weird wavy pompadour, so I can't go down in a window-cleaner's basket. Instead I hook into the rappel points and hack my generator into the in-coil system. It all works fine, and after working on the Empire State for so long I have no problem with heights.

From the slippery glass top I look out over the Colorado countryside. There are skyscrapers and suburbs then an endless flat plain of scrubby brown and green fields. This is Middle America, the plains, and it goes on forever. This new cairn will be visible for miles, so I better make it a good one.

I rappel down the building's side and work fast, running myself left to right along the windows like a dot-matrix printer, slapping the paint in place hastily but with deft familiarity. I don't work from sketches painted in the interior this time, because I'm not too worried about accuracy. A splash that looks jagged up close will look like a razor-straight line from a mile away. Distance forgives a lot.

I get high on the sway of it, spending the first day on the east-facing side swaying around between floors 48 and 40, covering most of the building's façade in yellow.

When it's done I set myself up to sleep in the dizzy heights of the top floor, along with my pal the security guard, hunkered down in an executive suite where probably the CEO stayed when he was puling an all-nighter. The TV in there is a hundred inches wide. There is champagne in the fridge and thirty-year-old brandy in the liquor cupboard. Sadly the ice machine in the corner doesn't work, and I can't be bothered to figure out how to hack it with the generator cables.

I lie on the massive bed in the massive silence of this stilted mausoleum to high finance, and laugh, with lukewarm brandy in one hand and a champagne glass in the other. I wasn't a big drinker before and I'm certainly not now. I sip at both and watch a movie on my laptop. It's the first in the Ragnarok series, picked up on DVD from a carousel in a gas station somewhere. In it our mythological superheroes are climbing all over buildings in Shanghai, fighting off aliens.

I'm not a huge fan but it is good fun. It feels good to watch it after so long and not twinge at all. The noise and light fills the room for a little while, and I can forget where I've been and what I've done.

The next day I do two more sides of the building, and wonder if my security guard has found his way down the stairs and out through the hole I smashed, or if maybe he's glitching round the top floor still, banging into walls.

The third day I finish with the north-facing angle and set up the cairn in the ground floor lobby, like a booth at comic-con, featuring my books and the digital file and the rest. I sign a few bits and bobs, authentic LMA merchandise, and intersperse these amongst the piles. I should get some T-shirts made.

I drive away. On the outskirts of Denver I look back along I-76 at my handiwork.

It's a giant yellow Pac-Man. I tried to do it like a stop-motion animation, though who will notice that I don't know. Starting at the east his mouth is mostly open, then clockwise he clamps it closer to shut, until at the north it's just a slim wedge of pie.

His eye is a black dot the size of a double-desk. It looks good. It's a bit of fun.

I rumble on.

I tell jokes to Io and she tells them back to me. I try to think of puns about zombies. Most of them revolve around the similarity of 'brains' to other words, like drains, grains, flames. I theorize aloud about why zombies have always been so interested in brains, and figure out it's probably because they haven't got any of their own.

"Remember, I sawed open that head?" I ask her.

"What head is that, Amo?"

"It was like a coconut husk."

"I like coconut ice cream."

I laugh. "Me too, Io, me too. Good luck getting that now, though."

"You're near a Wal-Mart. I'm sure they have it."

I'm impressed she knows where we are anymore. "That's a great idea."

We pull off the highway and into a Wal-Mart in the scrubby forests near Grand Junction, where the ice cream is rotten sludge in tubs, though that's not what I'm looking for. I've come for the astronaut's ice cream. I find it in dehydrated wafer-form, sealed in brick-like silver packages. There's no coconut but there are vanilla, strawberry, and Rocky Road. I grab a handful and on the way out pick up some cans of bolognese and a box of green tea.

It's a feast that night on the border between Colorado and Utah, camped out in my battle-tank with the bitter tang of the green tea's tannins in the air. Nostalgia overcomes me, and while chewing down bolognese I fire up the darkness in Deepcraft, slipping my goggles over my eyes.

Cerulean is there waiting for me. I turn on my diviner and go with him down the aisles, toddling along through the bicycles and the exercise equipment, circling around past the book machines and down narrow passages filled with large cardboard boxes containing all kinds of Barbie dolls.

Hank passes me but he's mute now, with his Internet feeds cut off.

The real Hank is out there somewhere, wandering with his darkness herd. The real Cerulean is out there too.

In the morning I drive on into Utah, replenishing my gas barrels at a Shell station because there's a tanker sitting on the forecourt, and that's a lot easier to siphon than the underground tanks. I get a pack of Big Red and some lukewarm grape soda and sip and chew my way into the desert.

The land turns brown and burnt red, in this our long approach through Mormon country to Las Vegas. To either side great sandstone buttes rise like the mittens in Monument Valley. It is a gorgeous, wasted land, as pure as driven sand, dotted with hardy green cacti and mountainous termite mounds. Scrappy shoots of dune grass crop up everywhere, and sand has begun to reclaim the road.

I pass through various National Forests, fed on water stopped up behind Bryce canyon to the north, and am enveloped in verdant Douglas fir and Bristlecone pine. I spot squirrels and turkey in the branches and the undergrowth, starting as I rumble by. I drink water from a fresh tributary stream, damn it is cold and fresh. I get on my knees and smell the sweet resin of the pine needle carpet. Just beautiful.

I drop more cairns, in Richmond and Beaver, in Cedar City and St. George. Of course I'm saving something special for Vegas itself. It's got to be grand, surely, for a place like that. I ask myself, what would Banksy do with all the world as his canvas? What would JR do? How far does fighting back against the man take you, being defiant against the new world order, when there's not a shred of that order remaining?

I'm not them, though, and I'm not in their world. I'm me, Amo, and I'll do what I've got in my head.

After Zion National Park I hang a left off the main track, and drive a few hours east for the first time since backtracking to the darkness. I've always wanted to see 'The Wave', a part of Coyote Buttes that has the most gorgeous sandstone escarpments, like the eye of Jupiter made flesh on planet Earth.

The terrain gets redder and harsher around me, Arapaho land, and I get misty-eyed and awed with it. Of course I've seen the Grand Canyon before, but there's something more intimate about this. Soon I pass through the parking lot and by the visitor's center. There I unhook the battle-tank from the JCB, loading the cab with a gas burner and some tea and bolognese, a blanket and an inflatable pool lilo, a pack of marshmallows, Graham crackers and Hershey slabs. With all that I take the JCB up the ranger trail.

It's already straining toward dusk as I ascend up into the wave. It is a perfect half-pipe of red and cream sandstone deliciousness, like freshly scooped raspberry ripple, so smooth and perfect I want to reach out and bite it. That all this was formed by water and wind just blows my mind. It feels as alien as Mars, and I am the last man alive to see it.

I park the JCB at the trailhead and climb one of the buttes by dusk light. The sandstone is slippery and a fine rain of sand shivers off at my touch. There are stairs cut into the rock and a rail bolted in, and I climb to a viewing platform atop a twisty crag, left behind when the softer sedimentary layers around it were worn away. So says the sign.

On top I set up my burner and sit on my lilo, and toast marshmallows on the open fire. They crackle and catch fire, quickly going black, melting the lovely inner layer to sugary goodness. I love this bit. I sandwich it with chocolate and crackers, watch the white distend and bulge through cracks in the black outer skin, and take that first luscious bite.

Oh my lord above, that is sweet.

The intensity brings back so many memories; hay rides with Aaron and my parents, my dad driving us in the little hay-trailer attached to his John Deere round the three acre wilderness farm he bought so we could play there and build proper tree-houses. We'd wade in the creek and catch crawfish, barbeque venison and have burgers, and tell stories by firelight while watching the fire crackle, munching on s'mores.

After a while we'd take the ride to the hilltop crest and lie back to watch the sky. There were always shooting stars, and we'd give them names and shout out when we saw them, sometimes pretending we'd seen one when none had come, just to tease along the others. My mom was the best at calling us out on that game, while my dad just nodded along and claimed to see them all.

I sigh and lie back. The tea and bolognese can be breakfast. I look up at the sky. Of course it's the same sky. These are the same stars, though the shooting ones aren't.

"They're not really stars," my dad told us once. "They're just little bites of interstellar dust, or the screws and nuts that come off falling satellites, burning up as they enter the Earth's atmosphere."

This awed us even more. That there was a layer of sky up there so hot that it burned, that interstellar dust was reaching out to our little planet across the gulf of space, then falling down upon us all like a fine rain, like fairy dust.

In the morning I head out, wordlessly, after the breakfast I promised myself. I hook the JCB back up and rev off, back to I-15, for the road through Las Vegas and out to the coast. It's the final leg now, and I'm excited about what I'll find.

Will anybody be there already? Will I find a copy of Ragnarok III tucked away in a producer's office, ready for distribution nationwide? Will it all be what I hoped, or am I going to end up swinging like dear Sophia within a week?

Whatever. I'm not worried. I feel good regardless of the outcome. I'll have done what I set out to do, and if it just leads to me dying there alone, then that's fine too.

I pull through the desert corner of Arizona and then into Nevada at the fastest clip yet, down largely empty roads. Soon Las Vegas dawns like an abandoned theme park from the wastes, and I blow into the strip hard, roaring between outsized casino-hotels with my music pounding, bound for the UFO, a massive silver saucer sticking edge-into the ground, surrounded by faux-rubble, like it crashed there.

They only finished building it a few months before the zombies; one of the largest hotel-casinos yet, surrounded by giant green alien sculptures. I saw it on the news, distantly, back when I could barely handle TV. It's where my next-to-last major cairn will go. I heard they screened movie-launches across its massive circular façade.

Everything is still and silent but for me, and sand blows down the streets in cute twisty zephyrs. I see the UFO dawn like a dark sun over the faux-city.

Before that though, I see the man in the road.

Two floaters trail behind him, on leashes tied about their necks. For a second I think I must be dreaming, I blink but that doesn't change the reality. He's there. He's real, and he turns and waves as I roll near.

I pull the JCB to a stop and race out to meet him.

23. DON

I run over and he runs to me with his pet zombies dropped behind, and we stop an awkward distance apart, sizing each other up.

"Jesus," he says. His eyes are wide and watery. His face is thin and he's tall, he's got almost a foot on me. Across his thick chest he wears bandoliers of bullets just like I used to. There's a sword in a sheath at his waist and a handgun, and a shotgun in a sleeve down his back like Ash in the Evil Dead. "I thought everyone was dead."

I laugh. "Me too. Damn, it is good to see another living person."

He holds out his hand. I spread my arms. We pull into a braced, manly hug. He stinks of old sweat and the sour saltpeter tang of expended gunpowder, but then I probably do too.

We pull away and we laugh in the awkward gap between us.

"Don," he says, holding out his hand. He has a southern drawl. We're both grinning like idiots. "I'm from Texas, I've been roaming all the highways for months, looking."

I take his hand and give it a firm pump. "Amo, from Iowa, though I've just come from New York."

He raises his eyebrows. "New York, in that rig? It must've taken a month."

I shrug. "Yeah. I was looking out too, for others."

His eyes narrow eagerly. "Did you find any? Are there others?"

I consider telling him about Lara and Cerulean, but despite the natural ebullience of meeting a survivor, I hold back. I don't know this guy at all. "No. Well, yes, but she was dead. A girl. She committed suicide before I reached her."

This casts a pall over our jubilant meeting. He runs a hand through his thick blonde hair. He looks to come from Scandinavian stock.

"And you?"

He shakes his head. "You're the first, man. Damn, it is good to see someone."

I nod. It is.

"And you said your name was ammo? Like, bullets?"

I hold in a laugh. Shall I tell this huge man that my name actually means love, and my parents were hippies? Maybe later.

"Sure," I say.

"That's cool. I guess I should've come up with something better than Don." He laughs sheepishly. Then he draws his sword. It looks like a medieval replica, maybe from a fantasy movie or something, with an ornate pommel and what look like runes carved into the shaft.

"Sword, maybe? It could be a good name. Here, you want to have a go?"

He swivels the blade smoothly, doubtless a practiced motion, and holds it out to me.

"I got the idea from that zombie TV show, you know, that black girl?" He jerks his thumb to the two floaters milling aimlessly where he left them, their leashes trailing. "Them too."

I notice they're both female. They're dressed as cheerleaders, in bright miniskirts and tight sweater tops that haven't faded with exposure to the sun. I think-

"Here," he says, pressing the sword closer. "The balance is perfect. Most of these things are made of zinc, and the tang, that's the bit of the blade that goes down into the handle here, is nothing more than a thin pin, so when you hit something, snap, the whole thing comes apart." He hawks and spits to the side. "This baby is real though, cold-rolled steel sharp as a straight-razor."

I take the sword by the handle. There are spots of dried blood on the blade, but the balance is fantastic. I give it a few experimental swishes.

"It does feel good," I say. "Where did you get it?"

His grin widens with pride. "I found it in some rich asshole's pad in LA. He had a whole wall full of them, like he was some kind of crusader knight."

"You've been to LA?"

"Sure. I go back and forth, you know, patrolling the desert. Scouting."

I swing the sword a few more times, then hold it out to him pommel first. For an instant I feel vulnerable, with the handle toward him and the blade pointing toward me. All he'd have to do is push and I'd be impaled.

The moment passes though and he takes the sword.

"Just hot shit," he says abruptly, while sheathing it again. "Just color me damn surprised to meet you. Ammo, what a name, and what a rig."

"And you walk?" I ask. "You just, kind of roam?"

He laughs. "Yeah, sometimes. Me and the girls."

We look at his floaters. They toe the ground and strain at the edge of their taut leashes. I notice he's tethered them to a nearby car. I guess he did that while I was getting out of the cab.

"So, you know they don't want to kill us right," I say.

"Sure, of course. I woke up when the plague hit and some nurse was leaning over me all attentively, you know? I was in a hospital, then. For a minute I thought she wanted to screw me, but then I figured it out. TV down, lights down, the white eyes?" He points to his eyes to help me get the point. "I figured it. I gave her what she wanted."

He grins. I smile back. What did he just say?

"So, Ammo. You say you're going to LA?"

I nod, then wish I could take it back. I'm not ready to tell him about the others yet. I ad-lib. "Yeah, I've got family there." I cast around for a part of LA I know. "Down near Muscle Beach. You know it?"

He laughs. "It's full of posers still! I guess they were having a full-moon party or something, there's a stage set up, the band's gear all up there, and all these idiots wandering around with only their bikinis and shit on like there's no better place to be than the beach."

I nod, absorbing this. I look back at his cheerleader zombies on their leashes. It's clear they're straining to get away, to go wherever the rest of them go.

"So what's with them?" I point. "It's not like the TV show, you don't need them to fend off the others."

He shrugs. "Company. I like to have them around."

"Where did you get them? They must've come out of some

midnight show in a casino, perhaps, with clothes still bright like that?"

His eyes narrow slightly. "Yeah maybe. I found them wandering in the desert nearby, and they came up with all the hugging that they do. Maybe they're sisters, I'm not sure, you can't really tell with the raisin faces. I figured I'd keep them. There's nothing where they want to go but other drifters, you know?"

I process this for a second. I put it to one side, that their clothes would not be so bright if they'd truly been wandering in the Nevada sun for three months, because it leaves a pretty distasteful taste in my mouth. Did he dress them like that?

I focus on the most interesting thing.

"You're saying you've followed them, the floaters? You know where they go?"

He laughs. "Sure I have. I guess you wouldn't have though, would you, not when you're making for your family?" His brow wrinkles. "But let me ask, why the convoy Ammo, pulled by that thing? You could've made it across the country in a few days if you took, like, a Lamborghini or something."

He's catching me in a lie. "Supplies," I blurt. "I didn't know what to expect. I didn't know they weren't dangerous until a week ago."

He stares at me. "Seriously? So you've been fighting the zombie apocalypse, like, all this time?" He gives a low whistle. "That sucks. I feel that. Of course they're not dangerous, not in that way at least. And you've not got any yourself, chained up inside? It's really all ammo in there?"

He looks concerned. I try to puzzle out the reason.

"Why would I have them chained up inside?"

He laughs again. "I don't know, man. Who can say what people do? Can I take a look inside, anyway?

"What?"

He points. "Inside the school bus, see what kind of gear you're packing. Call it professional curiosity, one survivor to another. I showed you my blade, show me yours. Plus, I've got some whiskey in my pack, we can toast."

I let my answer wait a second too long, maybe. I recover quickly, but still.

"Sure, yeah. I've got tea."

He laughs. "Tea! Brilliant. Yes, let's have some tea. After you."

"OK."

I lead us toward the battle-tank. He catches up and slaps me on the back. The sour stink of him is actually overpowering. "Don't be nervous," he says. "We're all good. I've been waiting for this moment for so long."

I laugh. "Who's nervous? I've been hogging my RPGs since the start, I don't want to go sharing them out now."

"You've got RPGs? Damn, I knew you didn't play about, Ammo. Walking around with no weapon on you, music blaring like you were the ice cream man come to town or something, I knew either you'd gone soft or you had to be packing some major heat. You sure there's no one in there right now, drawing a bead on me?"

"What? No, there's no one in there."

"Good."

We reach the bus door, reinforced with cut strips of sheet metal. I open a square cover in the tank's side, like the flap on a gas tank, and pull the lever. The door cranks noisily open.

"Love it," Don says. "After you, boss."

I climb in. It's the same as it always is, though my crates of comics are lying right there. For some reason I feel I ought to hide them away. This starts to feel like a mistake. There's hardly even any ammo or weapons in here at all, and I forgot I tossed all the RPGs away weeks ago.

"What the hell is all this?" Don asks, climbing in behind me. His head almost strokes the roof of the tank. In the confined space, the disparity between the size of us becomes far more apparent. He's huge, and his animal stench comes at me in waves like an assault. "Where are the guns? And what are these, comics?"

He thumbs the copies lying topmost on the crate. "Jesus, they're all the same. 'Zombies of America'? What are you doing with these?" He picks one up and leafs through. "New York," he murmurs, "the road West. Damn, is this you Ammo? Did you, somehow, make these?"

He holds the comic out by the cover, causing its own weight to pull at the binding.

"Yeah," I say. "I printed them out."

He looks at me. "Why? Just for your own pleasure?" He twirls his finger round next to his head. "Gone a bit crazy? That's fine, I understand. I've gone plenty crazy myself. It can be hard, you know, to keep a handle on things."

"I know."

He eyes me hard. "Do you know? From the look of this, and the lack of guns, it seems like you've had it pretty easy."

"I've had plenty."

He puts the comic down. "So where are the guns then? The ammo? I don't see anything. You promised me RPGs."

"I guess I threw them mostly away, after I realized they weren't dangerous. Let me see." I back up to the end of the bus, and rummage in the storage boxes there. I come up with a handgun. I turn back and find he's followed me halfway up the bus, closing in tighter.

"I've got this."

He nods, licks his lip. "Let me see that."

I stare at him. "Why?"

"Just let me have a look. Is it a police gun? Man I love those. Smooth recoil."

He advances a step closer.

"Hang on a second Don," I tell him. "Hold up. You're crowding me."

He stops and raises his hands. "Sorry. I don't mean it, I'm just, you know, so excited? Let's relax, you're right." He doesn't take a step back. "Where did you say your family live, down near Muscle Beach? A lot of apartments that way, are there?"

I massage the gun's handle into my palm.

"I've never been, to be honest."

He nods. He looks around the battle-tank interior. "Yeah, OK. It's kind of drab in here, you know? I'd cheer it up a bit, some color or something. You're an artist, why don't you paint it?"

"Let's drink a whiskey," I say. "Why don't you pour us a whiskey? There's glasses at the front. We can celebrate."

He grins. "You know, now I've got a taste for tea? You put the idea there, and now it's stuck. Can you make me some tea, Ammo?"

It's wonderfully awkward. It would make a great moment in a movie, because I just can't read him. Am I truly penned in, about to hand over my only gun to some psycho, or is this just friendly chitchat? Social nicety or bait on a trap? My finger slips silently through the trigger guard.

"What's with the cheerleaders, Don?" I ask. "You've got them on leashes. What are they for?"

He frowns at me. The moment ticks over. "Those drifters? I told you, company. It's lonely out here."

"But you dressed them. You must've stripped off whatever rags they were in, and you dressed them like that."

He shrugs, then grins. "So what if I did? What's that between you and me, a little titillation? A little company. You know they come to us in the night, what do you think they're looking for?"

I edge up against the hard plastic crates lying along the back seat.

"What have you been doing with them, Don?"

He laughs. "Seriously? Don't look so offended, Jesus. Do you really need me to explain this? And you're telling me you haven't? It's OK buddy. We all get lonely, we've all got natural drives, there's nothing wrong with that. They come to us and we give them what they want, and who doesn't feel used when they leave the next morning? Like a one night stand." He winks. "So I keep them around, my favorites anyway. It's no big thing."

I stare at him as the wave of understanding crests. It repulses me.

"You've been having sex with them?"

He laughs. "Well, sex is a bit strong. It's more a kind of masturbation, you know, since they don't really get involved. But we don't need to talk about that, if it freaks you out."

I can't not talk about it. "It's rape."

He laughs. "What? How could it be rape? They don't even think."

"They're in comas," I say. "You were in a coma too, right?"

He frowns. "A coma? Sure, like a year ago, but what's that got to do with this? And how did you know?"

"I was in one too." I gesture around me with my free hand. "That's what this is. You had terrible migraines afterward, but then it went away when the zombies came, am I right? You said you were in hospital, it was probably for the migraines, yes? Now these 'drifters', the ones you've got roped up outside and dressed like damn Barbie dolls, are people in comas. It is rape."

He frowns. "I don't think so. It can't be. They just lie there."

"And you've been killing them too," I say. I can't stop myself now, though I feel that I should. "When does that happen, if they disappoint you in the sack? I saw the blood on your blade."

He shrugs. "I put them out of their misery, sometimes, so what?

Don't tell me you haven't killed any."

"I've killed thousands! But that was before I knew what they were. You knew, but still you did this?"

His expression hardens slightly. His footing sets. I realize we're only a few steps apart.

"Stop being so damn sanctimonious," he says. "You don't know shit about them, 'Ammo'. You don't even know where they go, do you? You haven't got a clue, your precious 'people' in 'comas'. You want to know where they're headed? They walk into the goddamn ocean! They walk right in if you let them, after they've had their fill, after they've used you. How is that fair, I ask you? Poof, they're gone, and you're alone again. It's not rape or imprisonment, it's saving them! So I take a little pleasure in their company, where's the harm in that? I'm saving their lives, and they don't complain. You don't get to dictate to me."

My eyes blur with excitement and my body hums into a fight or flight tension. I try to calm myself but I can't. I imagine Blucy in his hands, straining to get away while he heaves his bulk onto her back. I imagine Lara, alive or dead, with him mounting her and leashing her and dressing her up in cheerleader clothes.

"They're dead," I say. My legs are shaking. "And you dressed them up. Those two girls, you put them in those uniforms. They didn't volunteer for that."

"So what? They're mine now, don't the leashes say as much? They may as well be goddamn cows I'm leading around. And it's not even as if the sex is very good, Ammo, you know? They're dry, man. It sucks."

"So stop doing it. Go cut them free. That's it. If you can't do that, get the hell off this bus."

He stares at me. "You're serious."

I nod.

"The last two survivors in all America, and you care about this? I'm not going to try and make you have sex with them. It's not a big deal."

"So cut them free."

He stares at me. I can tell he's making calculations. He's bigger than me by far. He only needs to cover a few steps and he'll be on me, then I'll be screwed. Seconds pass, and he decides. His expression twists into a snarl.

"Bleeding heart," he says, with disgust in his voice. "I knew it when I saw you. An artist. A sensitive soul. You're really saying you'll choose them over me?"

He takes a step closer. There's only a few rows of chairs between us now. I raise the gun and point it square at his chest.

"Get out of the bus, Don."

He laughs. "What are you doing, Ammo? Ammo from New York, headed for Muscle Beach, where there ain't shit but sand and shopping? We're just two guys having a conversation. You owe me some fucking tea."

"Get out of the bus now."

He shakes his head. "No. I don't think so. And listen, tell me this, Mr. Judgment who's never seen another living soul, who's Lara?"

Hearing her name come from his lips shocks me. He must have read it in the comic. He uses the moment to take another step closer. Dammit, we're almost within reaching distance. One lunge, and…

"You've lied plenty, sinned plenty too, haven't you? I get it, man, you think there are others out there, so you're trying to keep them from me? You want to send me off on some crazy back trail, because what, I'm not good enough? Because I got a bit lonely, because I took their advances to mean what they obviously meant? It's not my fault they always leave, is it? It means something to me. I'm not that guy."

I start to think I've made a mistake. This whole thing is a terrible mistake. "So back up," I say. "We can talk about this, Don. Maybe you're right. You just have to back up and we can be OK."

"OK? What the fuck's OK about this, Ammo?" He's getting red under his thick blonde hair now, and his voice is getting louder. "That's a goddamn joke. What do you think we're going to talk about now, after you've screwed everything up? You're going to judge me some more, then figure out how to humiliate me in front of your Lara? Dammit, if I want my girls, if I want your girls, I'll goddamn well have them, because there's not another thing in this world for me now. Do you understand that? This is all I've had, Ammo, for months! Then I meet you, I let you hold my sword, and you give me this, a gun in my face?"

"I'm penned in here, Don. Listen, I'm sorry, I over-reacted. Just back up. We can talk."

"Screw talking! You made the decision about me the second you saw me. You lured me up here so you could do this, and what are you going to do afterward, Ammo, write me into your comic as the psycho loser you met, tell all the world about my fucked-up sexual depravity? No way, my friend." He licks his lip. I feel it coming.

"I won't do that."

"Damn right you won't. You think that gun is going to stop me? You know how many times I've tried to kill myself, son? It doesn't work! I've shot myself full of holes, and always I just wake up. I'm strong and you're weak, and that's what the record will show. I'll burn your shitty comics in a heap, and I'll burn you, and I'll tell your precious Lara you died in a stampede because you were fucking the dead. How do you like that? You can either put that gun down now, or we can tango and find out who the real man is."

I angle the gun to point at his throat. He notices and smiles. "Not that weak, then," he says, and lunges.

His right hand shoots up and covers the barrel just as I pull the trigger. Blood spurts out, the bullet sprays through his palm and out the other side, ricocheting off his temple and sparking from the bus roof.

Then his bulk hits me and slams me back against the reinforced metal back wall. The supply chests dig sharply into my thighs and knock me off balance, tipping me to the side. He falls with me and there's blood dropping on my face. I fall into the narrow space behind the back seat, hemmed in, and he clumsily reaches after me, his ruined hand pawing me with blood.

I've still got the gun and I hold it up but this time he manages to bat it away, pressed up against the seatback. I pull the trigger and the bullet takes off the top of his thumb, more blood spurts out across my chest, and he howls.

"Enough," he shouts, and somehow claws the gun out of my hand. It goes clattering off the floor several seats over. He tries to get his left arm into the tight space to close around my throat, his eyes now burning with pain, but it's so tight he can't easily reach in.

I brace my shoulders against the emergency door and kick out at his legs. I catch one of his shins sharply with the ball of my foot, so hard it twinges my ankle and something clicks. It drives another bellow of rage from him as the leg flips back and he falls hard onto the seat back, his ruined right hand no longer enough to hold up his weight.

His cheek cracks off the metal rail, and if the gap between the seat and wall were wider he'd fall right on top of me, but it's too narrow for his thick chest. Instead for a second he's left lying suspended above me, blood dripping down from his head and a new gash in his cheek, gazing at me numbly.

His left hand pats at my chest weakly. "Why?" he mumbles.

I grab for the pistol at his waist and slide it out. He stares in horror and snatches down at it.

"Back off," I rasp, pointing it at his belly.

"No," he mumbles, and tries to grab the gun.

I put two slugs through his belly. He jerks and more hot blood splashes out, then his hand closes on the barrel and pulls it easily from my grip. He slides backward to slump in the tight aisle on his knees before me, turning the gun in his blood-slick hands, searching for the trigger.

I kick him in the face, there's a stiff crack and he jerks back, then I scrabble desperately behind me for the emergency exit lever. My hand finds it, yanks down, and the side wall opens outward, spilling me out several feet into the bright sunlight.

I hit the sandy asphalt with a crunch on my shoulder and neck, then tip ungainly backward across my face. I come to rest flat on my belly with a great view of Don in the shadow getting the gun in position. I roll to the side as he shoots, one, two, three shots, a fourth, and one of them catches me in the foot like a whipping snakebite. I look down to see blood spreading across the toe of my left boot.

"Come on, Ammo," he calls from inside. "Let's talk. You wanted to talk."

I lurch to my feet and start hobbling back along the side of the bus. From the delivery truck the sound of Counting Crows singing Mr. Jones peels out, the soundtrack of this ragged escape. I reach the JCB just as there's a crunch and he hits the road behind me, holding the pistol and pulling the trigger, but all it does is click.

He gets to his feet as I climb up to the cab, my left foot bloody and my right twingeing with every step. I can barely even hold my own weight going up. I make two rungs on the ladder then my leg gives out and I fall back, barely stopping myself from a full fall with my hand on the railing.

There's no time. He pulls the shotgun from its sheath on his back. I roll around the front of the cab just as the first blast roars out. It tears shreds of metal out of the side and draws fracture patterns on the glass. I hobble ahead, keeping the JCB between me and him, cornering and working my way back down the battle-tank.

"I just wanted to be friends," he shouts, his voice a pained gurgle. "Why did you have to be such a dick?"

I don't say anything. Another blast tears across the air beside me and I feel the breath of the shrapnel passing inches over my shoulder. I risk a glance back and see him rounding the cab. He looks like shit, pale-faced as a zombie, with blood and maybe his entrails hanging out of his blasted belly. If I can just keep ahead of him I'll be all right. He'll die of these injuries, I'm sure.

"We could have shared them," he shouts. "One cheerleader for me, one for you. It didn't have to be like this."

"You don't get it," I shoot hoarsely back. "How could I trust you with anyone else?"

I hobble on, one foot sprained and one shot through. I pass the end of the battle-tank and am closing on the ocean at the back of the delivery truck when he shoots again.

This time I feel it more than I hear it. My legs go out from under me, peppered by spray, and I hit the road hard with my face, cracking my nose and my lips sharply, too abruptly to get my hands up in front of me.

"I'm a good person," he slurs. "I am."

Ah god. I roll over and feel the acid sting of buckshot burn hotly in the meat of my legs. I'm twingeing again, it's rising to cloud my vision with gray, and I can't think clearly. Lara, I think, Cerulean, I'm sorry. I twist back to see my thighs and calves lying limply like torn fins behind me, and beyond that there's Don, humping wheezily closer, slotting fresh shells into the shotgun's breech.

"Should have listened to me," he says. He's moving by sheer will too. He's barely alive, there's so much blood pouring out of him. "We could have been pals."

I look forward and start to crawl. The asphalt burns hot against my palms and cheek, and I know I'm not going to make it. Like Sophia I'll be found broken and beaten, and this will be my legacy, our two bodies left entwined with no explanation or reason why. I don't want to die.

I'm sorry Lara. I'm sorry Cerulean. I'm sorry Sophia too, I've let you all down.

My vision clouds and I look up to see the ocean lapping near. They come over from the back of the truck, all withered faces and gangly limbs, half-dressed and gray, as eager as over-friendly dogs. I think of Hank in the darkness, barreling out to be close to me, and how happy he seemed to have me near. I think of all the horrible crimes I did against them.

"Please," I whisper to them. "Help me."

I roll onto my back. Don's over me now, leveling the shotgun, and the music is too loud for them to hear him, to even notice him.

"Please," I say again. He points the barrel right at my chest, and I know this is the end.

"Bleeding heart," he says, "bleed for me."

Then gray flesh flies over me and at him. He pulls up the shotgun and blows it to powder, but another follows in an instant, leaping over my ruined legs and taking another spray of buckshot that blows it to pieces.

My head falls back and I watch as more of them come, leaping over me like sheep over a fence, and I'm drifting. Four, five, six. I hear Don begin to scream, I hear the sound of rending and tearing, and when I look up briefly, I see the ocean for the first time as they feed on a fellow human.

They're eating Don. His arm lifts up from the midst of them, covered in his own blood, and one of the ocean bites into it, tearing a chunk of quivering meat free.

He screams throughout. They rear back with his intestines dangling like strands of spaghetti from their mouths, his bright red blood everywhere, splashing like a geyser. They're eating him. They're really eating him alive.

It could be me next.

I lie back and look up at the sky, where wisps of cloud twist and turn. One of them looks a little like Lara, or it may, because I can hardly even remember what she looks like. I never took a photo and it's already been so long. In my mind she merges with Sophia, another soul lost to the vast emptiness of this great country.

Don's screams fade, replaced by the gristly snap and crunch of the feast. My vision goes dark. If this is the end then so be it. Let my bones be a warning to those that come after me, a cairn itself, helping them forward and making them strong.

I'm not sad, I'm happy. I've done a good thing. Let the ocean join the ocean in freedom, and there swim for as long as they like.

INTERLUDE 3

The videos changed everything.

Lara watched them again and again, shots of Amo walking amongst the throngs of the dead, laughing and smiling. He touched them and they touched him, amidst the same Iowa cornfields she stood within, surrounded by gold.

She broke down many times. She'd killed her own mother and father because she'd thought she was putting them out of their misery, when she could have had this. They could have come with her on this journey across the country. They could have been together, or at least had a farewell. They didn't have to die.

She wept until she ran out of tears, then stopped.

"Enough," she said, and it was enough. She'd killed her parents, but Amo had killed thousands. He had that on his conscience and they'd forgiven him. Being amongst them had changed him. She could see it in the childlike wonder on his face in the video.

Now there was the comic. She held it in her hands like an artifact from a long-gone age, birthed through the apparatus of the old world, into the new.

Zombies of America

It chewed everything that had happened and somehow made it real, sucking the nutrition out of the cold reality and making it wholesome and palatable. It was better than an oral tradition. It was the beginning of a new history.

She leafed through the parts with her again. She was presented almost angelically, which made her laugh. She wasn't an angel. By some lights she was a failure, washing out at the legal bar, losing her way, becoming a coffee monkey and calling herself a barista to snatch back some modicum of credibility. Then for months after the event she'd hidden in her parent's house, while Amo was out there dealing with the world and thinking about others.

She'd never once considered doing something on the scale of greatness he'd opened up. She wouldn't have thought herself capable. But maybe now.

She looked again at the date he'd written on the blackboard in the car. It was cute that he'd taken it from a coffee shop, sort of keeping it within a strange kind of family. It was only a week ahead of her, August 14th. Making the comic must have slowed him down, bringing them closer together.

Her heart trilled. If he was truly driving in his JCB, clearing the road mile by mile, then perhaps she could catch him before he reached the coast.

Suddenly it seemed essential that she do that. She had to find him before he hit LA. If she pulled up to the Chinese theater and found him hanging there like he found Sophia, it would kill her too. She'd just string herself up right by his side, and that would be the ultimate message and lesson of this whole trip, for them and for any who came after; all of them hanging like mannequins in a long line, together at last. This was the future of the entire surviving race.

She ran back to the RV and jumped in. She tossed the comic in the passenger seat and tore off into the night.

She cleared Iowa into Nebraska in the early hours and slept a few hours in the back seat, no longer so concerned about nesting in somewhere safe. She woke before the dawn, to see a gray face at her window pressing close, lit by its white eyes and the light reflecting off the dash controls.

It terrified and thrilled her. Slowly, fighting against her every instinct, she wound down the window. The wrinkly screwed-up face

24. SAVIOR

I look up and see Lara's face again, hovering under the clouds like the shadow of a dark mother ship.

"Hi," I whisper feebly. I reach up and pat at her face, like creamy coffee.

"Jesus Amo, what happened?" she asks.

I smile, high on dying, blessed with this final angelic vision. I try to frame an answer but my lips don't work well.

All night I slept fitfully, too weak to move, too surrounded by the dead to care. They pressed close, breathing their hot bloody breath against his skin, stinking of shit and raw guts.

My legs were done.

I watched the stars and waited for the end. I tried to crawl with just my arms, like the snail man back in Mott Haven, but the pain blacked me out. I didn't make an inch.

I look down the side of the battle-tank, through the shifting gray legs of the ocean. All that remains of Don are his bones. His skull lies like a fat white pebble beside the barrel tube of his ribs.

Lara is here, saying something. I smile up at her.

"Water, please," I mumble.

Her face is wobbly, like ripples on the surface of a lake after a stone's been thrown. I try to say something more but I can't really make a sound. It is good to see Lara after so long, even like this.

"This skeleton, what the hell is this?" she asks. "God, look at your legs Amo, what happened?"

I don't really feel my legs anymore. They are long and far off.

"There was an indicator," I manage to whisper. She leans in close to hear. "It hit my shoulder."

She frowns, the movement of her brows barely visible, then she starts tugging at my shirt.

"Left," I whisper. She pulls at the shirt there, running her fingers over the little dimple the indicator had made. That has healed too, so fast and so long ago I barely remember it.

"This is ancient," she says. "Amo, I'm going to have to move you. I need to do something about all this mess."

"They killed Don," I croak. "He's right there. We need to clean him up."

Lara turns her head then spun back. "The skeleton? Wait, you mean the ocean killed him? You said they're not hurting us."

"Help him," I mumble.

"I think he's a bit past helping."

She fumbles in her pack and produces a bottle of water. She unscrews the cap and holds it to my lips, and I drink.

Oh, angelic horde, the taste of manna from heaven. I suck it in and it fills me like a river. I look up and then she's gone again. Of course. I try to sing a song, a tune in my head but I don't even know the name. The ocean bumble nearby, filling the space she'd taken. I read the label on the water bottle absently.

Fresh Spring Water Direct from the Alps!

It sounds delicious, so cool and clean. I close my eyes for a time, and when I come back she's come back too. That's good.

"This is going to hurt," she says. There's some kind of low trolley beside her, a long shiny metal thing with a cream-cake coating of white sheets atop it, low to the ground, grumbling on wheels.

A stretcher? I look past it and see the blurry white flank of an ambulance, with a striking red cross on the side. What? Something of logic creeps in past the dying daze in my mind, and I look again at Lara.

"Lara?" I whisper.

She nods grimly, then does something to my legs which just about kills me, and just as I realize that Lara is really here, Lara has come out of nothing and is really, actually here, a black wave of pain reaches up like a dark ocean and gobbles me down.

Getting him on the stretcher was the first of the hardest things she'd ever done. He was so damn heavy, even lifting his torso half on to the edge exhausted her. Getting his hips on nearly busted out her back. She tipped his legs as gently as she could after, though she was afraid of touching them.

He cried out then went unconscious. That was a blessing, but not if he died. Already fresh trickles of blood were seeping from the deep and crusted wounds in the backs of his legs. They looked like spray from a shotgun blast; similar to patterns she'd etched into zombies to date.

"Hang in there, Amo," she said, then belted him in and lifted the stretcher to waist-height. The spring inside aided her, and she rumbled him over to the waiting ambulance in seconds.

She'd found it after fifteen minutes of mad driving in circles, hunting beyond the Strip for a hospital. The first ambulance she tried wouldn't even start, but the second did. The doors opened and pulling out the stretcher was easy, as the legs kicked down to the ground.

Now she pushed the feet end of the stretcher into the back of the ambulance, onto the sliding rails, and it accepted them. The front legs bent back flush, and Amo slid inward like a smoothly oiled drawer.

She followed him in, cursing, crouching in the tight space. She'd done basic first aid for Sir Clowdesley, but that hadn't covered shotgun blasts. First she had to see what she was dealing with.

She raided the many little shelves in the ambulance's back, coming up with rolls of bandaging, surgical tape and a pair of needle-nose scissors. With great care she slit his bloody and tattered jeans down both sides, then peeled them away. Coming free from the blood scabs, they tore and started fresh flows.

She could wash them later. She tossed the ruined pants out of the back and started wrapping the bleeding crevices, softly at first then tighter as dark red continued to show through. She worked on the left leg then the right, lifting them and slipping the bandage roll underneath, taping it, doing it again until his lower half looked a mummy, stained with blotches of red.

She applied pressure. For a moment he woke and barked out something, then passed out again.

"What now?" she muttered, looking at her handiwork.

She tore through the cupboards again. There was a mini-fridge with bags of dark red blood in, but those had to have gone off now, and she had no idea what his blood type was. She kept looking until in one cupboard she found a rack of yellow-ish clear bags, complete with long tubes. Drip bags?

She grabbed one and pulled it near. It was written with all kinds of chemicals, but it had to be right, didn't it? They wouldn't keep weird, extremely specific stuff in ambulances would they? She checked it against the other bags there, three in total. They were all the same.

It had to be the good stuff. She hung one from the hook on a swing-out hanger, then started hunting for a needle. She'd never injected a single person before. Of course she'd seen it on TV, and had her own blood taken at health checks. It looked simple enough. She rustled through more drawers until she came up with a needle that looked like a fit.

She attached it to the drip end, piercing the inner sack. Fluid began to drip out. She caught some and licked it, yeah, it tasted salty and sweet, probably that was all right? She twisted the little plastic tappet to halt the flow then took hold of his right forearm. It was splashed with road-dust and blood. With an alcohol-swab she wiped it clean, then wiped her hands too, and the needle.

She searched for something to bring up his veins, and settled on his belt. It slid free from his legless jeans and she wrapped it tightly around his bicep, patted the underside of his forearm, and waited. Veins popped up. Taking her heart in her mouth, she fed the needle into his skin. It seemed good, so she opened the tappet, then a bulge started to form.

Nope. She pulled it out and picked a different spot, trying again. Again it bulged. Third time, near the crook of his elbow, she got it. No bulge formed. The drip fed down. He was getting fluids and basic nutrition.

She taped the line in place, belted him again into position, then climbed out, closed the back doors, and got into the driving seat.

Where the hell was the hospital again?

She stood over him, lying on the stretcher by the window of a clean and white first floor hospital room. Getting him out of the ambulance and into a room had been horrible with blood and stress. One thing she was grateful for was he'd remained unconscious throughout. Flipping him onto his belly had been easy though. Keeping the drip going, setting up a fan and a light with a generator in the corner, all that was easy.

Far harder was contemplating his legs. She just didn't know. Was it better to leave him as he was, or dig the shrapnel bits out and try to sew him up, or sew him up with them inside, or what? He'd lost so much blood, could he stand to lose more?

She stood by and watched two more drip bags go into him, dithering. She raided supply rooms for the tools she thought she might need: a gallon of swabbing alcohol and a fat pipette to drop it into place, antibacterial soap to scrub up with, surgical gloves, scalpels, towels, bandaging, surgical thread and curved needles, clean blue scrubs and a face mask, a helmet with a large magnifying visor, a surgical light hung over the bed, pounds of cotton wool-type blotting stuff, gauze, a shiny kidney bowl for slugs she extracted, a range of tweezer-like utensils for extracting, powerful and pungent disinfectant in serious brown jars, bottles of antibiotics in pill and liquid form, and a dozen more drip bags with tubes and needles to match.

She laid them all out on silver trays on clean white strips of gauze and tried to decide.

"What do you think?" she'd asked the few of the ocean gathered nearby, like an audience. They looked like doctors. They held to her elbows. She didn't have time to be afraid that they might eat her, like they'd plainly eaten the body on the Strip.

Using portable machines she took his pulse and his blood pressure. They both seemed low, but then she took her own and saw they were low too. She strung up a third drip bag, injected a syringe full of liquid antibiotics into it, and watched it flow into him.

It began to grow dark outside, but the desert heat was unremitting. He showed no signs of waking up. At last she made the decision, and rolled up her sleeves, drew her mask into place, and pulled the makeshift covers away from his legs.

They were a torn and meaty mess. There were scour marks where buckshot had grazed through the sides, long furrows where they'd burrowed in, and dark red wounds where they'd gone deep. They looked like a muddy battlefield, crusted with trenches and bomb-divots sprinkled with fragments of denim. She didn't know where to begin.

Sweat dripped down her nose and caught in the mask. It was hot under the lights and the fan did little to relieve the dry heat. She stripped off her shirt and bent to work, wearing just a sports bra and her scrubs.

She began with something easy, cleansing a shallow furrow around his right ankle. If she did it piece-meal, allowing the existing sealed scabs to hold, then perhaps he'd keep most of his blood in him. She began to think of his body as a precious bag, one she had to keep intact so the liquid inside wouldn't leak.

Cleansing the interior of the shallow line, like a seed-line plowed into a field, turned her stomach. There didn't seem to be enough skin left to seal it over again. Scraping away the crust of blood gently with alcohol and a cloth, she saw the raw pink and red of inflamed skin and muscle beneath. Was it infected? She couldn't tell. Fresh blood began to seep up like water bubbling through porous cloth. She splashed alcohol and disinfectant liberally, which mixed with the blood and ran pink down the sides of his leg, darkening the white stretcher sheets.

There didn't seem to be any bits of shrapnel in this gouge. She swallowed back her gorge and took up one of the threaded needles. It couldn't have been further from the needlework she'd done as a kid, but surely the principle was the same. Grabbing the edge of the skin was hard, and piercing it with the needle was tougher than she expected.

She pushed it through with a little pop. The thread ran through his skin like a shoelace through an eyelet, stopping at the crude knot. She scooped into the other edge of the wound, blotting furiously now with gauze to clear her view, and pulled the thread taut. The wound zippered closed, but in doing so cracked the scabs on other wounds on his leg, which began to leak blood through their caked platelets.

"Shit," she cursed. She hadn't though of that.

So it became an awful, bloody race. She needled the rest of that gouge in one long thread, then tightened it up like a corset before tying it off. Half a dozen other wounds, each deeper and more severe, were bleeding now too. She leaned back and saw that his face was white.

"What the hell," she muttered. It was too hard. She was going to spend all night on this, and lose him still. But what else could she do?

She already felt exhausted from driving through the night, emotionally drained, but it had to be done.

"Stop pussyfooting around," she whispered to herself. She bent back to his leg, and dived into one of the biggest, darkest wounds, trying a new theory. If she could seal those up first, then perhaps there'd be less blood leaking out when she pulled the smaller ones tight.

It was deep a hole dug squarely into his calf. There was only a shallow crust of blood over the top, and when she broke through it began to well up profusely. She felt sick. She dug into the hole with one of her pliers. She rooted around, grateful the only sound was his smooth breathing, until she hit something hard. Bone or metal? No way to know. She dug deeper until she got a grip then pulled. It shifted, but caught on something. To pull harder would do more damage, potentially tearing ligament or a muscle.

She pulled out and went at it on a different angle. She clamped it again, and this time it came free with a sucking breath. She held it up, feeling dizzy. It was a bead of metal as big as a nail head. She dropped it with a clank into the kidney bowl, had another root in the well to check it was alone, then sewed up the hole. It took only a few stitches to pout it closed, sealing off the blood flow.

Already his leg was looking better. Still there were a dozen gouges to deal with on that leg alone, and she could barely dare to look at the other, but order was beginning to come to the chaos. It wasn't so bad.

She got on.

By dawn of the next day, it was done. Both his legs were a forest of blue thread, drawing strange patterns across his disinfectant-tangy skin, painted a dark brown. The sheets were a mess of pale blood and dark clots. The air stank of iron and iodine. The kidney bowl was heavy with the weight of lead she'd pulled out of him, like extracted teeth.

She bandaged him up in a daze, seeing colors and shapes in the air. A zombie tugged at her sleeve. She rolled Amo carefully onto his side, stabilizing him with pillows. She refreshed his drip. His breathing was shallow and his face was drawn and pale.

There was nothing more she could do. She fed the generator to keep the fan going, then fell blood-smeared and sweaty onto a sofa, and passed out at once. If he survived or not was up to him now.

25. SURVIVORS

There's an ache in my whole body. I'm lying on my side. I recognize a hospital room. Hot light streams in through the floor-to-ceiling windows, overlooking low suburbs and orange desert. There's a red sofa by the window and lying upon it is Lara. She looks shattered, asleep, rumpled in a thin white sheet.

My mouth is dry, my eyes hurt. I try to roll onto my back but I can't, there's some kind of frame holding me in position. I crane my neck to look at it, but even that much movement starts something screaming in my legs.

A gray figure with a cratered gray face shuffles into view. A janitor, maybe?

"Hey," I say. My voice sounds like rustling sand.

He says nothing. A few others shuffle with him, two doctors, a nurse, and some girl in dungarees. It's weird but I can't complain.

"Thanks for coming."

They say nothing. I remember Don, and wonder if these ones may turn too.

"Not feeling hungry, are you?" I rasp. My throat hurts. My forearm hurts. I look down and see a drip line feeding in. The bag it connects to is half-empty, hanging over my head.

So Lara saved me?

I guess so. I feel dizzy still.

"Hey Lara," I try to shout. Am I laughing, it's hard to tell. I sound more like Muttley, a canine barking laugh. She turns in her sleep. She must've had a hard time, saving me. I should let her rest.

I got shot with a shotgun. I should let me rest. I close my eyes and sweet, nourishing sleep finds me again in seconds.

She watched him for three days and three nights, as he lay in a coma-like torpor in the hospital's eastern wing, by a window overlooking a therapeutic Las Vegas garden.

"Only old people and junkies," she murmured to herself, standing at the window. She'd had the thought many times, based on the types of floaters she'd released from their wardroom 'cells'. It was a wonderful kind of emancipation.

There were dozens of them trapped in rooms, old people whose hearts had given out while riding a roll in their casinos, young guys and girls with caved-in noses from too much heroin, and the wrinkled faces of zombies to boot, thumping sluggishly against their windows and doors.

She let them out, and let them follow her. In their rooms she studied their charts while they crowded around her. This one was Anne Gideon, she suffered from gout. She looked like she was well over that now. Here was Toby McTavish, broken leg in three places. It didn't show.

She wandered round the hospital, from the canteen on the second floor to the lobby and through the staff rooms, up to the roof, where she looked over the tawdry conglomeration of Strip buildings, a few blocks of cheap motels with their dark blue swimming pools away.

She checked in on Amo frequently. She rarely went farther than the hospital forecourt, for fear he might wake while she was gone.

She kept the drips going into him, and his body sucked them down. She dressed and salved his wounds twice a day, once in the morning and once at night. They seemed to be healing extremely quickly, more than normal, but what was normal now? She'd read about him shooting himself in the head and surviving. It was a new world.

The skin was tight and inflamed, but puckering in places around the stitches. Towards the end pulling the wounds closed had taken all her strength, with the constant worry she'd rip open some of the other stitches to make them all fit. There just wasn't enough skin left to cover all his muscle. She'd gotten most of it though.

He mumbled and stirred in his sleep. She stroked his hot forehead with a cool damp cloth.

He opened his eyes. He looked right up at her, and her heart leapt in her chest.

"Hey," he said.

Her jaw dropped. Tears at once raced down her cheeks.

"S'OK," he mumbled. He patted at her hand with his own. "Don't cry."

"I'm not," she said, though her eyes were streaming. "God, it's good to see you."

"You too." He was smiling, that same mischievous grin he'd given her at Rien, when he'd pulled her hand over and 'blessed' her with happiness. Now he was lying all torn up in a Las Vegas hospital. "You followed me."

She blinked away tears and laughed. "You made it easy. Cairns, Amo? The 'f'?"

His smiled widened. "A symbol for our modern age."

"And Pac-Man?"

He laughed, but it obviously hurt and he stopped. "A bit of fun. His mouth opened and closed."

"I saw that. Brilliant touch."

He closed his eyes then, and she thought perhaps he'd drifted back to unconsciousness, but then they opened again, a gentle, amused hazel.

"Good luck with the zombies," he said.

She frowned. "What?"

He laughed again, stopped again. "Good luck. You wrote it on a note in my room. You left it behind."

The memory of that came flooding back; such a strange, throwaway message, ultimately so prophetic. She laughed too.

"I guess we both had good luck."

He smiled and his eyes closed again.

"I'm glad. It's good. Poor old Don."

Then he was under. She watched him for a time, sleeping peacefully now. The color was back in his face. His breath came in deep, clear flows. He was alive, because of her.

She took photos. She went out onto the Strip and photographed the skeleton that had to be 'Don'. She took pictures of the cheerleaders tethered to the car, trying to piece together what must have happened. She tracked the blood trail and gouge-marks in the battle-tank's side to the back corner, where the emergency back door hung open.

The area behind the back seat was stained with blood. She rooted inside and found two guns scattered on the floor, one fully discharged, one two bullets short. There had been a struggle. She took photos and video.

She cut the cheerleaders free. Part of her expected them to come at her like the others must have gone for Don, but they didn't. They walked right past, heading west. They'd clearly had their fill of people. They faded into the heat-haze.

She gathered Don's bones up in a bucket. It was strange they all fit so well. She opened his pack, left inside the battle-tank, and looked through the contents. A bottle of whiskey, a Bible with half the pages torn out, a journal that documented mostly only the blandest of observations; the weather, the zombie count, how many roads he'd covered and where he might strike for next.

There was an occasional entry on his loneliness. It seemed to bite into him more sharply than it ever had into her. There were two passages of nothing more than harshly scribbled expletives written in capital letters, followed by passages of regret the next day.

She didn't understand fully what he kept the cheerleaders for, but she suspected. There were no lurid mementoes in his pack, no evidence, but she tried to imagine the exchange he'd have had with Amo, who saw the ocean now as good, living, willful beings.

It went badly between them. Perhaps it hadn't had to, but then how could she know? She didn't even know him, or Amo either, not really.

She buried Don's bones in the sand, and left his sword sticking into the ground like a headstone. He had been a survivor, like her. He'd been alone for too long. Perhaps they could have been friends. They all deserved better.

She closed up the tank. The floaters were all gone now. Las Vegas was a ghost town. Standing on the hot asphalt, she looked up and down the broad Strip, dotted with emergency vehicles and stretch limos pulled to the sides. So much life, lost. Evolved.

Back in the hospital, she found Amo awake.

My legs burn and all my efforts to sit up fail. Instead I lie on my belly and lean back, painstakingly unpeeling the bandaging. The skin down my legs is tarnished yellow with disinfectant, and a loop-de-loop train-yard of blue stitch tracks, following wounds that spray across like the beams of a lighthouse. My skin looks alien, body parts wrinkled and preserved in formaldehyde, and the sight throws me into shock.

I look away and breathe into my pillow for twenty minutes, willing the body-horror away. Soon enough the flop-sweat and nausea fade, and I look again. They are repulsive, but I can begin to admire the work Lara has done. It's pretty amazing, considering. I suppose baristas have very deft fingers.

I slump back, thinking hard. Don did this. I shot him in the guts and I sent the zombies to kill him. Do I regret that?

I'm not sure. I don't regret surviving.

I swivel slowly on the hard stretcher-bed on my belly, and reach for a bottle of mineral water on the side-table. The movement causes the drip line to pull tight, jerking me to a stop, and I watch as a flow of my own blood begins to feed back up into the line. What the hell? I watch for a second in fascination, as this life-giving tube sucks my own blood up into it, then I pinch the tube and the flow stops.

I pull the needle out of my forearm, and a little blood flows from the needle-hole but it peters out when I press my thumb on it. I toss the line away and it spits my blood onto the floor. It's OK, I'm making more. I tape up the hole then rotate slowly, so my head is at the tail of the stretcher, watching the door for Lara's return.

My back aches like a son of a gun, probably from lying sideways or on my belly for so long. I wiggle my feet. The movement of tendons in my thighs and calves feels like complex clockwork grating, but my feet move. I flex my knees, just the tiniest amount as the tightness in my stitches gets unbearable quickly, but they bend.

I lie there and wait. It's not long until Lara returns.

Hell, she is beautiful, maybe more so now. Her curly hair is tied back loosely, her eyes are as bright white as ever, and she smiles wide as she comes in, like she's really pleased to see me.

"Amo!"

She rushes over and drops to her knees, bringing her face next to mine.

"Hi," I say.

She kisses me on the lips. No tongue, but still it fires up an engine I haven't thought about for a while. She strokes my cheek as she pulls away.

"I'm so proud of you," she says.

I blush. "I just turned around on the stretcher," I say, displaying my trademark wit. "You could have done it too."

She laughs. She strokes my face. Then she kisses me again, this time with some tongue. It gets hot, and before I know it she's climbing onto the narrow stretcher and shimmying off her pants and her shirt.

"On your side," she whispers breathlessly, backing up into me. My paper boxer shorts come down, bristling against my stitches, and the heat of her skin against mine is overwhelming, the smell of her is intoxicating. My hands snake around to cup her breasts, and she arches her back.

"Condom," I whisper.

"Screw it, " she says breathily, craning her neck back to kiss me. I kiss her hard. I'm sure my mouth tastes like a shriveled sand pit, but she doesn't complain. She grinds back into me, and I seize her sheer brown hip and press myself into her. She gasps and so do I.

 God, this is worth it. It is the right choice to have survived and be here like this, with a beautiful survivor just as hungry as I am, aching for the touch of another.

We move together, breathing hard and grasping like we might fall if we don't hold on. Sensation rushes through me like salvation. It means we aren't dead, and there are things to live for still.

We finish together; she cries out and so do I. It is a release, and the start of something new. Neither of us is alone any more.

Afterward I lie with her nestled in my arms, breathing warmly. I love it. I love that this beautiful, resourceful woman who has surely saved my life, has chosen me.

"He was having sex with them," she says eventually. "Don."

"He was," I say.

The fan's breeze drifts over us, tingling off bare skin. The generator chutters smoothly in the corner.

"He was mad," she says. "You didn't want to kill him."

I know what she's asking. I don't have a good answer. "He came into the battle-tank. He got worked up. Maybe I worked him up, I'm not blameless here. I could have done it better. But I didn't know, not for sure. He had the comics, he could know about you, about Cerulean. I had to be sure. And he wouldn't back off."

"You fought in the back of the battle-tank."

I talk through it. I tell her about the floaters, responding and tearing him apart. It leaves us both in silence.

"Do you think they were defending you?" she asks eventually.

"I don't know. I honestly don't. Perhaps if he hadn't shot them, all they would have done was hug him? I don't know. I've never killed them in view of others, then let them come close. Perhaps he triggered a kill instinct they couldn't switch off."

"Or they were protecting you."

I frown up at her.

"You asked them to. You are their father after all."

I consider that for a time. "That would make you their mother."

She laughs softly. It sounds partly like a sob, and I pull her close.

"Maybe. I never had a coma, though. I suppose I was just a catalyst."

"You weren't 'just' anything."

"I was a vessel. It's OK, it could easily have been the other way around. Whatever happened that night, it inoculated me. I'm glad."

I nod. I consider saying something like, 'I saved you with my magic penis', but probably that's not a good idea.

"Ground zero," I say instead. "Right."

"Right."

We lie quietly. I stroke her bare arm. It's good.

I recover steadily. She brings me freshly un-canned fruit and bolognese. I still don't need to eat much, but I eat more than before. I drink more. We make love several times a day, lying on the stretcher. We graduate to a double stretcher, lashing the two together with drip-bag tubing, so we can sleep comfortably side by side.

The first of my stitches come out, and the wound holds. I rub the newly sealed skin repeatedly, fascinated and repelled by the bumpy ridges the stitches have left, like castle battlements.

"You won't be Miss California," Lara teases. She kisses me. "Don't wear tights."

"I had such plans," I answer. "The apocalypse has freed up my inner woman."

She chuckles. "Priscilla, queen of the desert."

I rub the healing wound until it feels like my skin again, no longer so horribly foreign. Welcome back, I tell it. The nausea fades.

More stitches come out. Lara's hand is steady and skillful.

"We learn this, for pouring milk," she says. "Carrying coffee requires a steady hand. It was a hard boot camp."

"I'm sure it was very rigorous. Coffee training has prepared you well as a surgeon."

She pinches my knee.

Spent stitches slip out of my skin with a little suck each time. Bright beads of blood prick up in the tiny gaps they leave. Lara dabs these down with iodine swabs, which sting. We leave the deepest few wounds a little longer.

Already I can flex my feet almost fully, rolling at the ankle. I can bend my knees halfway to forty-five degrees. I ask Lara to bring my laptop and drawing tablet, and she does. I start to work on the latest pages of my comic. There's no fulfillment center I know of round here, I don't know if we can print them out professionally, so I expect to just print them on the hospital machines and add the new pages as addenda to the back of the ones I've already got.

At the same time Lara goes out. She's working on my plan for the UFO.

"The walls will be slick," I tell her. "The heights will be terrifying at first. Double-check all your ropes, your cradle, your in-coil."

I don't tell her she shouldn't do it, or that she should wait until I'm fit and we can at least do it together. I can see that she needs to do this, and I need to be willing to share it. We started this thing, and now we have to see it through together.

A week passes. I work on my art and I recover. She comes back each evening splattered with paint but jubilant.

"You should see it," she says. "It looks amazing."

I pull her in and pull up her shirt to kiss her belly. "I will see it."

"I think it's your best work yet. Steady hand."

I rope her in tighter. My legs are sturdy enough that I can lie on my back now, with her straddling me. It's a whole different experience.

26. LA

In a week I finish the updates to my comic. Lara finishes her art. The last of the stitches come out, and I inch over to the edge of the bed, where I've been lying for nearly as long as I lay for my coma.

"Take it easy," Lara says.

Sweat beads down my back and my legs are already shaking, as I lower them carefully to the floor. I do my best to not let my thighs take my weight against the edge of the stretcher, but they take some and feel like they're being pinched sharply. I wince and she helps a little more.

We get me onto my feet. Without her I'd fall for sure, but with her I can just about hold myself up.

"It helps you've gotten so wiry," she says. "Like a zombie."

I grunt. With one hand gripping the drip bag stand like a walking stick, I slide a hesitant step forward. I make it.

"Hoorah," Lara says.

"Hoorah," I repeat. "Ok. Let's go see it."

"The UFO, now? Are you sure?"

"Yeah. We may need a wheelchair."

At the doorframe she rolls round with a wheelchair, heavily padded. Getting into it is hard, and twice it slides away while we're trying to drop my poor buttocks into it.

"Backstop it," I suggest, sweating and shaking hard now. "Stand there. Use your feet as chocks."

"I found the brake," she says, clicking it on.

I grab the elbow-rests and lower myself as slowly as possible onto the deeply piled pillows. I ride so high I feel like the princess and the pea. I need a seatbelt to keep myself in. My legs hurt, but the cushioning helps a lot.

She leans round and kisses me on the cheek. "It'll get better."

I focus on breathing. It's decent of her.

"Can you push? I can hardly move."

She pushes. We wend down the ward, and I peer through various rooms to the windows and the view of the city beyond. Las Vegas passes like images on a slowly spinning zoetrope.

We descend by a gradual slope at the end of the building. I try not to suck on my teeth at each little irregularity of the wheelchair's movement. This was Cerulean's life for so long.

"I've kitted out one of the wheelchair minibuses," Lara says. "The elevator works."

I nod thanks. I want to give a little more, but it's all I can do to keep from cursing her out every time the wheelchair's momentum changes. Of course it's not her fault. I'm the one who wants to see this, now. I bite down my frustration.

We pull through bright sunshine, and I relinquish my iron grip on the rests to shield my eyes. We pull over to the minibus, and she revs it up. The side door opens electronically, and an elevator platform unfolds and descends.

"Like the Delorean," I manage.

She chuckles. "Those doors opened upwards."

I laugh breathily. "Yeah."

She rolls me on, keys it to raise, and the minibus lifts me in. The drive is not far, and I cling to the minibus handles throughout. We pull round a currency transfer stall near to the Strip, and Lara leans back over the seat.

"Close your eyes."

I close them. I feel the turn. We'll be passing the spot where the ocean swallowed Don about now. I try not to think of how that makes me feel. The minibus stops.

"Keep them closed," she says.

The door opens, the side door opens, then she's wheeling me out. The elevator drops me to the ground, then we're rolling forward.

"Just a little further," she says.

"To the viewing platform," I answer. I keep my eyes closed, feeling part excitement and part annoyance, though I'm trying to repress the latter. This was my thing, and now I'm a spectator. This whole thing was my idea, and though I know better, and I want to share it with Lara more than anything, I also want it just for myself.

It's ridiculous. A week back I'd have done anything to see her face. Now I just want a little more time for myself. I snort.

"What's funny?" she asks.

I think I'll keep this one to myself. "Nothing. I was thinking about Jeo. Digital cairns and all that."

It's a white lie, as cairns are something I've been thinking about plenty recently. We used to let everyone know where we were, just by clicking a geo-location button. This cross-country slog has been pretty much the same thing, an analog trail across a once-digital world.

More people is what I wanted. That takes adjustment. I grit my teeth and adjust.

"There," she says. "Open them."

I open my eyes. For a few seconds I get used to the light, then I pick out the shapes of giant green and purple aliens, like stalky octopuses frozen out of water, holding ray guns, and beyond them her work.

It's better than I ever imagined. It is awesome, and it stands out starkly on the UFO's sheer silver saucer. It is a message from a modern-day hero that cannot be denied. Everybody who sees this will know what it means.

It is the silhouette of Michael Jordan, as seen on millions of shoes around the world, flying. His arm is up and touching the peak of the saucer, his legs spread across the widest point at the middle, and under his legs lies the famous strapline, adapted just above the dying brown palms in the brown grass fore-gardens, in letters a story high.

JUST LIVE ON

It staggers me. He's an outline only, drawn in thick yellow paint, but the work is exemplary, on the largest scale yet. It reminds me of white chalk figures carved out in English hillsides that survive for millennia. It is a new Mt. Rushmore for a brand new world.

"Shit," I murmur, feeling truly humbled.

All selfish thought of getting away from Lara for a minute, all peevishness about her taking this role away from me, fades in the face of how perfect this image is. It is inspiring, and across his middle she's emblazoned my tag, a touch I never would have been arrogant enough to add.

LMA

"You don't think it's shit do you?" she asks.

I look at her, thinking she must be joking, but she isn't. The nerves are plain on her face. I understand then, that this is about acceptance for her as much as it is for me. We both need to play a role in this thing, and I need to move over to make room. I can't complain. She has done her bit beautifully.

"God no, it's not shit," I say. "It's fantastic. I really mean it. I never thought a corporate logo would move me so much. Well done, Lara."

She smiles shyly. She pops down to kneel beside me, placing her arm awkwardly around my back. The added weight presses down on my legs and hurts like a bitch, but I am so high on awe that I don't even grimace. I suck it up and kiss her.

"I'm so glad," she says softly, whispering against my cheek. "I was worried."

"Steady hand," I say. "Draw that in your latte and smoke it."

She laughs.

"You should add your tag too," I say. "LBA."

She grins and points. "I did. You can just see maybe, across his shoe."

I peer. I see it.

"Well-deserved."

We dredge and sieve a nearby pool for sand and pond scum, until it's relatively clean. We take two days to relax, spreading out the work of filling up the UFO cairn with material. We drink cold piña coladas with freshly crushed ice, after hacking power to one of the icemakers, then think to add those same ingredients to the cairn. They can have coffee and cocktails, all those who follow on behind.

We lounge and sunbathe and recuperate. We drop in the warm pool water, now about halfway down the side thanks to evaporation, strongly redolent of chlorine, and walk up and down. It is rehabilitation for me. We take it in turns to carry each other around, held like rescued damsels, bobbing on the surface. We skinny-dip without shame.

At times we get drunk, giggling and trying on sunglasses naked in the lobby. We pose and lounge around like bohemians. We end up putting racks of sunglasses into the cairn, so others can share our fun. We print out my new pages on A4 and fold and staple them into the comics in fat stacks. We make love lazily on the pool loungers, listening to soulful crooning from the Rat pack.

"What if someone comes now?" Lara asks, "and they see us like this?"

"We'll have a toga party," I answer. "Set up some disco balls. Party at the end of the world."

She presses her hot chest against my chest. My legs hurt less now, even with her weight. Getting them in the sun seems to help. They tan irregularly, the newly forming scar lines remain a tight white, but the inflammation is fading.

"Do you really think there are others?" she asks.

"There have to be. I've seen two already. There must be more, hiding out there somewhere. Looking for us. They might be on the trail already."

She 'hmms' softly, starting to doze. I stroke her ringlet hair. It smells like coconuts, after we raided one of the expensive body-cream shops, and she had a crazy field day picking out a trolley full of beauty and cleansing products.

"It's not just for me," she'd protested when I rolled my eyes. "It's for the cairn."

It was a nice touch, I had to admit it. She made everything a lot prettier than I did. More welcoming and feminine I suppose. Mother and father, didn't somebody say that?

"Cerulean's out there too," I say softly, into her hair. She 'hmms' again.

Cerulean's out there.

After two days we pack up the convoy. I stand at Don's sword-marker grave, leaning on a fancy silver cane Lara found, and think about what I'd do if I found another person like him.

I don't know.

Perhaps if I'd just handed him the gun on the battle-tank, he would have looked it over and handed it back. We could have drunk whiskey or tea. I could have raised the issue of the cheerleaders later, shaming him less, adjusting his behavior gradually, and maybe he'd be here with us now, a valued member of the team. I could have helped him, maybe, and we might be friends.

But I couldn't know then. He might have turned the gun on me, and spent the next three days torturing me to death. He'd already let go of civilization the minute he started to have sex with the ocean. When he tied them up, when he dressed them for his own pleasure, when he raped them, he crossed a line. It didn't matter if anyone saw it or not.

I know better than any. There is a line out there in the wilderness, and once you cross it, the only way back is long, hard and lonely.

I turn and walk away. The ocean rendered judgment in the end, and for that I'm grateful.

The JCB only has one seat, so I sit on the battle tank roof on my beanbag, strapped to the ceiling, as we roll out of Vegas. I don't feel jealous or possessive of this work anymore, I don't need to be in the driving seat or the one making the cairns. It's open-source for the masses now, and I don't own it. I wave goodbye to the hero on the UFO, and wonder what he'd think, if he saw what we'd done.

A corporation raised him up for profit, it's true, but I don't care about that. He was a hero to millions for his skill and his dedication, a symbol of perseverance as potent as any other, and he's a hero and a symbol still. Him and Pac-Man both.

"Goodbye Vegas!" Lara cries out from the cab.

"Yeeha!" I shout out. She echoes it. We're on the final cattle-drive home.

The ocean follow us down to the sea. It takes a few days, and we stop and take shelter in mansions set back from the road along the way. Some of them have front grounds that stretch for acres in dead brown grass, withered for lack of water. I know California is notoriously dry.

I walk more smoothly every day, in and out of dark kitchens as big as my whole apartment used to be. I brew us green tea.

"No art," I say, shrugging apologetically as I hand her a cup. "No foam."

Lara punches me in the shoulder.

"Argh, indicator hole," I wince.

She laughs.

I make 'fresh' bolognese with dried pasta, vine-ripe tomatoes from a sheltered part of the yard, using salt, pepper and wild-growing basil, with chips of dehydrated soy in place of meat. It tastes better than anything I've ever tasted.

"We can have whole fields of tomatoes," Lara muses, while we lie back on a massive balcony and watch the sun come up over the country. "Grapes too, there's plenty in California. Wine. We'll start up agriculture again."

"Fields of bolognese plants," I say. "I hear the soil is perfect for them."

She snorts. "That would be cows."

I lean back and savor the moment. "Fields of cow plants then. They'll be so cute when they bud."

She doesn't even snort. "There must be some we can round up. Fence them in again."

"Yeah. If the ocean haven't eaten them all."

"True. They ate their way through all my neighborhood's dogs."

"I'd like a dog," I say. "I'll call it Buddy."

"I'll have a cat," she muses. "And a horse."

We cuddle closer and nap. We drive on.

Los Angeles is a low gray sprawl. We come upon its suburbs gathered in the base of a low valley like receding ice at the pole, spreading out into a steady gray plateau of malls, condominiums, office parks, warehouses, and windowless buildings that could be CIA black sites or storage lockers or film studios.

We push through, down the same snake of road that has carried us like a river from New York, expanded now to eight lanes. We go under and over numerous other highways, each of them jetting off to other cities, spread across the country.

We hit downtown and stop in a tourist shop for maps, accompanied by the usual herd of floaters; maps to the stars in the Hollywood hills, maps to the various beaches, maps that show the Walk of Fame outside the Chinese theater.

We pull off I-15 and turn north along the coast. Everywhere there are dribs and drabs of the ocean, skinny and shriveled and gray, stumbling along the boardwalk and down to the beach. There they walk steadily to the water, and in.

"Jesus," Lara says. "They're really doing it."

She stops the convoy and we get out. We walk down to stand amongst them on the shore. They pass by us like falling snowflakes, oblivious, driven by some strange internal drive.

"Do you think they're going to drown?" Lara asks. "Was Don right?"

"No," I say. "I don't know, but I don't think so."

We watch them file one by one, like shooting stars across the beach, flaming out in the surf. They don't try to swim, and they don't carry on the waves. They walk until they go under.

"Maybe they fill with water," Lara says. "Then they walk along the ocean floor."

"So they don't need to breathe?"

"Maybe not. They always have breathed, I know. But maybe they don't need to."

I squeeze her hand. "I hope so."

I really do. I don't like to think of all these people, drowning themselves a few hundred yards away from where we stand. Surely the beach would be scattered with their washed-up bodies, if they were just dying.

"They're going somewhere," I say. "Maybe a better place."

We drive on. The Hollywood sign appears on the hills. We go past the Chinese theater the first time round without really noticing it. I only notice the stars on the sidewalk, glinting in the sun.

We pull back and park. We get out and stand before it.

"This is it," Lara says.

I nod. I root around inside myself, wondering what to feel. There's nothing strong, though. I half-expect to see a line of people swinging by the necks from the entranceway, an image Lara shared with me, but there are none.

We are the first. I feel pride at completing this mission. I have come across the whole country. I have fought, and learned, and survived, and now we stand on the precipice of something wondrous, the end of the yellow brick road.

The Last

People may come.

It takes one generator to fire up the projector in the largest premier screen, and one to run the sound, and one to run the coordinating computer system in the central office. We perform a rude hack to get it all working, but it works.

It's all digital now. In the storage room by flashlight we sift through the solid-state black bricks that contain movies.

"Gone with the Wind?" Lara suggests.

"Put it on the pile."

"Ghostbusters?"

"Pile."

We heap them up. Already there's an audience of the ocean gathering in the theater, drawn by the sound and light. I guess these ones aren't quite ready to move on yet.

I keep hunting for the movie I've been waiting to see for years, one that was never screened, but must surely be ready. We don't find it in the theater, so we go on.

We find the studio that owned it, and dig through its campus. Every door we open releases floaters into the wild. We pass through cavernous dark studios, editing bays and offices, grand lobbies and storage rooms filled with old memorabilia, corridors lined with signed posters, busts of famous, long-dead actors, until in a central vault deep in the belly of the central building, I find it.

Ragnarok III. It comes on two bricks, and we carry one each.

"I don't even like these superhero movies that much," Lara says.

"It's not about liking," I say. "It's an event movie. We watch it like people used to go to church, to be together and listen to a sermon."

"That is dour."

"I do quite like them too," I add. "There's more spectacle than church."

We slot the first half of the movie into place in the Chinese theater's control room with a satisfying clunk, on August 23rd, 2018, at 1:15pm. It kicks into life with a pre-roll of ads and trailers. We pause it.

We make popcorn in a microwave. We decant fizzy soda from the machines. We alter the strip line boards at the theater's front, sliding in the letters of our message.

LMA/LBA PRODUCTIONS PROUDLY PRESENTS:

RAGANAROK I, II & III TRIPLE BILL

WELCOME TO THE WEST COAST, SURVIVORS!

We settle down amidst the ocean, in the premium loveseats at the back, and watch the movie. It is great fun. The world is nearly destroyed, our heroes battle each other then unite, and all is relatively well in the end, with just enough mystery and threat left to hint at bigger and darker stories to come.

Afterward we stand at the entrance at sunset and look out over the actual ocean. It laps at the beach only yards away. Floaters flow out around us, heading down to the orange-dappled water like a tide of gray gazelle. We hold hands.

"They'll come," I say. "Cerulean will come."

Lara squeezes my hand. "Of course he will. The Last Mayor of America is handing out free coffee, who can resist that?"

I squeeze back.

We stand and watch the burning eye of the sun sink into the Pacific. I wonder if this is what the ocean are following, like devotees of the sun god Ra. Round and round the world they'll go, like a tidal flow, endlessly chasing the great bright light in the sky.

It makes me smile. It's no different than wildebeest roaming the plains or salmon swimming upstream. It's just another natural cycle, turning with the world.

We stand there a time longer, sipping bottled beer and thinking our own thoughts while the burnt sienna sunset fades atop the ocean, when a noise comes from down the coastal road. It is unmistakably an engine, drawing near.

Lara turns to me with wide eyes. I smile.

We fire up the front generators that power up fairy lights all round the Chinese theater's façade. We watch the headlights meander up the coast, always growing closer. My heart hammers with hope.

One of my RVs from New York pulls up, followed closely by a classic red Mustang. A young man gets out of the RV. He's pale, his hair is dark and feathery, and he stands at the door looking up at us with a broad grin on his face.

I spread my arms. "Welcome!" I say.

There are tears in his eyes. "We didn't know if you'd be here," he says. He looks at us in turn. "Amo. Lara. Look at this."

The door to the side of the RV opens, and someone else gets out. It's a little girl with frizzy dark hair, wearing a cute blue and white outfit. She's followed by an older but hardy-looking woman and an Asian woman in camouflage gear. From the Mustang comes a somber Hispanic man. A floater washes past them and not a one of them draws a weapon or shows any sign of fear. I feel such pride.

Then someone else comes. The RV back doors open and my heart leaps in my chest. A wheelchair edges into view, then comes round the side.

In it is my friend, grinning like a madman, crying like all of us.

Cerulean. Robert.

I run down and hug him, shouting out his name with words of welcome spilling off my lips.

"Good job, Amo," he says in my ear, thumping my back.

"You too," I answer, barely able to breathe.

He introduces us to the others, each of them a survivor gathered along the way, on the road or in my cairns. We all hug and shake hands, we tell them our names though of course they already know, and we all cry together and laugh together and grin like idiots together.

"Welcome," I say. "We've got movies. We've got popcorn and fizzy soda. Welcome home!

Author's Note

Thank you for reading The Last! I sincerely hope you enjoyed it. As an indie author I'm keenly aware of how many great books there are out there, and I appreciate you taking the time to try this one. Would you consider reviewing it on Amazon and/or Goodreads?

It doesn't matter how many stars you give or how long/short your review is, as long as the review is honest. Honest reviews from readers like you are the lifeblood of indie authors, affording us visibility and social proof in a highly competitive market.

Thank you!

To show my gratitude, I'd like to offer you my free Starter Library of two post-apocalypse thriller ebooks- one of them is The Last, the other is titled Mr. Ruins. Mr. Ruins tells the story of an ex-marine after an apocalyptic global resource war, and his battles with a monstrous figure who wants to swallow his soul- Mr. Ruins.

You only need to let me know your email to get Mr. Ruins:

www.michaeljohngrist.com/newsletter-sign-up

In addition, I'm always looking for genre experts/beta readers to join my ARC (Advance Review Copy) Squad, who get free copies of all my books, a month before anyone else, forever, in exchange for reviews on launch day plus any beta-reading/typo-spotting you want to provide.

If you'd like to join the ARC Squad, please send me an email at michaeljohngrist@hotmail.com and I'll happily make you a member.

Now, read on for the first chapter of The Lost, Book 2 of the Zombie Ocean!

- Michael Grist

About the Author

Michael John Grist is the British author of the Zombie Ocean series and the Ruins War trilogy. He lived in Tokyo, Japan for 11 years, and now lives in London, England.

During his time in Japan, he explored and photographed abandoned places like ruined theme parks, military bases, underground bunkers, and ghost towns. His photographs have drawn millions of visitors to his website www.michaeljohngrist.com, and often provide inspiration for his books.

Other Works

Zombie Ocean
1. The Last
2. The Lost
3. The Least
1-3 Box Set
4. The Loss

Ruins War
1. Mr. Ruins
2. King Ruin
3. God of Ruin

Ignifer Cycle
1. Ignifer's Rise
2. Ignifer's Fall
Ignifer Tales (short stories)

Short fiction
The Bells of Subsidence - 9 science fiction stories
Bone Diamond - 9 fantasy stories

Non-fiction
Into The Ruins - Adventures in Abandoned Japan

THE LOST

Book 2 of the Zombie Ocean

7 billion zombies. 1 little girl.

When the zombie apocalypse claims America, only **1 in 10 million** survive.

Anna is one of them. She's a sweet five-year-old girl who hasn't left her sickbed for a year. She likes banana milkshakes and Alice in Wonderland.

She's alone against 7 billion undead.

Will she survive?

'Alice in Wonderland' meets the zombie apocalypse like you've never seen it before, bringing a haunting emotional weight to all the adventure, twists and gore.

THE LOST (CHAPTER 1)

Seven hours before the zombie apocalypse took away everything she ever knew, five-year old Anna lay in bed listening to her father read Alice through the Looking Glass.

"When I was your age," he said in the high voice he used for the Red Queen, "I always did it for half an hour a day. Why, sometimes, I've believed as many as six impossible things before breakfast."

Wrapped up in the tight covers, Anna listened to the words intently. Her Daddy had a cozy brown voice that always kept her calm, and this was one of the few stories she could hear without the hurt becoming too much. It helped that her small bedroom was dark, and the covers were dark, and her Daddy's pajamas were dark; all except the yellow lightning bolt on his back, but she was used to that.

Darkness helped. Quiet helped. Impossible things didn't, but if she couldn't even enjoy imagining those, what did she have left?

"Tell me an impossible thing, Daddy," she said.

He smiled down at her. He had a dark and stubbly face, lit by the low orange light from the side-table lamp. She knew he wasn't all that old, but there was gray in his dark beard, twinkling like Christmas snowflakes. His brown eyes were warm and full.

"I could quote just about anything in this book, I should think," he said. "Card-men? Bread and butterflies? The Jabberwock?"

Anna smiled and closed her eyes. Her Daddy was another thing that didn't hurt her head at all. After the coma the doctors said that anything she already knew would be all right, and wouldn't make her head hurt. But the only things she could really remember from that time were Alice, her Daddy, and a vague sense of her mother.

Her mother had gone though. Only her Daddy had stayed.

"What about ham-fly?" she asked. "Or potato-bird?"

The hurt kicked in, a persistent throb that quickly spread through her head.

"Alright button," her father said softly. "I think that's enough."

She opened her eyes. "Tell me one. Just one then I'll go to sleep."

He sighed. "You'll be up all night, Anna."

"I won't I promise, just one."

Her father frowned, and tapped her nose gently. "One, all right. Let's make it good." He leaned back and thought for a little while.

This wait was delicious. Most nights it was one of their routines: to make up something new, something to dream about, something to chew and digest and make herself stronger.

"OK," he said at last, "I've got it. In the rainforests of Peru, some of the women wear birds instead of clothes. Did you know that?" His eyes twinkled. "They pleat the feathers together into beautiful patterns. Why?"

Anna screwed up her nose. That idea hurt her head sharply, like a lump of freezing snow behind her face. It was new and vivid. "Not just for fashion?"

Her Daddy chuckled. "Probably for fashion, ladies do like fashion don't they, but what else?"

The hurt thumped. She screwed her tongue up in her mouth. "So they can fly into the trees and get coconuts?"

"Good guess. Yes. They fly up for coconuts, then fly up higher and plant the coconut seeds in the tops of the other trees. Why?"

Her head banged and her eyes throbbed. "To make an arch? A rainbow out of trees. So they hang down on vines like a canary in a cage? So they become birds."

"They become birds by dressing up in birds, exactly. Like the caterpillar in his chrysalis. It's what makes them happy."

Anna sighed, part in satisfaction, part with the hurt. Her father stroked her forehead.

"You're getting hot Anna. That's enough now."

It was enough. Too much, probably. She'd have to lie silently and still for hours now before sleep would come, thinking through Alice's familiar adventures to clear these new images from her head. But that was OK. She'd be able to add them in to her collection soon, as their newness faded.

"All right," she said, narrowing her eyes to hurt-reducing slits. "But can we draw the bird ladies tomorrow?"

He stroked her face softly. "We certainly can."

Their drawings were pinned up around the room, as evidence of the adventures they'd been on together. The bird ladies would fit in perfectly next to the cucumber-men that lived on the ice volcano. It was too dark to see them now, but knowing they were out there stuck to the plain black walls made her feel good, like friends hovering in the darkness.

"Good night then, sweetie," her father said, and tucked her covers tighter around her.

She peeked up at him through slitted eyelashes. "Can I please see the Hatter? Just for a second."

He sighed and paused in mid-rise. "I don't know, sweetheart. He's tired from his injection. You're tired."

"Just for half a second? It's part of our routine."

He gave a bemused expression, wrinkling his eyebrows like he couldn't believe this child was his. "It is routine," he admitted, "that's true."

"Just a quarter of a second. I want to pat his head."

"You'll be up all night. But all right, a quick pat on the head and that's all."

He eased himself up carefully and left the bedroom. Anna steeled herself. The Hatter was the newest addition to their family, and the hardest thing for her to be around, but still she loved him. He was so small and helpless. It felt nice that she might be able to protect him, like her Daddy protected her.

Her father came back holding the Hatter. He was small and black, a baby Dalmatian with eyes that could still barely see. He made a soft mewling sound as her Daddy laid him down on the sheets by her face.

He was beautiful. Just the smell of him, all fur and milk and laundry-fresh from his new basket, made her head thump harder. The way his little head quivered and his ears shifted angles enchanted her, while the hurt grew.

This was something to fight for.

"Can I?" she asked.

Her Daddy nodded. He helped her ease her slim pale tan arm out of the tight covers, and rest it lightly on the Hatter's downy head. He yelped. Anna melted and ached inside.

"Right here," her Daddy said, pointing at a small white bandage pasted on the Hatter's back, between his tiny shoulder blades. "The doctor made the injection here, so we can never lose him."

"A chip," Anna said, pushing hard now against the icy wall of hurt. "But not a potato chip."

Her Daddy smiled and tickled the Hatter's round little belly. "A chip, that's right. He could go anywhere in the world and we'd find him. He'd find us, too. He'll protect us both, Anna, when he's big and strong."

Anna rubbed the Hatter's ears. He leaned into her hand sleepily. She loved him so much already. She thought about asking if he could stay in the room tonight, but she knew she'd never sleep.

Instead she carefully retracted her arm, and her Daddy helped her slide it back into the covers. "Thank you," she said quietly.

"You're welcome, angel. Now sleep well."

He picked up the Hatter. He tucked her in. He kissed her forehead gently, stroked her hair, then clicked off the dim lamp and eased quietly out of the room.

Darkness surrounded her.

She lay very still and pushed back at the hurt. This was the final routine that ended every day; trying to claim for herself whatever strange new ideas they'd come up with. The birdwomen took a long time to swallow down, and they hurt, though she had techniques that helped: most of them involved telling herself variations on Alice's adventures.

She looked up at the glowing clouds on the ceiling. These were left over from before, so they were OK, but so much else had gone. Her TV was a dim memory; her dolls, once scattered round the room ready for the next tea party, were all tucked away in boxes. She never went outside. She hardly ever left the room. Even looking at the pictures in the Alice books was too much. The most she could handle were the stories themselves, spoken in her Daddy's cozy brown voice.

At last she fell asleep.

When she woke six hours later her Daddy was standing over her, lit only by the glowing white of his eyes.

"Daddy?" she whispered.

He lunged toward her. His right hand glanced off her forehead and his left caught in her pillow, while his white-eyed face plunged closer like a nightmarish worm.

Anna screamed.

His forehead thunked off hers and stars popped across her vision. Instinctively she recoiled, ducking her head into the covers and burrowing deeper. The covers were so tight she could scarcely breathe, but now he was slapping at the pillows so she scrunched herself up at the bottom like Alice in a giant's pocket.

She gasped in hot stifling breaths. It was so dark and she felt dizzy, then his hand slapped hard at her back from above and she shrieked, "Daddy stop it!" but the words were muffled by the covers.

The bed rocked as his weight flopped onto it. Anna instinctively froze.

Silence thumped in the dark like the hurt. She strained to hear above her own gaspy breathing.

"Daddy?" she whispered.

The bed jolted and something snaked across her shoulder. His arm nudged her back through the blankets, and then came a horrible soft clicking sound, matched by a tightening of the blankets. The terror redoubled as she realized what it was: his teeth biting at the sheets.

She screamed and started burrowing through the sheets to the side. Her foot found the mattress edge and she pushed at the sheets as hard as she could. They untucked a little. She squirmed harder, using muscles she hadn't used for a year, until her toes popped through into the cooler air of the room.

Her father pressed harder and so did Anna, widening the hole until she could pour herself through it like hot tea: her foot and leg went first, the other leg followed, then her hips and the rest of her body tumbled through and slumped awkwardly onto the carpet.

She lay for a second panting in the cool air. Clouds glowed above in an eerie white light. It was a dream; it had to be a dream.

Her Daddy's face popped over the edge of the bed like a horrible jack-in-the-box. She froze. It was her Daddy but not her Daddy; the black centers of his eyes were gone, covered over with shining white like Humpty's cracked eggshells. His dark skin had gone gray and his breath sucked in and out with loud raspy wheezes.

He reached down for her and she yelped, then unfroze and rolled under the bed. In four dizzy revolutions she cleared the underside, just as he tumbled to the floor with a thump. She stared in disbelief as he got on his belly and started crawling toward her. It was tighter for him and he came on slow, but he didn't stop.

For the first time since the coma she stood up. It felt incredibly high up, like Alice after biting the cake. The dark room spun and her frail legs wobbled below. She barely remembered how to walk, and she didn't have a clue what to do. Most of all she wanted to call for her Daddy, but he was right here chasing her, and-

CRUNCH

A horrible sound came from below, shaking the house and making her jump. Another followed then another, and her heart skipped a beat with each one.

THUMP THUMP

More hit. Her Daddy was still well under the bed so she chanced a trip to the window. She hobbled over on the scratchy carpet to the window and caught her balance on the wall. The black velvet curtains were tacked to the frame, protecting her day and night from the light of the outside world. Now she slipped her hand underneath the fabric and tore it away.

Outside it was night still, and the road was filled with people.

They were everywhere, hundreds of them in pajamas and sweatpants. They all had the same strange gray skin and the same glowing white eyes, and all of themwere trudging in the same direction down the road, like a river flowing to the ocean.

Then they stopped. Their heads turned as one, like flowers bending in the wind, and their glowing white eyes settled on her.

Her breath stopped.

They charged.

CRUNCH THUMP THUMP

They hit the house and glass shattered, the floor and wall shook, and Anna jerked away from the window to smack up against her Daddy.

"Aaah!" she screamed.

His hand came up to scrape her face and she ducked and staggered round him, running jerkily back to the bed. If she could just get back under the covers and close her eyes then this horrible dream would go away, she knew it. She started to climb up the mattress but her Daddy stopped her with a hand on her back.

She screamed again. He pressed closer trapping her against the bed frame so she couldn't move at all. Tears streamed down her cheeks.

"Stop it Daddy!" she wailed. "I don't like this game." He pressed closer still and his gray face with its white eyes loomed in and she thought she was going to die.

Then the Hatter barked from the other room.

She barely heard the weak sound of his bark over the crashing of people-waves outside, but her Daddy did. He stopped advancing at once and went very still. Anna went very still too, not even daring to breathe.

The Hatter barked again, more of a yelp than a real bark, and now her Daddy moved sharply away. He went through the bedroom door roughly, banging his shoulder off the frame.

Anna let out a quiet sob. The Hatter barked again and her Daddy was stalking now outside in the hall. He'd saved her, but now who would save him? She was small but the Hatter was much smaller. She'd made a promise to protect him.

She got up and started for the door, almost tripping over her big ankles. She could hardly run; her body wasn't used to fast movement at all.

"Wait!" she called over the crashing sound.

It was dark and she stubbed her toe on the edge of the bedroom door. The corridor outside was a dark foreign territory, a place she hadn't seen for months, half-remembered from an old dream.

The dim light of her Daddy's eyes receded down the hall.

"Wait Daddy."

He turned into his bedroom. Anna bounced along the walls after him, calling all the time. Her legs were not used to this, her balance was weak, but the Hatter needed her and this was her one job. She reached the doorway gasping, exhausted from the exertion, to find her father holding the Hatter up before him in both hands.

"Here he is sweetie," her Daddy would have said, "come pet him,

I'm so proud that you got out of bed."

But this was not her Daddy, and he didn't say any of that. Instead he lifted the struggling puppy to his face, opened his mouth, and bit down hard into the Hatter's soft and furry back.

Out Now

Printed in the USA
CPSIA information can be obtained
at www.ICGtesting.com
LVHW041914121124
796457LV00006B/134